What the critics are saying:

"Alexander ignites the pages with Book 1 of her Hot in the City trilogy. This promises to be one of those rare series where the reader is immediately ravenous for the next installment. (A) deliciously decadent story." *~Susan Mitchell, Romantic Times Bookclub, 4 STARS*

"FRENCH QUARTER is an unbelievably erotic tale that takes place in sultry New Orleans. Even though many scenes are extremely explicit, I found that Ms. Alexander wrote them in a very tasteful way. The incredible magnetism between Liz and Jack combined with their sizzling sexual adventures made FRENCH QUARTER one of the hottest and sexiest stories I have ever read." *~Jennifer A., Romance Junkies, 5 BLUE RIBBONS*

"FRENCH QUARTER is an outstanding [illegible] qual and I would highly recommend it to those in [illegible] ture like none other. It is an incredible [illegible] grossed with the characters that you [illegible]

~ Jennifer Ray, Road to [illegible]

"Ms. Alexander has creat[illegible] story of a woman who is awakening to her true self and [illegible] depth of her sexuality. Each incident is handled masterfully, with beautiful writing that draws the reader in, allowing you to feel every emotion Jack and Liz do. It is a perfectly crafted tale that is both extreme in its topics yet personal in its telling." *~MeriBeth McCombs, The Road to Romance*

"FRENCH QUARTER is a wonderful, explosive, erotic story from the first page to the last. New author Lacey Alexander has written an amazing debut novel that has blazing heat, mischievous exploration, and an inevitable fall into love. Don't miss this extremely erotic story. It will definitely add some spice to your life." *~Enya Adrian, Romance Reviews Today*

ELLORA'S CAVE
ROMANTICA PUBLISHING

FRENCH QUARTER
An Ellora's Cave Publication, July 2004

Ellora's Cave Publishing, Inc.
PO Box 787
Hudson, OH 44236-0787

ISBN #1-4199-5011-8

ISBN MS Reader (LIT) ISBN # 1-84360-797-2
Other available formats (no ISBNs are assigned):
Adobe (PDF), Rocketbook (RB), Mobipocket (PRC) & HTML

Edited by *Heather Osborn*
Cover art by *Dawn Seewer*

HOT IN THE CITY 1: FRENCH QUARTER

Lacey Alexander

I'd like to dedicate the Hot in the City trilogy to my husband,
with fond memories of
hurricanes in New Orleans,
daiquiris in Las Vegas,
and too much wine in Key West.

Chapter 1

A thin line of nervous perspiration trickled between Liz Marsh's breasts and into the black lace of her bra as she stood outside the slightly battered Royal Street door. She stared at the name, Jack Wade, stenciled on the old wood in gold letters beginning to peel. Taking another glance down at her transparent black blouse and short skirt, she wondered if she could go through with this.

But she really had no choice—she *had* to go through with it.

Even so, when she turned the doorknob and stepped inside, the last thing she expected to find was a dark-haired god of all that was sexual. He sat behind a desk that had seen better days, but he made it look good. Leaning comfortably back in his chair, he made her think of an animal lounging in his lair. His eyes were a shade lighter than midnight and seemed to pin her in place the very moment he lifted them.

She stopped, halted by the sheer magnetism, and reached out for the back of the chair that sat across from him. Not only was she suddenly more nervous than she'd been a few seconds ago, but she was wearing new heels, bought—however crazily—just for this occasion, and just a look from him made her feel unbalanced.

"Hello there." His voice was as rich as dark chocolate. "What can I do for you?"

What *couldn't* he do for her? That quickly, she found herself mentally penning a list that started with "kiss my lips" and descended to kneading her sensitive breasts and stroking the hungry little spot between her thighs.

This wasn't like her, not at all. Everyone knew Liz wasn't the sexy type. They might call her pretty. On particularly good days maybe even sophisticated. *And* conservative—she was a woman who played by the rules. Usually, anyway. No matter how you sliced it, though, Liz wasn't the sort of woman to experience heart-stopping lust for strange men on sight.

Maybe it was the dress. The shoes. The makeup. Maybe it was all working together to turn her into the woman she'd come here masquerading to be. Not that she'd arrived in hopes of finding a totally hot man whose very gaze colored him interested—no, that result was just an unexpected perk. She'd dressed this way because it had simply seemed important to look good—like a woman who could catch a man, *keep* a man—on this particular mission. The god raised his eyebrows as if to punctuate his question, which made her realize she'd never answered him.

"I want to hire you," she said.

"For?"

Given the way they were staring at each other, the question seemed all too loaded, and a slightly wicked grin tweaked the corners of his mouth, as if he knew exactly what she was thinking.

That's when she remembered why she was here. Despite how hot he was, she *hadn't* come to catch a man. She'd come to catch a man *at* something. "I need to find out if my fiancé is cheating on me."

Her hot god chuckled. "Sorry, *chere*. I graduated from those kinds of cases a long time ago. You wanna see Manny Goodman down on Decatur." He lifted a thumb, pointing vaguely over his shoulder.

"But I want *you*. Specifically."

Only as his grin returned did she realize she'd taken the double entendre still further. "Understandable," he replied, arrogance and sex dripping from him. "But like I said, I don't do those jobs anymore. Go see Manny. He does decent work. He'll find out what you wanna know."

Yet Liz didn't want to see Manny. It was nerve-wracking enough to actually be hiring a private investigator, and embarrassing to admit to a stranger that the man she'd planned to marry might be getting some on the side. She didn't want to go from place to place explaining her problem. Furthermore, her friend and neighbor, Lynda, had recommended Jack Wade. Ten years earlier, Lynda had hired him to catch her cheating husband in the act, and she'd promised Jack did good, quick, discreet work. The P.I. business seemed like one that might attract some shady characters, and because Lynda said she could rely on him, Liz wanted her search for a private eye to stop *here*.

What Lynda *hadn't* mentioned were his gorgeous-to-the-point-of-being-hypnotic eyes, his strong jaw, his broad shoulders, or the sexy hint of a Cajun accent in his speech. He was the sort of man that made her want to touch him. Already, she experienced the urge to run her hands down what she knew would be a hard, muscular chest, to unzip his jeans and see if the bulge she couldn't help noticing was as promising as it looked from her current vantage point. Maybe it wasn't *just* reliability that made her want to stay.

Resuming the persona she'd come into the office displaying, she leaned over and braced both hands on his desk, giving him an excellent view of her considerable cleavage. The bra was her own, but the blouse was borrowed from Lynda, and the button between her breasts strained to come undone. "Look," she said softly, "this is very difficult for me. And you're the guy I want for the job. If it makes any difference, money is no object." She leaned even farther, giving him a still better view, her own seductive moves making her breasts feel swollen and sensitive within the cups of her snug bra. "Now, what will it take to get you to help me?" Peering down at him, she bit her lip slightly and felt a surge of wetness in her panties. She was struck once more by how unlike her this was—not only was she filled with uncharacteristic heat for him, but now she was using her body to manipulate him. It made her feel sexy and powerful.

"Why me?" His voice came low; his eyes turned glassy with want.

"Because I heard you're good. And I *need* somebody good, somebody who can do this job well, and quickly."

Just then, the door opened behind her.

"Hey, I just—hell, sorry, man. I thought you were alone."

Liz spent a split second wondering just how tight her skirt stretched across her ass, just how high it rose on the backs of her thighs, before turning to see the man who'd come in. Tall, blondish, a bit lankier than Jack Wade, he was tan and classically handsome. A neater haircut would have made him a perfect Malibu Ken doll, but she instantly liked the rough edges she saw. Like Jack Wade, this guy hadn't shaved today. But whereas the P.I. wore a simple polo shirt, his friend sported shorts and a tee that made him look laid back and comfortable in his own body. Despite his loose-fitting clothes, she could see the sinewy muscles in his arms and legs and couldn't help wondering what it would feel like to have them wrapped around her. Liz couldn't remember a time she'd ever been aroused by two men at once, so as her body ached, almost painfully, she counted this as another new, unlikely experience.

"Hi," he said to her, a smile playing about his lips. "Sorry if I interrupted something."

"No. I mean..." She glanced between the two guys who were currently filling the room with more testosterone than she'd ever felt before. "I'm a client of Mr. Wade's, that's all."

The blond tilted his head back with an, "Ah," but his amused expression said he wasn't sure he believed her.

Jack Wade chuckled again. "You're makin' quite a presumption there, *chere*."

Liz bristled at his words. Something inside told her she'd come too far to turn back. To walk out of his office now without "winning" would feel like a huge defeat. Because this wasn't just about business any longer—it had definitely become sexual; it had invisibly turned into an issue of something like...conquest. She'd dressed provocatively because telling a guy your fiancé was probably cheating seemed like the ultimate embarrassment, and she'd thought she could handle it better if she made the P.I. think her fiancé was a total idiot to look elsewhere for gratification. To walk out now would make her feel she'd failed at that, too.

"Maybe I am," she said. Then she leaned back over the desk again, not caring what kind of view she gave the Ken doll if it meant seducing Jack Wade into taking her case. She licked her lips and gazed into those dark eyes of his, letting her voice go husky. "But I don't think so. I think you're too curious to turn me down." About what, she didn't say, but she wasn't talking about the case.

"Is that so?" His voice was just as gravelly.

"Yes, that's so." She rose back up and turned to the Ken doll. "Don't you agree? Don't you think Mr. Wade should give me what I want?"

The blond man looked as aroused by her as she was by her own boldness. "Oh *yeah*. I think he should give you whatever your pretty little heart desires." Then he looked past her to the P.I. "Quit giving the lady a hard time, Jack."

Jack Wade looked back and forth between the two of them, appearing half-annoyed, half-amused. Finally, his gaze settled back on Liz, turning her warm and a little wetter than she already was. "Darlin', I'm findin' it hard to believe a guy would cheat on a *jolie fille* like you."

A rush of gratification washed through her at the compliment—she knew little French, but was fairly certain he'd just called her a pretty girl, and his sexy tone alone turned the words more suggestive.

"So why do you think he's steppin' out?" he added.

Of course, this brought Liz back to reality, back to the reason she was here, and it bit sharply into her excitement. "The usual signs, I suppose. Repeated claims of working late, *very* late, and coming home looking more rumpled than a man should get at the office. Little to no explanation when I ask why he has to work so much, and he acts like I'm nagging him when I express concern." She paused, thinking how thin her suspicions sounded. "Maybe it seems as if I'm jumping to conclusions, but it's just a feeling I have, and I need to find out if he's really working or if he's going someplace else."

As the Ken doll stretched out quietly in a chair in the corner, Jack Wade took notes on a small pad of paper. "How often does this happen?"

"Lately, nearly every night of the week."

Jack nodded, made another note, and then asked for a few more specifics centering on her fiancé's place of business, normal working hours, and route to work.

Then he looked up at her. "Just so you know, nine times out of ten, if you think they're cheatin' on you, they are. Might save you some time and money to just go with your gut and turn the guy loose."

But Liz only shook her head. "I need to know for sure."

"All right then. I'll need your name and a number where I can reach you discreetly."

"Liz," she said. "Liz Marsh." She recited her work number, watching him jot it down.

"Liz," he repeated, letting the "z" sound roll off his tongue. "I'll be in touch with you very soon, Liz," he promised, but his eyes said more, like he was talking dirty to her, and she felt more desirable than she had in a very long time as she thanked him for his help and exited out onto Royal Street.

The day felt balmier than usual for March. Or maybe, she thought, it wasn't balmy out here at all. Maybe it was just the fresh and unexpected heat running thick through her veins.

* * * * *

Late that night, Jack settled into a small booth at Club Venus, one of the French Quarter's classier strip joints. Lots of brass and mirrors and plush burgundy fabrics turned the otherwise average bar into a "gentlemen's club." Five or six mini-stages set about the extravagant room so that wherever you looked, you found a lovely *fille* gyrating out of her clothes to a barely there g-string. On the stage closest to him, a beautiful brunette, mid-20's probably, twirled around a brass pole in a short, tight dress, displaying firm breasts with dark nipples thrusting through thin white fabric, tan legs that went on forever, and strappy fuck-me shoes with five-inch heels and at least an inch-high platform beneath her toes.

A waitress wearing a gold lamé bikini that barely covered her soon approached. "What can I get you?"

"Vodka on the rocks," he said, watching as her thong-clad ass jiggled its way back toward the bar.

His gaze returned to the brunette, who now peeled the top of her dress down to reveal a predictably gorgeous pair of large round breasts, nipples still standing at full attention. Letting the bodice fall to her waist, she swung her hips slowly back and forth to the beat of a sexy song and ran her hands over her ample curves, lightly pinching her nipples as she moved. He enjoyed the show she put on, but found himself thinking of another lovely lady with long tawny hair—his new client, Liz Marsh. A warm rush of blood flowed to his cock as he imagined *her* up on the stage, doing a slow sexy grind just for him.

Merde, it had been a long time since he'd found himself thinking with his dick, but that was exactly what had happened today. He'd quit taking cheating cases years ago—they were the bottom rung of the ladder for a self-respecting P.I.—and he wouldn't have taken hers, either, if not for the way she'd used her eyes and body to seduce him. He couldn't help wondering if she'd noticed the imprint of his hard cock trying to burst past his zipper. And if she'd happened back by his office a little while after she and his friend, Ty, had both left, she'd have found him unzipping his strained blue jeans, leaning back in his chair, and taking his hard shaft in hand, all with thoughts of her.

On his desk, with her skirt pushed up to her hips, that tight blouse unbuttoned, that sexy black bra undone. Wrapping her legs around his body while he sank his hungry cock into her sweet wet pussy. Panting, moaning, crying out as he drove into her moist heat. He'd slid his fist up and down his long, swollen shaft, envisioning every dirty detail and wishing like hell it wasn't just a fantasy. It hadn't taken long before he'd found relief, but damn, thinking of her now, watching the girl on the stage and envisioning Liz Marsh in her place, had him hot and hard again.

Another thing Jack hadn't done in a long while was mix business with pleasure—or, in this instance, a hard bout of good old-fashioned lust. It was amateurish and he wasn't an amateur. He'd opened his business as a wet-behind-the-ears kid of twenty-one, and fifteen years later he made a very respectable living, generally taking—and solving—cases the police couldn't. The families or other people involved in the crimes often got fed up with a lack of answers from the authorities, and came to him with cases of theft, blackmail, missing persons; he'd even cracked a few murder cases. In a city like New Orleans, there were plenty of mysteries to be solved and secrets to uncover—just like the Mississippi, it was a river that never ran dry. And it wasn't that he'd never slept with a woman he'd met through his job, but somewhere along the way he'd grown up; he'd decided fucking the customers was unprofessional, and he hadn't done it since.

Not that he knew for sure if he'd sleep with Liz Marsh. But he knew if she gave him the chance, he would. Already, it had become a fact, something he wouldn't bother denying. He'd liked the open, mutual lust flowing between them far too much to pretend he could just turn it off like a leaky faucet—hell, it had kept him half-hard all day.

So watching the stripper tease her stretchy dress up over a very round ass, then skim her hands over it as she danced, turned him as solid as a stone pillar by the time the scantily clad waitress brought his drink.

Sipping at the vodka, he indulged himself, watching the rest of the number—the sexy brunette finally shimmied free of the dress, leaving her in shoes and a flesh-colored g-string that barely concealed her crotch. She crouched down to allow the guys near her little stage to tuck money into the thin elastic string at her hip before continuing the slow, provocative dance. She caressed her own curves—breasts, hips, inner thighs—and licked her lips, clearly as aroused by her performance as they were.

That's when he spotted what he'd come here for—Todd Darcy, his new client's fiancé. Liz had provided him with a recent photo, which he now pulled out of his pocket to do a double-check. Damn, this was too easy.

All he'd done was hang around outside the guy's office building around five, the hour Liz had informed him was her fiancé's scheduled quitting time. Around 5:15, Todd had exited onto the downtown street wearing a shirt and tie, suit jacket tossed over his shoulder. His first stop had been a small café on Jackson Square, close enough to walk to from his office. Jack had meandered inside behind him, taken a seat, and watched Todd eat a po' boy and drink a bottled water. It gave Jack a chance to study him.

The guy was handsome, he guessed, but in an all-too-average way. Light brown hair, cut short to match his yuppie clothes, thin build, nothing spectacular. Certainly not spectacular enough for a woman like Liz Marsh. And his eyes…there was something about them Jack didn't like. He'd learned a lot about reading people over the years, and Todd Darcy looked like a man possessed…by something.

By six, Todd was striding through the Quarter, making a beeline for Bourbon Street, unaware he was being followed. He'd slipped into Club Venus so quickly that by the time Jack had paid his cover charge and come inside, he'd not been able to spot Todd in the dimly lit room, which sported a reasonable size crowd of mostly middle to upper-class men, despite the early hour.

So he'd taken a seat, knowing he'd see Todd sooner or later, and now, here the guy was, pushing a folded bill into the stripper's g-string, and looking so lost in lust that Jack felt a hard pang of sympathy for Liz Marsh. It was one thing for a guy to spend an occasional night out at a strip bar with his buddies, but one look told Jack this guy had it bad. Now he knew what Todd was so damn possessed by. He was like those guys addicted to Internet porn, only it was strippers that fed Todd's hunger.

Rising to his feet, Jack reached into his pocket for a tiny camera hidden in a lighter. He made a slow, casual trip around the room, stopping at various spots to discreetly photograph his quarry as Todd gaped lustfully up at the next *fille* to take the stage, this one starting her dance in a clingy pink miniskirt and matching camisole.

Half an hour later, Jack sat nursing his second vodka, enjoying the female entertainment and keeping an eye on Todd.

What the hell did Liz Marsh see in this guy? Maybe he made a lot of money. Or maybe they were childhood sweethearts or something.

Hell, could be anything, he supposed, but without even taking into consideration that the guy lied to his fiancée to come to a strip club every night, Jack wasn't impressed with him.

He also found it hard to believe Liz couldn't keep the jerk happy in bed. Her sexy outfit had revealed enough to tell him she had a killer body, and her mannerisms had told him she wasn't afraid to use it. What kind of pleasure did Todd get from strippers that he couldn't get from Liz and her delectable curves, her sweet, pouty mouth?

Damn, a split second before Ty had walked into his office, Jack had been tempted to kiss her. Inappropriate as hell, especially given the reason she was there and that she was engaged to be married, for God's sake, but she'd been leaning so close, a musky, feminine scent emanating from her. Those pretty berry lips had been telling him she needed somebody good, while her lush breasts strained against the filmy fabric buttoned over them and—*merde*, how much could a man be expected to resist? What he wouldn't have given to take those soft mounds in his hands, to kiss their taut nipples, to suck them until she begged for more. Hell—clearly, his fantasy after she'd left hadn't given him nearly as much of her as he needed, since it was growing now, expanding in his head. He wanted to spread her thighs, sink his fingertips into her warm wet cunt, feel her fucking his fingers, getting wetter and wetter for him, until she came on his hand.

He let out a heated breath, pulling himself back to reality, remembering why he was here. Work. He had a job to do for Liz Marsh, and a fiancé whose angle he needed to figure out. Taking a deep breath, he refocused his attention on the little weasel across the room.

Maybe Todd had a thing for strippers because it was forbidden. Maybe the lure of doing something "naughty" was what drew him. At the moment, Jack thoroughly understood that lure, if in a different way. Still, if you were into the forbidden, Jack supposed, there was *no* woman—not even Liz Marsh—who would be able to keep you happy.

Pulling his mind back to the present, Jack saw Todd speaking with one of the girls who'd just finished dancing—a blonde co-ed-looking type with small, high breasts and nice legs. Still seated in one of the plush chairs surrounding each stage area, he mooned up at her as she stood next to him, flirting for money. Jack pulled out his camera and took a shot from his seat.

He watched a folded bill exchange hands just before the co-ed lifted one knee over Todd, straddling his hips. As the next song began to pump a hot slow rhythm through the sexually charged room, the co-ed began a sensuous dance as she hovered over Liz's fiancé. Jack decided this was well worth grabbing on film for Liz and made another trip around the room to be sure he got enough angles to capture Todd's face and to make it very clear what he was doing.

An hour later, Todd had paid three hot women for lap dances before disappearing with two more into a back room. Although Jack couldn't follow, he snapped a few shots of the nearly naked women leading Todd through the door labeled "private dances."

Even as badly as he felt now for Liz Marsh and as much as he was not looking forward to telling her what he'd learned, he hoped like hell she'd want to let him take her mind off her troubles. Admittedly, sitting in the club watching comely strippers dance down to tiny g-strings had gotten him hot, but it was his fantasy about Liz that truly had desire burning from his chest down to his rock-hard erection.

* * * * *

Just hearing Jack Wade's deep voice on the phone the next day had made Liz wet, even as she sat in her cubicle at the downtown ad agency where she worked, surrounded by other co-workers.

"I need to meet with you," he'd said.

She'd attempted to still the heat flowing through her veins and tried to sound halfway professional. "At your office? I could come at lunch."

"See you then."

Now she stepped out of the taxi she'd hailed a few blocks away, in too much of a hurry to walk. Anxious to see what Jack had learned about Todd's whereabouts last night, she nearly burst through the door of his office, but stopped short, remembering how sexy she knew Jack had thought her yesterday afternoon, and wanting to be that way for him again.

She was wearing a business suit, but fortunately the white blouse beneath was rather sheer, enough that she kept her black jacket buttoned all day whenever she wore this particular piece of apparel. Now, standing on Royal Street, she slipped the jacket from her shoulders and looked down to glimpse the white lace of her bra showing through, the fabric clinging nicely to her curves. Her skirt had ridden up her thighs a bit in the cab, but she didn't tug it down. Finally, taking a glance at herself in the shop window next to Jack's door, she pulled the clip from her chignon and let her hair fall wild and wavy about her shoulders.

Feeling adequately sexy and nearly as anxious to see Jack Wade as she was to find out about Todd, she went inside.

He sat with his feet propped on the corner of his desk eating a sandwich. As the door closed behind her, he lowered his feet to the floor, set the sandwich on a paper plate, and sat up straighter.

"Hello, Mr. Wade."

His look bordered strangely between lustful and gentle. "Call me Jack."

"All right, Jack." She sat down in the chair across from him. "What have you found?"

He let out a long sigh. "I know where Todd goes every night and what he does. I took pictures for you." He handed a stack across the desk to her. "Unfortunately, they're not very good quality. The room was dark, but the camera I used should've worked anyway. I can only guess I got a bad roll of film."

Liz thumbed through the photos. At first she wasn't quite sure what she was seeing, but through the shadowy lighting, she soon made out bare breasts, nipples pointing, and realized she was seeing a naked girl in a man's lap.

"I know it's hard to tell," Jack said, "but the guy in the picture is Todd. I followed him to Club Venus on Bourbon last night. He got lap dances from several strippers before takin' two of 'em to a back room for a private dance."

Liz blinked and looked at the picture again, trying to absorb what Jack was telling her. The guy in the picture didn't look like Todd to her. Of course, she could barely see his face, hidden in shadow—it could have been any man. But Todd wasn't the type to patronize a strip club. If anything, he was Mr. Straight Arrow, as clean cut and straitlaced as a guy comes. The very idea that he was doing something he wasn't supposed to had been a hard conclusion to reach, but now that she had, she'd expected to discover he was seeing some urbane executive like himself—some thin-faced, thin-lipped, glasses-wearing, briefcase-toting, hair-in-a-severe-bun, high-powered woman who'd turned Todd on by climbing the corporate ladder at a record-setting pace. Or maybe seeing someone like her—the *regular* her, not the lusty, sexy, see-through-blouse her that Jack Wade knew, but someone with even more of the prim and proper qualities Todd valued. In fact, she'd even convinced herself that was why he'd strayed—because she wasn't sophisticated enough, or prim and mannered enough.

"Are you sure it was him? Because this isn't Todd's style."

Jack appeared to be pained on her behalf. "I'm sorry, *chere*...but yeah, I'm sure. I followed him every step of the way from his building."

"Did you see him come directly out of his office *inside* the building?"

He blinked. "*Mais,* I saw him come out of the building, not his exact office, but I recognized him right away from the picture you gave me."

She drew in a deep breath. "Because a lot of men look like Todd. He's not exactly unusual—your basic suit and tie guy. And in a building that big, a lot of men could look like him at a glance."

Jack slowly tilted his head. "Darlin'," he said gently, "I really am sorry. I know this must hurt, but I'm sure that's your fiancé."

Liz pursed her lips. It wasn't that she was hurt, exactly—it was simply that she didn't believe him. Lynda had promised her he was good at his job, but what if he'd slipped? If Todd was spending every night with strippers grinding in his lap, well, that was more than enough reason to call off the wedding, but the photos were so dark and this behavior seemed so uncharacteristic...

"I'm sorry, too, but I'm afraid it's going to take more than a set of dark pictures to make me believe this is him."

Across from her, Jack sighed. "When I saw how the pictures came out, I was afraid you'd feel this way."

"I don't mean to doubt you," she said quickly, "but..."

"*Oui?*"

"Given how unlike him this seems, I'm just not sure I'd believe it unless I saw it with my own eyes."

"*Mais,* then," Jack said slowly, appearing to be thinking through the situation. "I'm busy tonight, but presuming Todd 'works late' tomorrow night, why don't you meet me at, say, nine o'clock, outside the Blue Moon Café, and we'll go to Club Venus together?"

Something in Liz withered. "Me, in a strip club?"

He raised his eyebrows. "If you wanna see for yourself."

"Well, I've never..." She decided to let that rest—she didn't want him to think she was any less worldly and wild than he currently did. "I presume women *do* go to this particular club on occasion?"

He gave a short nod. "I'm sure there'll be a few other women there."

She tried to hide her nervous swallow. "All right then. I'll see you tomorrow night." Rising to go, she glanced down at the pictures still in her hand. "May I have these?"

"Sure. If you look at 'em and decide you're convinced before tomorrow night, let me know and we'll cancel."

"All right, but...I'm not expecting that to happen."

With that, she turned and walked back out onto the street, nipples and crotch tingling for more reasons that she could easily identify. She should be upset, she thought, or livid, or *something*—at Todd. Instead, though, she was concentrating on the way Jack Wade had made her feel. All hot and crumbly inside. The flesh between her thighs heavy and aching. Something about this man made her feel so dirty—in a delicious way.

As for Todd, there was a part of her that almost *wanted* to find out he was cheating. She'd once thought she loved him, but now she doubted she ever had. She'd had worries and misgivings for a while now, yet her reaction to Jack Wade these last couple of days had shored up her certainty. She couldn't truly love her fiancé and at the same time want to get naked and sweaty with Jack Wade.

But she still didn't think the guy in those pictures was Todd. And she needed more solid evidence before she broke off the engagement. Their lives were too closely intertwined. Todd was from a good family and their parents got along famously—their fathers had even gone into business together, financing a chain of dry cleaning stores back home in Maryland. As far as both their families were concerned, Liz and Todd were as good as married already. So it would be a lot easier, a lot more cut and dried, with proof that he'd done something wrong, and the pictures Jack had taken weren't good enough.

Liz's heels clicked down the street toward a nearby deli—she wanted to grab a quick salad before heading back to the office. As she sat eating at a small corner table, she thought more about the pictures. When she'd eaten her last bite of lettuce, she lay down her fork, dug the photos back out of her purse, and looked through them, more carefully this time.

The man in the prints was slouched deep in a small, plush chair, head leaned back, mouth open. Even without being able to make out his face, she could see the raw lust in him. Soon, however, her focus shifted and she found herself studying the women in the pictures. One was large-breasted with big, pointy nipples which dangled teasingly above the man's face. Her body was so lush and curvy that something seemed sinful about it, even in the still, dark photo. Another had smaller breasts, perky with hard pink nubs at their centers. She looked lithe and acrobatic, in some shots rising up on her knees, in others grinding her crotch against the man in the picture. Despite the shadowy quality of the images, this particular girl looked like a blonde and Liz had the impression of her being young—twentyish. A third stripper was ultra-slender with medium-sized boobs, pretty and pert. She might be a redhead. In the fuzzy darkness, she looked very attractive, sensual. In some of the shots, she touched her breasts or tweaked her large nipples, in others she leaned her head back, looking impassioned. In one picture, she rubbed between her legs.

Looking at something so blatant, dirty, and sexual between strangers began to turn Liz on against her will. Her crotch hummed and her panties felt damp. The women were so lovely, so sexy, so bold and hot. She wondered if Jack Wade had enjoyed watching them writhe on top of the guy in the photos, enjoyed watching them touch themselves. She wondered if he'd gotten hard, if he'd gone home wishing he had a woman—or maybe he'd *gotten* a woman. For all she knew, he'd had a private dance himself.

A vision of the difficult-to-see redhead straddling Jack Wade's lap rose to her mind. Had the woman perhaps thrashed about on him, making him hard? Had he gazed up at her, watching her work, letting himself get lost in lust? The image was wildly arousing, even as she felt a mild pang of jealousy—irrationally, she wanted him to lust only for her.

God, what if he was married or something? It was the first time the thought had even occurred to her. He'd been flirting with her, undressing her with his eyes, but married men misbehaved all the time. And she hadn't noticed him wearing a ring—but some men just didn't.

Please don't be married, she thought. *Please be available.*

And...for God's sake, what about *Todd*? Why wasn't she even thinking about Todd? He might actually *be* the guy in the pictures, yet she'd gotten more caught up in looking at all those round, pretty breasts, smooth stomachs, and curving hips, and wondering if they'd excited Jack Wade the same way they were exciting her right now.

And to think, tomorrow night she was actually going to Club Venus with him. She was going to watch all this with him, live. One part of her was petrified—what if she was repulsed by what she saw there, what if she wanted to run screaming into the street away from the lewdness? But another part of her—the part she was just discovering over these past couple of days—was anticipating it.

Shoving the photos back in her purse, Liz emptied her lunch tray and went into the bathroom to freshen up before catching a cab back to work. Standing before the mirror, she fastened her hair back from her face and touched up her makeup. Then she noticed that through the sheerness of the blouse and the lace of this particular bra, she could actually see the dark shadow of her nipples.

Normally, she'd have been mortified to think she'd been walking around the streets that way. But instead, an undeniable and naughty warmth stole over her as she found herself hoping Jack had seen them, too.

Chapter 2

That day after work, Liz met Lynda, back in the Quarter. Lynda ran an antique shop on St. Peter, but she lived out in the Garden District, just next door to the historic home Liz and Todd had purchased when they'd moved there together six months earlier. Todd had accepted a relocation to his investment advisory firm's New Orleans office without even asking Liz. Looking back on it now, that seemed to have been the beginning of their problems.

Even so, she'd gone along with him, quitting her advertising job and finding a new one upon her arrival, packing up and leaving everything she knew in Maryland, where she and Todd had both been born and raised. If only she'd been smart enough to question the move more, maybe protest, not always be so easy to get along with.

But she'd never really been taught to stand up for herself—her parents had been strict disciplinarians and Liz and her two younger sisters, Diana and Carrie, had been expected to obey their parents' rules, to always do what was expected of them. Diana had been a rebel, but Liz and Carrie had both allowed themselves be poured into the mold their parents had created for them. And somehow, without quite planning it, Liz had let that carry over into her adult life.

But she had a feeling that finally, at thirty, that was about to change. Todd was cheating on her…or something, and whatever it was, it would provide the ammunition she needed when she told her parents she wasn't going to tie the knot with him. It wasn't that she couldn't simply decide not to marry him on her own, but she wanted to make this easy on herself, wanted to hear as little argument from her family as possible, so she could simply get on with the business of living once this was over.

Before moving, she and Todd had shared a happy, respectful—even if lukewarm—relationship, so pulling up her roots when he asked hadn't seemed like a large sacrifice. Only now that he seemed to be changing did Liz realize that perhaps she should have made her decisions more carefully. Having so much time alone in the evenings to contemplate his whereabouts and examine the core of their relationship had finally opened her eyes, made her want to be a more independent woman. And getting to the bottom of Todd's evenings away from home was going to be a big start.

Although Liz and Lynda had little in common, they had become fast friends. In fact, Lynda was the only person Liz had chosen to share her suspicions with. Now, they were meeting in order to...*initiate* Liz into the wild nightlife of Bourbon Street. Liz had never even ventured toward the red light district since moving to the Big Easy, and even as the newly awakened wild side of her was almost itching to see what went on in a strip club while at Jack Wade's side, she needed a pep talk from Lynda; she needed to know what to expect.

"So," Lynda said, locking up her shop and tossing her waist-length blonde hair over her shoulder to look up at Liz, "that Jack's a hottie, isn't he?"

Had Lynda read her mind? Liz couldn't help letting out a small giggle. "*Very* hot, as a matter of fact. Which you might have mentioned to me, by the way."

Lynda flashed a mischievous grin. "I thought you'd enjoy the surprise. And I bet *he* enjoyed your sexy little outfit."

Liz felt heat color her cheeks, but decided not to lie. Lynda had never liked Todd anyway, and she especially didn't like him now, so Liz didn't mind letting her friend know she'd flirted with another man. "Well, if the way he looked at me was any indication, yes, he did."

"Don't those dark, penetrating eyes just go all through you? And don't those little bits of Cajun he peppers his speech with just make you wet? Doesn't everything about him just make you want to hold him down and have your way with him?"

"Well..." she began, uncertain exactly how *much* she wanted to confide in Lynda, "I suppose that..."

Lynda laughed. "Oh come on, Liz, quit trying to keep secrets. You wanted to fuck his brains out right there on the desk, I know you did. I did, too, the moment I met him. So just tell me."

Liz couldn't help laughing, too, and finally said, "Okay, I admit it—I've never met a man so...fuckable." Dear God, where had that come from? Certainly not from her usual vocabulary. Must be Lynda's influence on her, she decided.

As they strolled up the cracked, broken sidewalk of the French Quarter toward Bourbon, Liz was struck once more by how unusual her reaction to him was. Remembering the way she'd felt as soon as he'd laid eyes on her was nearly enough to make her cream her silk undies again. Now that she took the time to thoroughly recall that first meeting in his office, she'd had the same sensual reaction to his blond friend, too, instantly thinking sexual thoughts, wishing for a physical connection—although her attraction to his friend seemed somehow *linked* to her desire for Jack in a way she could scarcely understand. She'd never experienced such emotions—it had been almost as if she'd become another person.

"In fact..." she added, deciding—oh, what the hell, why not just be totally honest? "Part of me is almost tempted to..."

Next to her, Lynda smiled. "Good. You should."

"Well," Liz reminded her, "I'm still technically engaged to Todd."

Lynda shrugged. "Whether he's banging some high society chick in the back of her Rolls Royce or paying strippers to wiggle around in his lap, we both know he's doing something he shouldn't be, and we both know that once you find out exactly what it is, you're going to dump him. In the meantime, I say all bets are off. If you want to let Jack Wade into your panties, go for it."

Liz cast her friend a skeptical look. "If you haven't figured it out already, Lynda, I haven't exactly had a lot of wild affairs. A few relationships where sex was involved, sure, but..."

"Doesn't matter. All you have to do is follow your urges, honey. It's all good. And if you find out that creep is cheating on you or paying for simulated sex with strippers, you definitely need to let go, let loose, and live it up. Lose all your inhibitions."

Liz wished she were as bold as Lynda. She knew from late night talks over bottles of wine that since Lynda's divorce ten years ago, she'd taken the very advice she was now giving Liz—she'd sought out wild times, wild sex. She'd been with another woman on more than one occasion, she'd told Liz, and she'd even once taken part in an orgy. Each time she'd told Liz one of these stories, Liz had secretly shivered with excitement, wondering what it was like to be that daring.

And Lynda's lack of inhibitions was the exact reason Liz had known Lynda could help her with sexy clothes when she'd wanted to look good to go hire a P.I., and why she knew now that Lynda was the perfect person to fill her in on Bourbon Street's sin dens.

Together, they perused the clubs that lined the street. It was broad daylight and many of them weren't yet open for business, but some had pictures in glass cases outside their doors. The cases displayed photos of naked girls—some had shots of girls kissing and touching each other, and one smallish building even exhibited numerous pictures of a man and woman actually having sex. "They really do that in there, on a stage?" Liz asked, a little taken aback.

Lynda smiled at her naïveté. "There's not much they *don't* do down here in N'awlins, honey."

When they reached Club Venus, Lynda said, "You'll be fine here. It's one of the more sophisticated establishments, basically just a classy strip joint. Pretty girls taking their clothes off for tips, that's basically all you get in here. Well, and lap dances, of course."

"Of course," Liz said, remembering Jack's pictures.

Linda tilted her head. "So, what if you go and Todd isn't there?"

"Simple. I'll tell Jack to go back to the drawing board."

"And what if Todd *is* there? Will you confront him, run out crying, throw a drink on him, what?"

Liz considered the options. "To be honest, I don't really know. I guess I'll find out when the time comes." The truth was, she was still thinking more about watching erotic dancers with Jack Wade than about her anger at Todd, and before she knew it, the moment would be at hand.

* * * * *

The following evening at nine sharp, Jack strolled up Bourbon Street wearing a pair of khakis and a sports jacket. He spotted Liz Marsh from a distance. She stood outside the Blue Moon Cafe looking hotter than the Vieux Carre itself on a ninety-eight degree day. Her dress was the color of warm cream, silky, and it hugged every curve from her breasts to her knee. Like yesterday, her hair fell in tawny waves around her face. And damn, she wore high-heeled, fuck-me-now shoes like the ones he'd noticed on the sexy, dark-haired stripper the other night.

"You're actually going to Club Venus with that hot babe from the other day?" Ty had asked when he'd happened into the office earlier and they'd discussed their plans for the evening.

"It's business," Jack had replied.

"I'd like to have *that* kind of business," his friend had laughed, and had gone on to tell him that if he decided he didn't want Liz that he could pass her right over. He chuckled now at the thought, thinking—*no way, bon ami, she's all mine.*

Not that he had any idea where things with Liz would go. As sexy and inviting as she was, when the shit hit the fan with her boyfriend, she might be too shattered to even think about fooling around with another guy. And Jack was no mender of hearts. He was looking to have a good time with her, not dry her tears. Either way, though, he was beginning to think Liz wasn't all that madly in love with old Todd and that maybe he had a very good shot at getting to know her better.

He approached her with half a grin. "Hello there."

She returned the smile with the same sultry look she always seemed to cast his way. It made him forget about business a little more. "Hi," she said, a sexy lilt in her voice.

Part of him wanted to ask if she even cared about her fiancé, since from where he stood, she looked very ready to have some fun with him, but instead he decided to just see where it all led. "Ready?"

"Yes."

They walked together toward Club Venus, but he warned her to be on guard—if either of them were to see Todd on the street, they'd need to duck out of view quickly.

That didn't happen, though, and they were soon stepping inside. "Enjoy," the doorman said after taking Jack's money, and Jack placed a hand at the small of Liz's back to guide her into the plush room of sin.

The place was more crowded than the other night, because it was later in the evening, and while he watched Liz looking around, focusing on the various stages where the women danced, he slipped a college-aged kid fifty bucks to give up the table he shared with two other guys. It was the same small booth in the back where he'd sat the other night, more secluded than tables closer to the various stages.

He took Liz's hand, motioning her toward the small semicircular booth.

"Like a drink?"

She drew her eyes from the main stage where a buxom blonde had stripped down to a Stetson and chaps, breasts bouncing as she danced, then lifted her pretty gaze to him. Damn, he wanted her—right here, right now. Maybe bringing her here wasn't a smart idea. He'd intended to keep his pants zipped—at least until the case was finished, until he'd proven to her what she wanted to know about her fiancé—but at the moment, he wasn't sure he could stick to his own rule.

"A screwdriver," she said. "Tell them to make it strong."

He grinned. "Gotcha."

As Jack ordered their drinks from a gorgeous young girl in a tiny bikini, Liz kept watching the dancers. She knew she should be looking for Todd, or maybe a guy who looked something like Todd but wasn't him, yet she couldn't pull her eyes from the lush flesh being paraded all around her in the room. She'd felt herself surge with moisture upon first seeing Jack and now she felt it even more; her mound pulsed with heat as she watched the women play with their breasts, teasing the audience by wiggling their g-strings. Her own breasts felt large and achy, and when she dared glance down at herself in the semi-lit room, she saw her nipples jutting out, even through the bra beneath her dress. Of course, the dress was Lynda's, and that meant it was a little snug over Liz's bigger chest, and feeling the fabric stretch to hold her in only added to her arousal.

She and Jack didn't speak much. He paid for both their drinks, asked her if she needed anything else. *Sex*, she thought. *I need you inside me so bad.* But she didn't say that, of course. She just kept watching the girls wriggle and sway and gyrate and tease, watched the breasts and legs and asses parade past her, let herself get drunk on the raw sensuality filling her senses. Before long, her eyes were drawn away from the stage—to darker corners where nearly naked girls danced in men's laps, jiggled their chests before their eyes, rubbed themselves while the guys watched, while *she* watched. The entire room was dripping with undiluted, unrefined sex.

"*Chere*," Jack said.

She looked up at him, let herself get lost in his eyes and felt her whole body melting, wanting to be touched by him, wanting to dance in *his* lap.

"You might want to brace yourself," he told her.

She blinked, the words stopping a little of her sensuous melt.

"I see Todd," he said near her ear. "Over by the bar, along the wall."

Liz looked. She instantly saw Todd, too. A busty blonde, à la Pamela Anderson, hovered over him. She tweaked her nipples and licked her lips while she swayed in liquid rhythm to the music. Todd watched her, looking intoxicated with lust.

"That's him, isn't it?" Jack asked.

She nodded, still watching.

"I'm sorry, *chere*."

"No, don't be. I'm glad I know." Still, she focused on the scene across the room, trying to absorb it. She really *was* surprised Jack had been right—really *hadn't* believed this could be Todd's indulgence of choice.

"I know this must hurt," Jack said. He slid one strong arm around her, gently caressing her bare shoulder.

"No, actually, it doesn't." The words were as surprising to her as they probably were to Jack. She knew she didn't love Todd, probably never had, but she'd still expected seeing him in the act—of cheating, of having a naked woman in his lap, whatever—to inflict some pain. Humiliation. The same embarrassment that had had her dressing sexy to go hire a P.I., the embarrassment of knowing for *sure* she wasn't enough for him. But that wasn't what she felt.

"Really? You're okay?"

She drew her eyes from Todd and the blonde to look at Jack. God, he was hot—he hadn't shaved today, and those dark eyes of his were suddenly so kind, so tender. He actually cared how she felt.

"It's...almost a relief," she told him. "It means...I'm not tied to him anymore. I have no reason to be loyal to him...to feel any guilt if I..." Her voice trailed off, but their gazes stayed locked.

It took a moment before he spoke. "What do you want to do now? Confront him? Leave?"

Practically the same question Lynda had posed, and the answer was one Liz couldn't have predicted. "No," she said softly. "I think I want to stay a while."

Jack looked intrigued. "Why?"

Her breath turned thready. "I want to see more, want to know what it's all about. If Todd can do this, so can I."

He tilted his head. "You're not...tryin' to condone his behavior, are you? Somehow hopin' you'll decide it's all right? Because it's not. Once you commit to a woman, you don't lie to her, and you especially don't lie to her about havin' naked chicks bounce around on your lap."

She gave him a thoughtful look, fascinated. "Why, Jack, I'm surprised. You hadn't struck me as such a...moral guy."

A wicked grin crept across his face. "Don't be too impressed by my morals, *chere*. I'm as much an alley cat as the next guy." The grin faded back to seriousness. "But I'm not married or in a relationship, and that's what makes it different. If I was in a relationship, I'd be honest, about anything and everything."

"So if, say, you and I were in a relationship, and you wanted to come here and get a lap dance, you'd ask for my permission?" The passion in her veins was on the verge of turning her playful, despite or maybe *because* of Todd. She was free now, free to do whatever she wanted, to let go of her inhibitions like Lynda had advised.

"Absolutely," he said, an air of teasing in his voice.

"And if I said yes?"

His voice went low, smoky. "I'd ask you to come and watch."

"And if I said no?"

He leaned slightly closer. "I'd ask you to give me one instead."

She cast a sexy smile. "What time is it?"

He checked his watch. "Almost ten. Why?"

"It's almost time for Todd to leave. He's always home before eleven."

Jack straightened slightly. "And you need to be home before he gets there?"

She shook her head. "No, I just need him to be gone from here, out of my sight, off my radar screen. As for getting home before him—I'm happy to let him wonder where *I* am for a change."

He smiled back, clearly liking her tactics, then sobered. "So, you and this guy—you love him?"

She shook her head. "I thought I did, but that faded. Since then, our engagement has felt almost like an obligation—there's family involved, joint business ventures, you name it. To them, not loving him wouldn't have been enough. I needed a reason, hard evidence, and now I have it because I've seen it with my own eyes."

"Good," he said. "You deserve somebody who can keep you happy."

Her heart warmed a little at the words.

Then, as if almost on cue, the big-breasted blonde extracted herself from Todd's lap across the room, and he stood up. Liz and Jack both watched. Wearing a lecherous grin, Todd gave the girl some money, whispered something near her ear, and started toward the door. For Liz, it felt like being released from jail. Not only did she owe him nothing now, but he was no longer here to watch her if she wanted to play.

"Tell me about a lap dance," she said to Jack. Suddenly, she no longer cared if she didn't appear experienced. Perhaps, she thought, because she also suddenly wanted to change all that, wanted to *get* experienced.

"What do you want to know?"

"How much does it cost? How does it work? Is there touching involved?"

He looked taken aback, aroused, before explaining. "You have to ask the stripper how much it costs—usually twenty dollars or so. You pay the girl, then she straddles you and dances. You can't touch, but she can touch you. They generally don't, but they can."

Jack pointed to a nearby table where a young guy was getting a lap dance from a pretty girl with round, sexy breasts and long brown hair—she looked particularly impassioned by her work.

Together, she and Jack watched and Liz could have sworn her body temperature was steadily rising. The gorgeous stripper leaned down over the guy, teasing him, her beaded pink nipples so close to his mouth that Liz wondered how he kept himself from nibbling on them. The stripper's hips ground into the guy's crotch, making the spot between Liz's thighs tingle hotly.

"Have you had them before?" she asked, still studying the intimate act.

Jack stopped watching the lap dance to look at her. She pulled her gaze from the stripper and met his eyes. "Yeah," he said on a heated breath. "Why?"

"Just curious." She took a sip of her drink and looked back at him, feeling daring, wanting—for once in her life—to just do something she felt like doing without weighing it, questioning it, or worrying about it. "Do women ever get them?"

His gaze remained steady. "I've seen women get 'em on occasion."

"I want one," she said, her voice low.

She could tell she'd surprised him once more, herself, too.

"Really?"

She nodded. Before now, she'd never desired another woman, but sitting here watching them had excited her, made her wonder what it felt like to touch or be touched by another girl, as Lynda had. Of course, Jack had just told her *she* couldn't touch them, but she simply wanted to do as Lynda had suggested and follow her urges, and her urge at the moment was to have a woman's curves hovering over and around her. More than that, her urge was to have Jack watch.

Jack's voice came even lower and huskier. "Did you have a particular girl in mind?"

"Her," Liz said, pointing to the same brunette they'd been watching give a dance at the next table. She looked at him. "Can you arrange it?"

He nodded.

Jack couldn't believe Liz wanted a lap dance. Her voice was so breathy asking him about it, her full lips so pouty and kissable, her eyes so wild with curious passion. As he rose to approach the same hot brunette he'd been aroused by the other night, his cock stood so stiff it was almost painful.

As the stripper finished working over the younger guy, rising off him and accepting her tip, she turned to where Jack stood waiting. "How much?" he asked.

"Is it for you?" she inquired and her eyes told him she wanted him to say yes.

"Afraid not." He pointed toward Liz, gaze focused on the main stage now, where a stripper circled her pole in a Britney Spears schoolgirl outfit. "It's for my…girlfriend."

The brunette offered a small smile that made him think she wasn't disappointed, after all, and that she liked doing women as well as men. "Twenty."

He handed her the money and added, "By the way, she's kind of…a virgin at this."

The stripper flicked pretty deep brown eyes from Liz to him. "Your idea or hers?"

"Hers."

Her smile widened. "Good."

Together, they returned to the booth where Liz waited. Before sitting back down, Jack pulled the small round table back so the dancer could reach Liz.

The stripper looked at Liz like Liz usually looked at him—her eyes brimming with desire. "Hi, my name's Felicia." Her voice was as smooth as silk.

Liz's eyes dripped with sensuality and a hint of uncertainty. "Hi." Her nipples jutted hot and pretty through the slick fabric of her dress.

A new song began, and without further ado, Felicia placed one knee on the seat of the plush burgundy booth next to Liz's hip before straddling her completely. "Just relax and enjoy," she said to Liz, who sank a little deeper into her seat as Felicia began to move.

Wearing only her requisite flesh-colored g-string and another sexy pair of fuck-me heels, she began to grind her pussy in hot, tight circles just an inch or so away from Liz's. She caressed her big, beautiful breasts while Jack and Liz both watched. She tweaked her nipples and swayed them over Liz until they brushed against her chest. Liz let out a small gasp of passion and it was all Jack could do not to take his cock in his hand. Like most guys, nothing aroused him quite like the sight of two girls getting it on with each other, and he thought he'd never seen anything so lush and sensual as the dance taking place next to him.

Felicia wore a dirty little smile, clearly pleased she was having the desired effect on both of them. Jiggling her bare breasts against Liz's once more, the stripper lowered her pussy directly on Liz's and began to grind. Oh yeah, he'd been right—Felicia liked doing girls. Her gyrations were hot and slow and sexy as hell, and Liz was beginning to grind back. While they rubbed themselves together, Liz's eyes roamed Felicia—from her face to her breasts to the bit of fabric stretched over her cunt where it pressed into Liz's crotch. He barely noticed when other guys in the vicinity began to watch, too—he couldn't have torn his eyes from the two women if his life had depended on it.

The grinding of pussies through fabric continued and Felicia now rubbed her breasts flush against Liz's, all while simulating a dance. Liz looked drunk with passion and when Felicia rose to a full sitting position—their crotches still pressed tight together—and began to squeeze and caress her bare breasts, Liz murmured, "Mmm, yes." That's when Felicia lowered her hands to Liz's lovely globes, kneading them as she swayed and moved. Liz let out a ragged sigh and looked down, watching Felicia mold her soft flesh through the dress. Jack could have sworn her nipples popped out a little more and that she worked her hips harder against the stripper's.

But then Felicia began to cool things down, gradually, and Jack recognized the end of the song approaching and knew Liz's pleasure was about to come to an end. Felicia ceased touching Liz's pretty breasts through that creamy dress and resumed kneading her own. Her grinding motions against Liz's pussy lightened, lightened, until finally she lifted herself up, disconnecting their crotches, finishing the dance that way.

When the song ended, Felicia lowered a soft kiss to Liz's cheek then slowly got to her feet. The guys at the next table gave a few low whistles and catcalls, and Jack tried to catch his breath as he tucked another twenty into the string of elastic at the stripper's hip. "Thanks, babe, that was fun," she said to him, then sauntered away across the room.

Jack slowly lowered his gaze back to Liz, who was sitting up straighter now, her breath coming heavy. Jack thought in one way this felt like the calm after a storm, as if Felicia had somehow just rained thick lust down upon his sexy, *jolie* Liz, and then vanished quick as a summer downpour. Only he didn't feel very calm and he suspected Liz didn't, either.

He wasn't going to mince words. "*Chere*, that was the hottest damn thing I've ever seen."

Her cheeks flooded with color. She looked tense, excited, intoxicated. "You liked watching?"

"Oh yeah." He nodded.

Her eyes lit with heat and Jack took it as an invitation. "I liked *knowing* you were watching," she said.

The very words made him want to groan, made the skin around his cock tighten even more. He'd intended to wait 'til her case was done before making a move on her, and as far as he was concerned, it had reached a conclusion a little while ago. Good thing, because nothing could have stopped him from being drawn into the sexual web he felt spinning tight around him. He lowered his voice, leaned in closer to her. "Did you like rubbin' against her breasts? Her pussy?"

The color in her cheeks deepened, but she didn't shy away from the question, keeping her gaze intense upon him. "Mmm, yes. It was...incredible."

"What do you want to do now?" he asked, praying she'd ask him to fuck her.

"I could use a drink," she said. "It's hot in here."

Despite himself, he smiled. It wasn't hot in there at all—unless you were getting a lap dance, he supposed. He flagged over another waitress in a gold bikini and ordered more drinks as he slid his arm warmly back around Liz's shoulder. Just the mere feel of her breast against his side added to the fire coursing through him. He turned and whispered in her ear. "Do you have any fuckin' idea how hot you've got me?"

She pulled back just enough to smile at him. "Mmm hmm."

He lowered his chin. "Did she make you come?"

Her smile softened into something more provocative. "No."

"Were you close?"

She bit her lip, nodded.

A little more blood rushed to his cock. "You want me to finish the job, *chere*?"

She gave a coquettish look. "Not yet."

Merde. Was this woman trying to drive him out of his mind with frustration? "Why?"

She paused, thought. "Because this is the most freedom I've ever felt in my life. I don't want to rush the night. I want to stretch it out. I want to feel *everything* tonight. I want to make it last."

He grinned. "Just because I get you off don't mean the night's over, darlin'. I'd be happy to make you come again and again."

Just then their drinks arrived and Liz took a long sip, turning her attention back to the main stage. Three naked girls stood in an enormous tub washing each other with soapy sponges. She seemed immediately entranced, which did nothing to relax Jack's arousal. He didn't think he could stand it much longer.

Questions swam through his mind. He hadn't misread her, surely? She wanted him as much as he wanted her, didn't she? Yes, she did—he knew she did. Her provocative words played through his mind once more. *I liked knowing you were watching.*

The girls on the stage swayed to music while they washed each other's breasts and stomachs, after which they proceeded to move their sponges over each other's asses and pussies, all the while giggling. Jack reached beneath the table, which he'd moved back in front of them after Liz's lap dance, and found her knee. He didn't linger there, letting his hand slide smoothly up her inner thigh, past the lacy top of a stocking, stopping only when she clamped her legs together.

Her look was scolding but playful. "What do you think you're doing?"

This made it clear—she *was* trying to drive him out of his mind. "Makin' you feel good, *chere*. If you'll just spread your legs a little bit." He concluded with his best wolfish grin.

Her scolding expression didn't fade, but under the table, her legs opened slightly and he slid his hand to the crotch of her panties. The tips of his fingers were instantly damp. He breathed low in her ear. "You're so fuckin' wet."

She kept watching the girls on the stage get their breasts and asses soaped, and simply smiled, enjoying the titillations.

"So fuckin' juicy," he whispered, beginning to stroke her through the wet silk. In response, her legs parted a little more. He took the opportunity to pull the fabric aside and touch her without any barrier. His fingers drifted over light pubic hair before he slid his two middle fingers into her warm slit.

To his pleasure, she let out a small moan at the touch. No one looked and he was glad—he didn't want to break the moment.

"Wider, so I can rub you," he instructed.

She kept watching the soapy female bodies on the stage and did as he said, spreading for him.

"Good girl," he whispered.

Then he stroked into wet, soft flesh and felt even more moisture surge over his fingers. His cock strained so hard against his zipper it hurt. He felt the hard nub of her clit against his finger and worked it in a circular motion. She gasped lightly and he whispered, "Is this the right spot, baby?"

"Unh," she said, still watching the stage.

As he moved his fingers over her in hot little circles, she began to move with him, lifting her hips, thrusting her sweet little pussy forward at his hand.

"I'm gonna make you come so good, *chere*," he murmured near her ear. "Gonna make you come so hard."

She finally stopped watching the show and leaned her head back in passion. The musky, salty scent of her arousal rose to greet Jack as her wetness encased his fingertips entirely. He moved his fingers in smaller, tighter circles over her clit, responding each time she sped up her thrusts or slowed them down. There was more speeding up than slowing down, though, and it didn't take long before her fists curled tight into the plush fabric at each side of her, and though she managed to stay quiet, her cunt clenched tight around his fingers, her breath came hard in his ear, and her thrusts turned nearly jackhammer fast.

"That's right, baby, that's right," he murmured as he watched the ecstasy wash over her face.

Liz felt like rockets were being set off at the juncture of her thighs. The pulses rose like flames inside her, each one higher, hotter, than the last. *God, yes, yes, yes. Mmm. So good.*

When she opened her eyes after the waves of heat and pleasure had subsided, it was like waking up from a dream. Only this wasn't a dream—it had all really happened. She couldn't quite believe how wild she'd gotten, the way she'd followed Lynda's advice so very well.

Next to her, Jack was wearing a sexy smile. Though strippers still shimmied and swayed on all the stages around them, it was suddenly as if Jack and Liz were the only two people in the room. "How was that?" he asked.

The truth was it defied words. "Very...very...good," she finally said.

Wearing a heated grin, he leaned forward until their foreheads touched. "I wanna fuck you," he said softly.

She wanted that, too. So, so much. The orgasm hadn't made her any less eager to have more of him, now. "Where should we go?"

He thought for a moment. "I live at the other end of Bourbon."

That sounded like a long walk, even too long to wait if they took a cab. "Too far."

"My office is a couple of blocks away."

"Okay," she said.

Despite the fun she'd had at the club, she was happy to step outside into the cool night air, on Jack's arm. The street bustled with crowds, people drinking, smoking, laughing. Music blared from open doors of dance bars. Jack took her hand and led her through the people; they walked quickly, and she wondered if he was feeling as frantic as she was, like each second was an eternity, like her pussy was empty and begging for him more with each step. Her *pussy*—she could scarcely believe she'd thought of it that way; it was so unlike her. But the wild events of the night had loosed something new and brazen inside her soul.

She glanced up, drawing his gaze down, and thought she saw the same sense of urgency in his dark, piercing eyes. "*Merde*," she heard him bite off with clenched teeth, and then he was drawing her into an alley, deep, deeper, between timeworn, windowless brick walls, past empty wooden crates, until he finally stopped and put his arms around her, pulling her close against his warm body. "I need to kiss you," he breathed.

That's when it hit her hard—they hadn't even kissed yet. "Please," she said in response and his mouth sank onto hers, molding as perfectly as if they'd been lovers for years. His tongue slipped between her lips and she met it with her own. The kiss was fierce and long, brimming with need, but soon softening into something deep and sensual and swallowing. His body pressed hard against hers—one particular part harder than the rest.

It made her want to touch and explore him and she let her hands roam across his broad back, his chest, his sexy butt. His hands traveled her body, too, caressing her bottom, her back, sliding from her waist up to the sides of her breasts. Ribbons of electricity snaked through her as he caressed them, kneading them just as Felicia had done, but his hands were bigger, stronger, more possessive, and she *wanted* to be possessed by him. His rough massage of her breasts made her unable to hold in her moans, made her yearn to somehow thrust the mounds deeper, harder into his touch.

"I can't wait, baby," he murmured against her ear, dragging kisses down her neck. "Office is too far away."

He pushed one strap of her dress off her shoulder, and she leaned her head back, wanting to make her sensitive skin totally accessible to him. His kisses sprinkled across her shoulder and down onto her chest until he freed her breast from the fabric concealing it. He licked at her beaded nipple, then suckled it, making her moan. Was anyone else around, anyone watching this? She didn't know and hardly cared. All that existed were her and Jack. All that mattered was that she wanted him inside her, deep and long. All that mattered was relieving the needy ache between her thighs. All that mattered was fucking him.

Chapter 3

Still kissing her breast, Jack's hands dropped to her hips, lower, inching her dress up. He had to get to her, had to have her, had to thrust his hungry cock deep inside her before he died of frustration. He leaned her back against the brick wall, found her round ass with his hands, all while he nibbled on her beautiful breast. She was wearing a thong and while he squeezed her ass in one hand, he used the other to pull the elastic from the center. He dug into the panties from behind to find her deliciously wet pussy, and then pushed two fingers up inside her. God, he loved the way her warm passage took his fingers.

She cried out and he moaned. She moved on his fingers, so warm and slick he could barely stand it. From the front, he ground the hard column of his lust against her soft, hungry cunt, his body working from need rather than decision. She rubbed herself against him just as urgently, thrilling him with her aggression. She got wetter and wetter, fucking his fingers, filling him with a gratification that came with getting her hot, keeping her hot.

He shifted the hand on her ass upward, all the way up into her hair, pushing it back, so he could see her face. "You drive me fuckin' wild," he said through clenched teeth.

"Unh!" she cried suddenly, pumping harder against his hand, her sobs of release echoing through the alley and filling him with a supreme satisfaction until they finally faded into the night. God, he'd made her come again, that fast.

"I need you, Jack," she breathed afterward, kissing him as she talked. "I need you in me."

Then her hands were at his belt, his zipper, fumbling, working fast, finally freeing him. He yanked hard on her thong and it tore free. She cried out again and he knew ecstasy was just a heartbeat away.

He thrust his cock into her warm, tight little hole and found heaven. "*Ca c'est bon,*" he breathed. *It's so good.*

It wasn't as if Jack hadn't been with a lot of women. He was about as far from a choirboy as you could get—he was a guy, after all, and he lived in a very hedonistic city. But he couldn't remember a time he'd felt this desperate to have a woman, this needful, this crazy to get his cock inside her. And now that he was there, damn—it was like he'd just won the race, climbed the mountain, reached a place where he belonged.

He fucked her slowly at first, looking down into her big green eyes, whispering, "You're so hot, *chere*. So wet for me."

She looked back, her face weak with passion, seeming only able to whimper the word, "Yes."

"I've wanted you from the first moment I saw you. Did you know you made me hard that day? So hard, baby." He thrust deep into her warm pussy, to make her feel *exactly* how hard she made him. "You got me so stiff that day I had to get myself off, and while I did it, I imagined somethin' just like this—me inside you, fuckin' you so slow, so deep. But it's even better than I was able to imagine, darlin'. So damn good."

He tried to keep their sex slow, make it last, make her feel every inch of him sliding in and out, but his dirty talk had their desire reaching the same fever pitch as when he'd first plunged into her and before he knew it, she was crying out with each deep thrust, and he was matching her groans, and she was so warm and wet around his cock that he knew he wouldn't last long. He pounded into her soft, slick cunt with all the strength he had, wanting to own her—*thrust*—wanting to make her scream—*thrust*—wanting to make her feel thoroughly well-fucked when they were through.

And then with a giant stroke he came—shooting off long and hard inside her and releasing a deep moan into her shoulder, where he buried his head for the length of the orgasm. Ah, *merci, cher petite fille.*

When he came back to himself, he lifted his head, looked down into her eyes—pretty, strangely innocent. He leaned his forehead against hers. "How ya doin'?"

Her voice was light, soft. "Good."

For reasons he couldn't explain, he suddenly wanted to be gentle with her. "Sorry I couldn't make it all the way to the office."

She shook her head. "This was…good." She gave another head shake and laughed. "I'm usually more eloquent, but…"

He grinned. "But I just fucked your brains out so you can't think clearly?"

She returned the smile. "Something like that."

"Come home with me." He ran his fingers through the strands of her silken hair and wondered why he'd said that. He'd meant it—he'd wanted her to come to his place, fall asleep with him—but it wasn't his common reaction to sex, no matter how hot. He was real good at keeping things distant, being aloof. Usually.

"I think," she began slowly, "I should probably go home and...break up with Todd."

"Fuck Todd," he said. "Give him a night to worry."

He gazed down on her pretty face, watched her thinking it over. Finally, she looked up at him. "Do you always invite women you barely know back to your place? I thought guys liked to be careful about that sort of thing."

She was right—guys did. *He* did. Always. Before now.

He told himself this meant nothing, then tilted his head. "Look, I'm thinkin' you don't know this idiot fiancé of yours as well as you thought, and for all we know, he's some kinda maniac. He probably went home a little drunk, and if you come in lookin' like you've been out with some other guy... I just don't think it's a great idea."

Thinking it over, Liz nodded. Jack made some good points. Breaking up with Todd wasn't going to be pleasant, but doing it late at night when she probably reeked of sex, and certainly *looked* like a woman who'd gone out seeking that kind of action, probably wasn't the wisest move. "All right," she finally said.

"We can pick up some donuts at the all-night bakery on the way."

"Donuts?" she asked with surprise, putting her dress back into place while Jack zipped up and tucked in.

"*Mais*, I dig carbs after sex," he said, laughing at himself.

Liz laughed, too. How the hell had this happened? She'd behaved like the total slut she *wasn't*, and still she felt incredibly happy and alive—and this man had even invited her back to his place? As they exited the alley hand in hand, she said, "I don't usually...do the things I did tonight."

"I know," he said as they started up Bourbon.

"*How* do you know?"

"The sexy clothes and sultry looks are very seductive, *chere*, but as the evenin' progressed, your innocence showed."

She protested in mock anger. "I'd hardly call myself innocent."

"Not after tonight," he offered in retort, laughing.

"By the way," she said, "just so you know, I'm on the pill."

Next to her, his eyes fell shut and he looked as if he'd been caught at something. "Yeah, about that." He lowered his gaze to her. "I definitely should have taken the time to get out a condom, but..."

"But what?"

"But my only thought was gettin' inside you as fast as humanly possible."

Her face flushed with heat as her eyes met his.

"Anyway, no worries. I'm safe. I've always been real careful about that sort of thing."

"Up to now, you mean," she said.

He gave her a soft grin. "Yeah, up to now."

They talked more as they walked toward Jack's place and Liz thought of all the years she'd kept this wild, sexual side of herself hidden—perhaps even from herself. Yet tonight she'd driven Jack to the same heights she herself had experienced. She wasn't sure where things with him would go or how long they would last—hell, maybe by tomorrow he'd be ready to say "so long"—but no matter what the outcome, she was incredibly glad she'd found this hot sexy man who could set this side of her free.

* * * * *

Upon reaching Jack's place, they sat out on the wrought iron balcony overlooking the quieter end of Bourbon Street. A sweet night breeze blew over them as they ate the donuts they'd picked up on the way and talked more. Liz used the opportunity to tell Jack a little about her family's expectations and how set they were on her marrying Todd. "Frankly, I think if I'd have moved away from Maryland on my own or with anyone in the world other than Todd, they'd have done everything in their power to make me stay. But since it was Todd's idea, they were all for it."

Jack also told Liz more about himself. He'd been raised in nearby Terrebonne Parish, and his mother was a tenth generation Acadian whose family traced its roots all the way back to French Canada in the

1700's. "My *grandemaman*, she lived in a little house on stilts back in the bayou—couldn't get there without takin' a pirogue. She knew all the old Cajun stories and traditions. But my *maman* wanted to leave the swamps, so she and my dad packed us up and moved us into town."

Jack had trekked to the Big Easy to attend Tulane at the age of eighteen, he then told her, where he'd majored in Accounting. "I loved the city, but by the time I graduated from college, I was disillusioned by big business and decided I wouldn't be happy in the corporate world, so I started my detective agency. Been in the same location since day one. I've got a lucrative business and could afford to fancy things up if I wanted, but I think in a place like the Quarter, people don't always like flash. The tourists maybe, but the tourists aren't the ones payin' my bills. The folks who live in New Orleans are drawn by things that are old and authentic, traditional, so that's how I keep my business."

"What about your parents?" Liz asked, taking the first bite from a big glazed donut.

"What about them?"

She grinned. "What are they like? I told you about mine—controlling and rigid. Tell me about yours."

"Not a lot to tell," he said, tearing a chocolate frosted donut into two pieces. "They divorced by the time I was twelve. I was an only child, and I stayed with my dad. Saw my *maman* on weekends, but she wasn't a typical mom. By the time she left us, she wanted to leave more than the swamps—she wanted to leave Lou'siana altogether. So she took off for New York around the time I started at Tulane, and I haven't seen her since."

Liz was stunned, saddened, but now all the more impressed with Jack's success and obvious sense of confidence. "What did your dad do?"

"Before we left the bayou, he was a fisherman—brought in crawfish and redfish and whatever the restaurants would buy. Later, he started drivin' a bus." He grinned. "Not a lot of dough rollin' in for me and *pere*, but we did all right together."

"See?" she said. "There *was* something to tell."

Yep, Jack thought, there was, but this was a good time to stop. He wanted to be with her, touch her, take her to bed—and yeah, talking was okay, could be a part of that, but not too much. Another rule he lived by. And he might have already broken his rule about sex and clients, but he wouldn't break this one. If his dad had taught him anything, it was about self-preservation, never giving up control. Jack could almost hear his father's voice even now. "You let a woman get to you, son, and you end up without any control, over you, over her, over your whole damn life."

Jack had watched the heartbreak his dad had gone through during the divorce, and though he knew he shouldn't let the fate of one marriage govern his whole life, he had. Because it had been easy. Because Jack had never met a woman he'd had a particularly hard time keeping at a distance. He respected women—hell, he was crazy about women, from their bodies to their brains—but he made it a point never to open up to a woman too much lest she think it meant he wanted a relationship.

And he didn't. Relationships worked great for plenty of people, but he wasn't interested. He liked his life fine the way it was—had always liked it. His job was his life, and *femmes* were like...a hobby, a pastime. If his work was his sustenance, women were dessert.

As for why he'd invited this particular female home with him, it was like he'd told her—it didn't seem smart to let her go home to her fiancé right now. And hell—he wasn't ready to be apart from her just yet, and he didn't think she was ready to be apart from him, either. That simple. Sitting there studying her in the dark, his mind drifted back to the intimacies they'd shared together tonight. God, what a woman. First writhing against that sexy stripper at the club, and then fucking him in the alley. He wasn't sure he'd ever experienced sex so gritty and raw, his desire rising from deep inside him like some twenty-first century caveman. His cock began perking to life in his pants again at the memories.

He got caught grinning at her across the little table where they sat. "What?" she said. "Glaze on my face or something?"

He chuckled his reply. "No, *chere*. Just thinkin'."

She smiled. "Thinking what?" Her naughty expression told him she'd already figured out the answer.

He lowered his chin and hoped she saw the hunger in his eyes. "Thinkin' I want to fuck you again."

She cast a coquettish look, took the last bite of a donut, washing it down with the milk he'd supplied, and quietly got up from the chair where she sat, meandering to one end of the balcony. She faced the breeze, putting her back toward him, and he understood that the simple gesture was an invitation.

Jack approached behind her, stepping up close enough for his erection to rub against her ass through their clothes. She wrapped her fists around the top of the wrought iron railing, waiting.

Reaching around, he skimmed fingertips up her thighs, under her dress.

He leaned near her ear. "Is your sweet little pussy wet for me, baby?"

"Why don't you check?" she whispered, turning her head to draw him into a kiss. As he pushed his tongue into her mouth, he cupped her mound fully in his hand, glad he'd torn off her panties earlier. *Oui*, she was wet, nearly dripping.

He pressed his fingers to her center, where he knew she was pink and aching for him. With his other hand, he reached around to toy with her nipple through the fabric, sliding his hard-on more fiercely against the delicate crack of her ass.

Liz heard her own breath come heavier until she was panting, writhing against him. She wasn't sure she'd ever felt anything so exquisite—every move brought pleasure, from his sweet stroking fingers in the front to his stone-hard rod in the back.

"Fuck me," she heard herself whisper on the breeze.

"Tell me again," he said softly in her ear.

She said it louder. "Fuck me."

She kept moving against his hand, the pleasure there mounting. Was he rubbing her harder or was she grinding more intensely against his fingers?

He didn't ask her to say it again, but she did anyway, wanted to, this time with more force. "Fuck me, baby. Fuck me." His fingers, moving in hot circles, were so good, so perfect; she was getting so close, *so close…* "Oh God, baby, fuck me."

"I'm fucking you with my fingers, *chere*."

She moaned and thrust against his touch, harder, harder, his fingers seeming to sink deeper against her clit as they stroked her—warm, swift, sure. The pleasure grew and gathered inside her, working itself into a hot, tight little ball that—oh God, yes!—finally exploded, breaking over her like a tidal wave, making her cry out over and over, without a thought to the attention it might attract. Each heated vibration was more shattering than the last, so powerful that her body spasmed and if Jack hadn't wrapped his other arm around her waist she might have collapsed on the balcony from the sheer intensity of her bliss.

He kept rubbing her, slowing when she began to slow, letting his fingers go still when she stilled, too. She finally panted her exhaustion, numbly leaning her head to one side when she felt Jack's kisses on her neck. "So sweet, baby," he whispered. "So sweet." Then his voice changed, got deeper, more forceful. "Now I'm gonna fuck you with my big hard cock." And he did—using both hands to slide her dress up to her hips and holding her there while he thrust inside.

"Oooh," she moaned at the entry. God, he filled her. With his...cock. Yes, his cock. Another word she'd never used before, but Jack was changing her, uncovering something in her she'd never known, some part of her that brought the raw and primal to the forefront, that made such words sound as natural and hot and loving as any others.

His voice was back to breathy when he spoke into her ear. "Tell me how you want it."

"Hard," she said. "Fuck me hard." She was getting good at this. Good at saying exactly what she meant, at talking a little bit dirty.

His thin, masculine chuckle was laced with arrogance. "Think you can take it?"

"Oh yes."

And mmm, did she ever take it. Jack pounded into her with hot, powerful thrusts, each one making her release a small cry. She felt each brutal stroke all the way to her fingers and toes. She loved the feeling of being fucked with such primal abandon, loved the way each sweet plunge seemed to fill her with him more and more. Her cries involuntarily turned into a word that came on each thrust. "Yes. Yes. Yes. Fuck me. Yes."

Her legs grew weak with the force of his sex and she gripped the rail even tighter lest she crumble to the balcony floor. Never in her life had a man fucked her with so much power, with such driving force that it seemed to be turning her inside out, numbing her mind to any thought but the pleasure that each deliciously rough stroke delivered. He never stopped, just kept fucking and fucking and fucking her, filling her with his cock again and again, and her pleasure was just beginning to be laced with weariness, a sense that she might soon collapse from the sheer force of his thrusts, when he said, "Baby, I'm comin'. I'm comin' in you."

His deep strokes slowed just slightly as he pumped his release into her, and she almost *felt* the thick pleasure of his orgasm through his long, throaty moans. Finally, they went still together, and he was hugging her from behind, resting his head on her shoulder, whispering, "So good, baby. You're so fuckin' good."

She barely had the strength to reply, but managed to look over her shoulder and cast a small smile before saying, "I'm so fucking *tired*. You've worn me out."

She relished his satisfied little grin. "Mmm," he growled, squeezing her body closer to him, "then let's go to bed."

* * * * *

The following morning, Liz took a taxi to the home she and Todd shared, but she waited until she thought he'd be gone to work. Her biggest fear was that she'd pull up and find him still there, frantic, with FBI agents and SWAT team members and God knew who else, because she was missing. Jack had offered to go with her, just in case Todd *was* still there, but she'd refused. She'd gotten herself into this mess by being a complacent do-gooder for the first thirty years of her existence—now she'd get out of it by taking charge of her life.

To her great relief, when the cab pulled up outside the Greek Revival home, the driveway was empty—Todd was gone. Once inside, she got undressed—very aware that she wasn't wearing any panties—and took a long, luxurious shower. She'd never spent as much time thinking about her body in her whole life as she had the last few days, so while showering, she paid attention to it. She watched the soap sudsing on her breasts, felt her own sensual response as she ran the bar over her smooth stomach, up her arms, down her thighs. She thought about how sticky her inner thighs had gotten at various points last night—both from her juices and Jack's. Suddenly, every touch to her skin felt brand new.

After calling her boss to claim she'd overslept and would be right in, she chose her work clothes for the day carefully, as she had plans to meet Jack for dinner. So while on the outside she wore a conservative plum-colored suit, underneath she put on a lacy demi-bra of lavender along with a matching thong and garter belt with nude stockings.

As she caught the streetcar on St. Charles and took a seat, she felt positively naughty. The sensations of the tight, binding lace beneath her professional clothes felt like a delicious little secret she kept from the other passengers, a secret she couldn't wait to reveal to Jack.

Unfortunately, though, she had a long day ahead before seeing him, so she'd just have to think of it as a reward, something to look forward to. Luckily, she liked her job and thus far had been a model employee, so coming in late today wasn't a big deal. The event she truly dreaded was calling Todd. And she couldn't put it off. In fact, now that the time had come to do it, she didn't want to postpone breaking up any longer—she wanted to close that chapter of her life and get back to having fun with Jack. So as soon as she got caught up on her morning tasks, she picked up the phone at her desk and dialed his office.

Damn, voicemail. But then, maybe that was a blessing in disguise. She hadn't planned to actually break up on the phone anyway, only to arrange a meeting with him. So she said, "Todd, it's me. I need to see you. Meet me at noon today at the Red Rooster." It was a small downtown diner where they sometimes grabbed quick meals together.

At twelve o'clock sharp, Liz was seated in a booth with a cup of coffee. Todd walked in looking hurried and a bit frantic, but she supposed she couldn't blame him, considering that she'd been out all night, had left a cryptic message not bothering to explain why, and that he had no idea she knew about his extracurricular activities.

He spotted her immediately and took long strides to the booth, sliding in and placing both palms on the table, as if to keep his emotions down. "Where the hell have you been?"

"That's not important," she said calmly. "What matters is that *I* know where *you've* been."

His pale brown eyebrows knit. "What are you talking about?"

"I saw you last night, Todd." She kept her voice devoid of emotion, and it wasn't difficult—she suddenly felt so indifferent toward him. She couldn't believe she'd ever agreed to marry someone who clearly held her in such little regard. "I saw you at Club Venus."

His mouth dropped open. He ran a hand back through his hair, took a moment to think. "Okay, yes, I was at Club Venus last night. A little happy hour with some guys from work—no big deal. We finished the project we were working on, so decided to reward ourselves. I was going to tell you when I got home, *but you weren't there*."

Liz released a tired sigh. What a liar. She'd have to be more direct. "Okay, how about this? I saw you pay a woman to dance naked in your lap. And I know that two nights before—and probably *every* night for the last two months—you indulged heavily in that particular pastime. I know because I thought you were having an affair, so I hired someone to follow you."

Now his eyes were as round as plates, gaping at her blankly. She decided to take the opportunity to press onward.

"I'm breaking off the engagement, Todd." She'd taken off her ring before last night, but she'd worn it to work today specifically so she could return it to him. Slipping it off her left hand, she laid it in the center of the table.

"Let me get this straight," he finally said, sounding a bit manic. "You're breaking off our engagement because I've gone to a strip club a few times to unwind after work?" He said it like she was crazy and unreasonable, as if he hadn't lied to her, as if it had indeed only been a *few* times. And as if getting lap dance after lap dance without having mentioned it was a perfectly acceptable way to run an engagement.

"Well, actually, there's more to it than that," she said. "For one thing, I've realized I don't love you, and for another, I've met someone else. But neither of those things probably would have happened if you hadn't started lying about working late so that naked women could wiggle around in your lap, so I guess that going to a strip club to 'unwind' did indeed lead to this."

Todd looked absolutely livid. "You're seeing another man? Cheating on me?"

She gasped her disbelief. "Not before I found out what *you* were up to, so don't act as if you've been wronged."

"Who the hell is it? I'll kill him."

She rolled her eyes. Compared to Jack, Todd was scrawny. "That doesn't matter," she said, getting back her composure. "The important thing is that our engagement is over." She looked at the ring she'd placed between them. "You'd better put that in your pocket before it gets lost."

Todd began shaking his head. "No, I won't accept that ring, Elizabeth." She cringed—she'd always hated that Todd insisted on calling her that, and she suddenly hated it even more now; it sounded so Puritan. "Because we're not breaking up."

Another sigh of exhaustion escaped her. "We just did."

"No, you can't break up with me, I won't let you. We're going to have the perfect life together and I still intend to have it. We'll be fine, you'll see. You'll just have to be patient with me."

She had no idea what he was blathering on about. She shook her head. "What? Patient with you?"

He nodded. "Okay, I'll admit it. I'm having trouble not wanting other women. But you'll just have to be patient while I get those feelings out of my system. That's why I've been going to Club Venus, darling, for *you*. So that I can go into our marriage with a pure heart and won't ever have to cheat on you."

"Dear God." She almost laughed. Did he actually think that explanation would make things better?

Then again, maybe he was so accustomed to the old, complacent Liz that he'd thought he could get away with *anything*.

Well, she was tired of arguing with him about whether or not he "accepted" her breaking up with him. She'd hoped they could have a civil discussion about this, maybe work out living arrangements over lunch, but clearly she'd been too optimistic. "Look, Todd, we're through. Understand?"

He shook his head vehemently. "No, we're not. We're going to have the perfect life, you and I. You're supposed to be my perfect wife."

"What?" she said, confused by his rambling.

"The first night I took you home to meet my parents, my dad pulled me aside and said, 'She's the one, son, the one who'll make a perfect wife for you.' And I realized he was right. You're going to make a wonderful mother to our children, Elizabeth, and you always handle every situation appropriately, and you listen to what I say and do what I want..." His eyebrows knit tightly again. "Or at least you used to."

God, he'd wanted to marry her because she was a doormat. And because his daddy had given her his seal of approval—probably because he recognized what a Stepford Wife she would make, as well. Liz let the tiniest smile leak free, wondering what Todd—or his father—would think if they could have seen her last night. Would they have found it "appropriate" for her to get a lap dance? Would they think it was "appropriate" for her to get fucked on an open balcony for anyone to see while she begged her lover for more?

"You know what, Todd?" she said with a knowing smile. "If you knew the *real* me, you'd *never* want to marry me. So trust me, I'm doing us both a favor."

His eyes clouded with bewilderment. "The *real* you?"

She simply laughed. "Goodbye, Todd," she said, and then she got up and walked away, out of the diner, up the street, feeling the stretch of lace against her skin and the blessed sense of freedom to which Jack Wade had opened her.

* * * * *

That night she met Jack at Pat O'Brien's in the Quarter for dinner. They were seated in the courtyard at a pleasantly secluded table behind the fountain. She sipped on a hurricane as they both ate sweet southern-style slices of pecan pie for dessert, and she told him about her encounter with Todd and what she'd figured out about herself.

"That day when we first met, in your office, I was only *pretending* to be sexy and wild. I was so embarrassed about the idea of Todd cheating on me that it helped somehow if you found me attractive and wondered why he'd do such a thing."

"I've got news for you, darlin'," he replied with a knowing look. "You can't pretend to be sexy. You either are or you aren't. And you definitely *are*."

"That's what I've figured out, I guess." A bit of her old sheepishness tried to sneak in, but she pressed on anyway. "That it *wasn't* just an act, that now I truly *want* to be wild...and I want to take you on the journey with me." She even went on to admit she'd been wearing Lynda's clothes in order to look like someone she wasn't. "But then I discovered that I actually *was* that woman, the wild, seductive one you met."

She hadn't actually *planned* to tell him all this; she just heard herself doing it. Somewhere along the way, she'd started feeling he was very easy to talk to. Jack wore a typical sexy grin as she explained that he was just the man to help her find that wanton, sexual side of herself.

"Can I ask you a question?" he said across the small table. He reached out, giving a soft, casual caress to her hand where it played with the stem of her glass.

"Sure, anything." She had nothing to hide with Jack any longer—and the hurricane was going to her head, making her feel all the more happy and open.

He tilted his head, looking sexy as hell. "What made you want to be with that woman in the club?"

The question—not to mention his hungry look—made her a little wet in her lacy panties. "I suppose it was watching all those beautiful female bodies. Seeing them through men's eyes. Your eyes. I never realized just how lovely women were before, so soft, so curvy and lush. Watching them dance out of their clothes, make themselves so sexual, excited me."

His eyes lit with fire and she knew he liked her answer.

He leaned a little closer. "Wanna know a secret?"

She flashed a wicked smile, nodding.

"I've always fantasized about havin' a woman who wanted to be with another woman that way. A woman who was secure enough in her sexuality to do what feels good. A woman who wanted me to watch." The last word came in a raspy whisper.

His words melted through her like the warm caramel in her pie and she found herself unable to tear her gaze from his.

His eyes glazed with desire. "What do *you* fantasize about, *chere*? Tell me one of your favorite fantasies."

She sighed, thinking. She hated to admit it, but… "Before a few days ago, I'm not sure I really ever *had* fantasies. Or if I did, they were sweet and romantic and…dreadfully average. Sunsets and tender sex on the beach after wine and cheese, that sort of thing."

"And now?" He raised his eyebrows.

She smiled even as she felt a light blush rise to her cheeks. "Well, this afternoon, at work, someone was talking about Mardi Gras parades. And out of the blue, I found myself fantasizing that you and I were naked on a big Mardi Gras float, wearing nothing but glittery masks and beads."

He leaned slightly forward. "Tell me more."

She leaned closer to him, as well. "You were sitting on a red velvet throne."

He chuckled. "It's good to be king."

"And I was sitting in your lap, riding you, and you were kissing and sucking my nipples through all the beads I wore."

She took his silence, together with his intense gaze, as encouragement to go on.

"I could feel all the people watching us, being turned on by seeing me fuck you, by watching me move on you. And at the same time, it felt safe, I felt anonymous, because they couldn't see my face behind the mask, and because we were up above them, on the float. I could tell somehow that they were all as excited as I was and that they wanted me to come. And I could feel the beads—I wore them around my neck, around my waist, around my wrists and ankles—all rubbing against my skin and making it as if I was being touched all those places. When I did come, I screamed, over and over again."

"Just like last night on my balcony," he reminded her with a smile.

"Right," she said. "And the crowd watching the parade cheered my orgasm."

He kept grinning, his chin propped on his fist. "What then?"

"We got off the throne and went to a special sort of platform, also upholstered in red velvet. I climbed onto it, on my hands and knees, and you fucked me from behind."

She thought she saw fresh heat in his eyes when he said, "I'm likin' the sound of that, *chere*. Hot."

"The crowd liked it, too," she confessed with a small smile. "They could see you moving in and out of me that way. They began to throw beads up onto the float in praise. And when I looked out at them, they were all beginning to undress and touch themselves, or each other, while they watched you fucking me." She bit her lip, remembering the fantasy, sinking deeper into it. "And you were fucking me so hard, so good. It made me crazy. I was screaming with each stroke."

"Go on." He wasn't smiling anymore, just looking aroused.

"Well, by the time you came, *everyone* was coming. People in the crowd were moaning along with us. And you were reaching around underneath me, rubbing me…you know, there."

"There," he repeated, gently teasing her. Somehow, those intimate words came easier in her mind than from her throat, she discovered.

She grinned in reply. "Yes, there. And your hand, plus your orgasm, plus watching all the spectators come, made me come, too, really long and hard and satisfying, like nothing I've ever felt before."

The fire in his eyes simmered to a smoldering heat, something quiet but ever so scorching. "*Merde*," he breathed.

She flashed a vixen's smile. "So, what's *your* biggest fantasy?"

He grinned. "I already told you. Meetin' a hot, sexy *petite fille* like you."

She laughed. "You've totally corrupted me."

His eyes narrowed playfully. "You love it."

"Yes," she agreed. "I do."

He shook his head lightly and took a sip of his drink. "Darlin', no one would ever guess that under that prim, pretty business suit—"

"There's a garter belt and lace?"

He lifted his eyebrows in question, and in reply, she crossed her legs to one side, and slowly eased her skirt up to reveal the top of one stocking.

"You been wearin' those all day?"

She nodded.

He leaned closer, clearly ready for more sexy banter. "Did they make you feel hot and sexy while you worked?"

She nodded again.

"Good." Then he lowered his chin lightly. "I can't wait to see *everything* under that skirt. And I'm so damn glad I'm the man who gets to go on this excitin' little trip with you."

She considered her new sexual journey over a long sip of her drink. "You know, I suppose there were hints of the sexual being inside me all along—I just didn't recognize them. I mean, I wasn't a *total* stick in the mud—I *liked* sex before this. I'd just never...had the kind of mind-numbing sex I had with you last night. I'd never...done it someplace where people might see. I'd never...talked dirty before."

He grinned. "Why don't you talk dirty to me some more right now? Why don't you quit callin' your pretty little pussy '*there*' and call it exactly what it is for me?"

"And rush things?" she asked with a playful smile. "No, baby, I don't think so. I think, just like last night, I want to stretch things out and make them last. I'll talk dirty—dirtier than I did last night—when you make me want to."

Damn, Jack thought when Liz rose from her chair and sashayed away to the bathroom. He watched the sexy sway of her ass and murmured under his breath, "What a woman." He still couldn't quite believe she was real. But he was sure as hell glad he'd done whatever he'd done to help unleash the sexual animal inside her.

Now, it was all he could do to sit here and finish his dessert. At the moment, he had no interest in food; all of his interest lay in getting her out of that suit so he could see the sexy lingerie she'd worn for him. He wanted to kiss those pretty breasts he'd gotten only a short taste of last night. He wanted to lick her lovely little pussy dry.

After that, he wanted to fall asleep in her arms, just like he had last night. In a strange way, that had been as good as the rest of what they'd shared—the perfect ending to a perfectly wild evening.

Fall asleep in her arms? Had he really just allowed himself to want that? He'd gone from pussy-licking to *sleeping*? Damn, he must be losing it. Or hell, maybe he was getting old—he wasn't a young kid anymore, and good, hard fucking wore a guy out. So maybe it was natural for falling asleep with a woman to become part of sex now.

Even so, he shook his head. That explanation sounded ridiculous. *Was* ridiculous.

But he wasn't going to let himself worry over something so minor. So he liked falling asleep with her. So he'd liked seeing her sleepy eyes first thing this morning. Big fucking deal. It meant nothing. This was just good, hot fun, nothing more.

By the time she returned from the bathroom, their check had arrived, so he asked her the question burning in his mind. "What now, *chere*?"

She looked primed and ready for action when she gave her head a provocative little tilt. "Why don't we check out the action on Bourbon Street?"

Jack couldn't wait to see what surprises the night held.

Chapter 4

They wandered through the growing crowds just as the evening began to come alive. Every night on Bourbon was a party—neon lights pointed the way into dance clubs and karaoke bars and sex shows and shops that sold colored beads and souvenirs. Every type of music, from rock to blues to Zydeco, could be heard spilling from open doorways. Daiquiri bars offered drinks to passersby who watched mimes and clowns on stilts meander the thoroughfare, which was closed off, admitting only pedestrian traffic.

Just as Liz had never been to this part of town in the daytime until her visit with Lynda, she'd certainly never been here after dark before meeting with Jack the previous night. It was as if a whole new world had opened to her. Jack held her hand as they wove through groups of people, some walking, some just standing around talking and drinking hurricanes or daiquiris or tall glasses of beer.

Although every sight and sound was entrancing, the places that drew Liz's attention the most were the sex clubs. At the door of one establishment, a pretty girl in nothing but a pair of filmy panties and matching bra stood handing out coupons for discounted drinks inside. At another, the windows were shaded but offered strategically placed silhouettes of shapely girls, their curves smooth and bare—one dancing erotically, another gliding back and forth on a large swing. After her unexpected experiences last night, not to mention how excited Jack had seemed by her daring, the forbidden allure of the clubs had Liz's pussy pulsing at a maddening rate.

Just then, her gaze landed on an adult store. Like Bourbon Street's other illicit pleasures, Liz had never had occasion to venture into such a place. "Have you ever been in one of those stores?" she asked Jack, slowing their pace to peek inside. She caught sight of vibrators in packages hanging on the walls and a mannequin wearing bits of black leather.

When he saw where she pointed, he gave a short laugh and she knew her naïveté was showing. "Uh, yeah, darlin'," he said as if it were a given.

She smiled at his amusement. "Well, *I* haven't and I want to go in."

"Let me lead the way," he said, and they entered the wide open doors.

Liz's eyes were drawn to boxes of triple X-rated DVDs and videos—on the box covers, naked women kissed each other or wore leather and wielded whips and chains; on one a cheerleader bent over revealing her bare, shaved mound. Other videos appeared to be for gay men—one pictured two nude, handsome, well-endowed men in a light embrace, their penises touching.

"Have you ever been with another guy?" Liz asked Jack on impulse.

He followed her eyes to the video box, chuckling. "No, *chere*, afraid not."

She looked up at him. "Have you ever thought about it?" After her encounter with Felicia last night, something which had been far more pleasant and seductive than she ever could have imagined, she couldn't help wondering if Jack had ever experienced similar stirrings. Suddenly, everything around her, the very air, seemed weighted with sensuality and she was filled with questions and desires that had never before occurred to her.

He still grinned. "I can tell you want me to say yes, but the truth is, I haven't."

She gave a playful shrug. "Don't worry—I won't hold it against you." She concluded with a wink.

Meandering farther through the store, she stopped by a wall display of glow-in-the-dark condoms; below it were shelves of edible undies and body paints. Without warning, she turned and slid her arms provocatively around Jack's neck, pressing her curves flush against his body. "What if I asked you to?"

His hands snaked around her waist and he laughed. "What?"

She cast a sexy smile and lowered her voice to a hot, husky purr. "What if I wanted you to be with a man while I watched? Would you do it?"

His answer came in a teasing tone. "I don't know. What would I get in return?" His strong touch dropped to her ass and he pulled her in tighter against his solidness. Through their clothes, she felt his cock growing hard against her warm slit.

She gazed invitingly into his dark eyes and licked her lips. "Anything you wanted, baby."

"I've got a better idea," he said, his erection getting more and more prominent.

She had the urge to wiggle against him, but given that they were in a fully lit store with other people around them, she resisted. "What's that?"

"Why don't we quit talkin' about me with other guys and start *doin'*, me with *you*. Why don't we go back to my place?"

The heat in his eyes filled Liz with a new but already familiar power, and she couldn't help brandishing it a little. On a whim, she whirled away, out of his arms, casting a mischievous grin. "Not yet. I'm not quite ready to call it an evening."

He dropped a quick glance down at his crotch. "Well, *I* am."

"I noticed."

"I'll bet you did."

"It'll keep."

"You *hope* it keeps," he laughed.

"I've told you before, I don't want to rush." She took his hands in hers and whispered up to him. "I love the way this feels. Everything I touch, smell, eat, drink, see—adds to my arousal, stretches it out. I want to keep stretching it and stretching it."

His look bordered between entertained and frustrated. "Is this your version of foreplay?"

She tilted her head and flashed a smile. "I suppose."

"All right then," he said, stepping past her to a long wall containing every color, size, and style of vibrator and dildo imaginable. "Let's look at these. Which one would you pick?"

She was embarrassed to realize that just the sight of all those phalluses made her hotter and wetter. Maybe Jack was right—maybe they should go back to his place and fuck each other senseless all night long. Clearly, she was ready to have his long, hard cock inside her.

But no, she'd meant what she said. She wanted to stretch it all out, make it last, see how hot she could get, and then let him reap the rewards.

So she studied the vibrators on the wall and let out a laugh, once again struck by disbelief.

"What's so funny?"

She pulled her gaze from the fake penises to him. "I've never even really seen these things before, let alone used them. And here I am, standing here like a seasoned sex toy veteran, trying to pick one out."

"Well, madam," he said, suddenly pretending to be a store clerk, "let me show you some of our most popular models."

She smiled boldly at his little game. "All right."

"Many women like this simple gold unit. Easy insertion, attractive tool. Some of our more adventurous customers, however, go for this one." He pointed to a flesh-colored vibrator with tiny nubs all over it. "It provides extra stimulation to the vagina's inner walls." He was speaking at a normal level, clearly not caring if anyone heard.

"Go on," she said as if she were nothing more than a discriminating shopper.

"The purists often go for this natural looking one, with realistic head and shaft, and even balls. And then we have this little number—also realistic but with an added feature. This little nub here rubs against your clitoris and gets you off."

"What else can you show me?" Liz asked, practically breathless by now. The very mention of her clit had it practically humming.

"*Mais*," he said, dropping his voice slightly and stepping in closer as if to share a secret, "we do have one more, our best seller, in fact. But not every woman can handle it. It's very big and very powerful." With that, he drew her into a corner, glanced around to make sure no one was watching them, then took her hand and placed it over his cock.

Liz went weak with how large and hard he felt. She realized it was the first time she'd touched him there, even though their intimacies had already gone much further than that. But since they were doing things a little backwards, and a lot hedonistic, she figured it only made sense that this first time she touched him should be in a brightly lit sex shop.

God, he felt big. Definitely bigger than Todd. It reminded her what he felt like inside her, and that she'd known the first moment he'd entered her that he was definitely the biggest she'd ever had, that he was filling her deeper and stretching her boundaries farther than ever before. What she felt through the fabric right now had her heart beating out of control and her cunt throbbing. With her hand hidden safely between their bodies, she stroked her palm upward. He drew in a breath of pleasure as he gazed down at her. Loving that look in his eyes, wanting to pleasure him much, much more, she began rubbing her hand slowly up and down the large shaft. He kept looking down at her, breath grown heavy.

As she caressed him, her knuckles brushed over the front of *her* crotch, as well, sending scintillating little darts of pleasure outward through her whole pussy. "I feel it, too," she said, wondering if he'd understand what she meant.

He glanced downward, past their chests, to where their bodies met, her hand in between, before biting his lip and raising his eyes to her face. "Let me take you home, *chere*," he whispered in a smoky voice.

She wanted him just as badly as he wanted her, but she still resisted with a simple shake of her head. She continued rubbing his cock, lightly grazing her slit with each stroke.

This time he spoke through slightly clenched teeth. "I *said*, let me take you home. *Please*, darlin'."

This time her refusal came with a wicked little smile. "Not yet."

"If you're not careful," he said, his eyes filled with sensual threat, "you're gonna end up gettin' fucked in an alley again."

Her smile widened. "Is that supposed to scare me? Because it's only turning me on more. I *loved* that urgency, *loved* not being able to make it one step farther."

She kept rubbing, aware that it was torture for them both, but still wanting to push their arousal closer and closer to the edge. He narrowed his eyes on her slightly. "No, it's not supposed to scare you. But I wanna take my time with you, baby." He gently stroked his fingers up and down her arms through her suit jacket, soft caresses that tingled from shoulder to elbow. "I wanna go *so* slow, make you feel *so* good for *so* long. And if we don't get to a bed soon..."

"*This* is taking our time. *This* is going slow. Just *my* way."

She watched as he drew in a deep breath, looking as if he was trying to accept the fact that she was calling the shots and he wasn't going to win. Again, part of her wanted to give in—his promises were deliciously tempting. But everything about this public sort of foreplay was so different than anything she'd experienced before that she still wanted to soak up all these new titillations with him, for him. He made her want to try new things while he watched, made her want to tease him—but only because it would make the end reward even sweeter. She knew that by the time they made it to a bed, the things they did there would be all the more exciting and satisfying.

"All right, Miss My Way," he said. "What now? Just stand here and fondle us both to death in front of the vibrators?"

"No," she said, "come with me," then she abruptly separated from him and drew him by the hand out of the store and back onto rollicking Bourbon Street. Only now it felt different, the air even more supercharged than before. She knew it was only her, only her body responding to what they'd been doing in the store, yet still she reveled in it, and wished she could bask in the hedonistic feelings even more. Though the cut of her suit jacket showed her shape and her skirt was fairly short, she wished she was wearing something sexier, skimpier. All this freedom made her want to show her body off the same way she had the other times she'd seen Jack.

Without delay, she led him back to Club Venus, just a few doors down.

"Do you have somethin' specific in mind for why we're here, or are you just..."

She smiled up at him. "Following urges," she finished for him, loving how much he'd tuned in to this new, reckless side of her. All her life she'd been a planner, but for once, she *liked* not knowing for sure what would happen to her behind these doors tonight.

Inside, the scene was much the same as the previous evening—lush, shapely women did sexy dances in various states of undress while lusty-eyed men took in their every move.

It was Friday night, though, so even more crowded—no tables were available and many men watched the action while standing. Jack led Liz to an empty spot where he leaned back against a wall and wrapped his arms around her from behind. When she settled against him, that glorious erection of his eased into the crack of her ass. She couldn't help looking over her shoulder at him and exchanging a private little smile. Like back in the store, she felt the overwhelming urge to rub against him, wanting to feel him even more, but she resisted—for now, anyway.

When she turned back to watch the strippers, Jack leaned down to whisper in her ear. "Tell me which ones you find most attractive."

She cast a sideways grin. "Why?"

He returned it. "Because I dig it when girls like other girls. I can't help wantin' to know exactly which women do it for you."

As Liz studied all the beautiful, sexy strippers shedding their clothes to reveal tantalizing curves, Jack pulled her even closer, snuggling his cock tighter into the valley of her ass. One arm wrapped full around her, beneath her breasts, pressing warm against the bottom of them. His other hand caressed her hip in slow circles that grew wider until each revolution brought his palm over one side of her ass then nearly around to her crotch. Lord, she wanted to wriggle against him—the little fissure of her asshole had never felt more sensitive.

But no—stretch it all out, she commanded herself. Experience *everything*.

"Well?" he said. "Which ones?"

Finally, after taking long, slow looks at each of the women performing for them, Liz made her selections. "Felicia," she said, pointing to a stage where the stripper danced in only a white micro-miniskirt and towering strappy shoes, caressing her ample breasts, rosy nipples hard and pointing.

"And, I suppose, that girl." The second pick had been difficult—most of the women in Club Venus were stunning—but Liz had chosen a petite blonde with slender hips and breasts that were smaller than Felicia's but still round and pretty with pale pink crests. The red Spandex dress she'd once worn was now gathered around her waist as she moved sensually around a brass pole in matching red heels.

"Nice choices," he purred in her ear, and she thought how strange it should feel to be telling a man which two *women* she was most attracted to, but with Jack, it was easy. He accepted this brazen side of her even more effortlessly than she did, and it made exploring this new facet of her sexuality all the more sweet.

Just as the current song came to an end, Jack eased himself out from behind her. "I'll be back in a minute, darlin'."

"Where are you going?" she asked, but he was already gone. She instantly missed his nearness, but figured he was headed to the bathroom or the bar. As a new set of girls took to the numerous stages sprinkling the room, Liz watched and enjoyed, but she really wanted Jack back. Somehow, watching the female entertainment wasn't as arousing without him there behind her, watching with her.

A short moment later, he appeared back at her side, taking her hand. "C'mon. *Allons*."

He wasn't pulling her toward the door, but deeper into the club. "What's going on?" she asked, following. "Where are we going?"

He stopped and looked back at her, a wholly sexual expression etched on his handsome face. "*Mais,* little Miss My Way, I decided *I'm* takin' charge for a while."

"What did you do?"

"I got you a surprise," he said, leading her farther.

Up ahead, she noticed doors marked "Private Dances," and at that very moment, Felicia and the blonde slipped inside one of them. Liz's heart rose to her throat. Despite last night, she wasn't sure about this, hadn't planned on doing anything with anyone here but Jack. And yet…hadn't the unknown beckoned to her when she'd entered Club Venus a little while ago? Hadn't not knowing for sure what to expect made her all the more excited?

"What did you do?" she asked again when they stopped just outside the door.

He cast a wicked grin. "Just told 'em what I thought you'd like."

Liz's stomach went hollow with a combination of excitement and fear. Even after last night, what lay inside seemed so forbidden.

"By the way," Jack said in a low, sexy voice, "in here, you can touch 'em back."

Every nerve in her body seemed to prickle as she looked up at him. "I'm nervous."

The tilt of his head seemed almost scolding. "You? I don't believe it. I don't think you have a nervous bone in your body."

"I was beginning to think I didn't, either. But everything else that's happened has been so spontaneous, with no time to think. And this seems…so orchestrated." Liz couldn't be sure what she was afraid of. Was it because there were two women instead of one? Or because they were both so gorgeous—was she intimidated?

An expression of concern took over Jack's handsome face. "I thought you'd be into this. But we don't have to go in there if you don't want to, *chere*."

Suddenly, she felt like he'd picked out a gift for her and she didn't like it. The fact was—she might love it, she just wasn't sure yet. She braced her hands against his chest. "Tell me something. Will it excite *you*? Will it do as much for you as it probably will for me?"

He looked incredulous. "You have to ask?"

She nodded earnestly.

He ran his hands up her arms, stopping at her shoulders. "Baby, it'll excite the holy hell out of me, probably more than anything ever has." He stopped and took a deep breath, and it was clear the very idea was heating him up.

And that was all Liz needed to know. One look into those dark, passion-filled eyes and she was more than ready to discover the pleasures that waited behind the door. Knowing it was as much for his delight as hers took away all her fear, even turned her eager. In one sense, she knew Jack so little, yet in another, she trusted him, and she wanted to share pleasure with him so much that it felt like they'd been together for a very long time. "Then I want to do it."

He used the crook of one finger to lift her chin. "Are you sure?"

She nodded and felt the fresh excitement rumbling in her chest. "Very."

Twisting the doorknob, she walked into the room, which was small but even more plushly furnished than the rest of the club, with a rich burgundy sofa and chair, expensive-looking lamps, and mirrors all around, on both the walls and the ceiling. Both girls sat on the sofa and smiled when Liz and Jack stepped inside. They'd put their clothes back on—the blonde in the skintight red dress that stopped sinfully high on tan thighs and was thin enough that her nipples jutted prominently through the fabric. Felicia wore the white mini and a small white Spandex blouse that tied in a knot between her bulging breasts. Both of them looked like sex on a stick.

"Hi there," Felicia said, tilting her head as she gazed into Liz's eyes. "I think we met last night."

Liz nodded. Her breasts felt heavy, her pussy tingly, as she remembered how intimate she'd been with this woman just twenty-four hours earlier. "Yes."

"I'm glad you two came back for more," she said, then motioned to the other woman, who looked like a living Barbie doll. "This is Morgan."

Morgan nodded hello, a sensual little cat's smile on her red lips.

Rising to her feet, Felicia took Liz by the hand and urged her to sit down on the couch between the two women. Jack took the chair a few feet away. Liz's entire body pulsed with anticipation.

Reaching toward a small sound system on a table at the sofa's end, Felicia pushed a button, releasing soft, sexy music into the air. Only then did Liz realize she could no longer hear the sounds of the club outside the room, that the space must be soundproofed, which made it seem even more private.

Turning to Liz, Felicia licked her lips, painted a pale, sexy pink tonight. Her eyes brimmed with seductive fire. "Just sit back and relax, sweet thing," she said. "Let us do all the work."

Liz's heart seemed to lurch as Felicia reached for the opening of Liz's jacket. She hadn't worn a camisole underneath, so the suit jacket was fastened from her chest to below her waist. One by one, the sexy brunette undid the buttons.

When they were all free, Morgan slipped the jacket off from behind, the move revealing Liz's lacy lavender bra. The cups, cut to cover only from the nipple down, held her large breasts high and firm. "Pretty," Felicia whispered, her gaze on Liz's chest. Then Felicia gently dug her fingers in both cups and flicked them down just enough that Liz's nipples popped free. The quick touch had felt like a delicious lick of flames and Liz's cunt reeled. The simple act of having her breasts exposed to the three other people in the room thrilled her deep in her womb.

Pushing to her feet, Felicia began a slow, sensual dance only a few feet in front of Liz. Liz watched each move of Felicia's delectable body, getting caught up in the liquid motions, drunk on the steamy rhythm. From the corner of her eye she saw Jack watching the scene, and feeling his eyes on her increased the tempo of the heartbeat throb in her pussy.

From behind her came Morgan's tender touch—feathery fingers on Liz's shoulders eased her back into Morgan's soft arms. Liz let herself settle there, relaxing, basking in the softness of another woman. Felicia's dance grew more provocative—she ran her hands over her breasts and round ass, and she teased Liz with the temptingly short hem of her tight little skirt. Morgan's arms settled briefly around Liz's waist, but soon her hands rose to gently cup the bottoms of Liz's aching breasts, and then her thumbs began to play over Liz's hard, pointed nipples. Waves of pleasure washed over her cunt like a tide coming in and out, in and out. The delightful sensations echoed from her breasts through her entire body.

Every ounce of her being was caught in a deep, languid pleasure and the whole time, even as she kept her gaze rooted firmly on Felicia's dirty dance, she kept thinking, *Watch me, Jack. Watch me.*

Finally, Felicia teasingly undid the knot on her top and cast it free so that her big, lovely breasts were bare for both Liz's and Jack's hungry eyes. Felicia ran slender fingers over the two perfect orbs, then down over her smooth stomach and still swathed hips. Morgan kneaded Liz's breasts now, full in her small, soft hands, and Liz heard her own breathy sounds, heavy and weak.

It was at this point that Felicia pulled a simple ladder-back chair from a corner of the room, turned it around, and straddled it. The move made her skirt rise to her hips, revealing that she was naked underneath—no g-string. The vision of her shaved slit, opened slightly, revealing a bit of pink, was electrifying.

Next, Felicia resumed her sexy dance on the chair, pussy gyrating hotly as her breasts jiggled. Her expression said she was as turned on as Liz, just like last night.

Finally, Felicia abandoned the chair, but her stretchy skirt remained high on her hips so that she was effectively nude. She approached the couch and bent over, reaching for the side zipper on Liz's skirt. She slid the zipper down, reaching to tug at the skirt's hem. Liz lifted, letting Felicia pull it off, leaving her in only her lavender lingerie.

Felicia's hands glided from Liz's knees up over the tops of her stockings and garters, past her hips and tummy, not stopping until both she and Morgan were fondling Liz's breasts. Liz watched their hands mingling there, Morgan firmly kneading and massaging, Felicia toying with her nipples, raking her fingertips over the hard beads, then pinching them and gently pulling at them, driving Liz wild. Liz spared a quick glance to her lover in the chair a few feet away to find his eyes glued on her, his gaze lust-filled.

Next, Felicia climbed onto the couch, straddling Liz's hips and beginning to dance, as she had last night. Her pussy—now tantalizingly bare and smooth, large pink clit peeking from between the folds—hovered just above Liz's scant lavender panties. Liz's breath came even heavier; she was nearly panting...and *wanting*, so badly wanting the woman who lingered seductively over her nearly naked body.

And then Felicia sank her pretty cunt down onto Liz's lace-covered one and began to grind. It was a grand relief to finally feel the weight and pressure of Felicia's body where Liz burned and ached the most. Her pussy had gotten so very swollen and wet, desperate for stimulation, and now the dark-haired stripper was rubbing against her, riding her, taking her where she needed to go. Liz didn't hesitate to push back, working her mound against Felicia's. So intoxicated on sex that she no longer thought, only felt, Liz reached up for Felicia's breasts.

Round and soft in her hands, she squeezed and caressed as Felicia rode her and massaged her breasts, too. Liz twirled Felicia's nipples, hard and erect between her fingers, following the urge to sit up slightly and rake her tongue over one beadlike crest. It felt like a pearl on her tongue, so innately feminine and sensuous. Both women purred and Liz did it again, this time to Felicia's other breast.

The sensuous stripper moved her pussy in hotter, tighter circles and Liz matched her, getting closer and closer to the edge. When Felicia leaned low over her chest, raking her bare breasts lushly over Liz's, it happened—the climax shot through her quicker than she'd expected, making her cry out in joy and relief.

The orgasm had been so long in coming that it was especially thick and intense. Each wave of pleasure engulfed her entire body and sent a fresh surge of moisture to her swollen mound. She pumped at Felicia's pretty cunt, each thrust pushing their breasts gently together until Felicia spasmed, too, crying out in passion, and Liz knew she was coming, as well. They moved together, their rough lunges hard, hard, hard against each other, before slowly becoming softer, lighter, until their grindings were so delicate they were almost beginning to excite Liz all over again.

She flicked her gaze to the man a few feet away. Their eyes connected with beams of pure liquid heat. Her orgasm had been a hundred times more incredible knowing Jack was there, watching her come, watching her writhe against another woman.

Finally, Felicia backed off Liz and both let out slow sighs of recovery. Liz sat up and turned to find Morgan, still completely dressed in her tight mini, looking just as beautiful and sexy and only slightly spent. It gave Liz an idea. Jack had just given her an astounding gift, something she never would have experienced any other way, and now she wanted to surprise him, too.

She leaned up to whisper to Morgan. "Dance for him."

Morgan's pretty blue eyes met hers, shining with uncertainty.

"Start out just dancing, stripping, and then give him a lap dance. Whatever you feel like doing—okay?" Liz said.

So as the music continued playing, Morgan rose up on her incredibly high heels, stepped over to where Jack sat, and began to sensually sway her curves directly in front of him. He flashed a quick glance to Liz and she smiled, saying, "*I'm* back to taking charge again."

"Mmm," he said, and clearly understanding he was supposed to sit back and enjoy this, he turned his eyes on the delectable Morgan as she slid thin red straps from one shoulder, then the other, slowly pushing the dress to her waist. Liz thought she enjoyed looking at Morgan's pretty pale breasts as much as Jack did.

Soon Morgan was easing the already ultra-short hem of the dress upward until it revealed that, like Felicia, she wore no panties, no flesh-colored g-string like out on the floor. A tuft of pale brown hair floated above a smooth-shaven pussy that she settled over Jack's crotch.

Liz hadn't been certain how she'd feel watching another girl give Jack a lap dance, but she quickly discovered that she *loved* watching her man receive the pleasure she'd decided he should have. He refrained from touching Morgan, keeping his hands gripped on the arms of the plush chair, but let his eyes slide up and down her body as she worked over him, caressing her own breasts, gyrating her hips.

Next to Liz on the couch, Felicia lounged comfortably, half lying down, lightly touching herself as she watched, raking her fingertips through her naked slit. Her eyes went glassy as she licked her full upper lip. The lush, erotic vision stole straight into Liz's pussy, making it pulse with excitement again. God, the forbidden pleasures she was experiencing with Jack, *because* of Jack, were almost overwhelming at moments, leaving her to wonder how much exhilaration her body could handle.

As she shifted her gaze to the sexy lap dance, her breasts turned heavy, missing Felicia's stimulation and compelling her to reach up and caress them herself. She massaged her soft globes and twirled her nipples between thumb and forefinger, all while she viewed the sexy lap dance. A glance from the corner of Jack's eye told her the sight of her touching her breasts upped his excitement.

Morgan continued to dance on Jack's lap, heated gyrations that crushed her crotch against his cock, firmly rubbing, raking over the length of the column Liz could see outlined through his pants. Jack looked fully intoxicated with lust as he watched the stripper grind against him. Although his only thrusts against her were small, gentle, his knuckles had gone white on the arm of the chair and Liz suspected it was all he could do not to push back harder. His soft, low groans added to the tension gathering and swirling in Liz's pussy as she continued to tweak her nipples, mold her breasts. She wondered how long he could last, and just when she was sure he would come, he placed his hands at Morgan's hips and gently eased her back from his erection.

"Stop," he whispered, breathless, looking up into the blonde stripper's eyes. "This is incredible, but I don't wanna come." He shifted his glance to Liz. "I wanna save it all for you, *chere*."

Chapter 5

By the time Jack and Liz caught a cab to his place at the other end of Bourbon, his senses were on overload. She continued to blow his mind with her eager willingness to please them both in such hot, sexy ways. He hadn't been lying when he'd told her watching her with two women would excite him more than anything ever had—that's exactly what had happened. But he was glad his instincts told him that at the end of the evening, she'd want only him—and he was glad when she'd finally suggested going back to his place where they could be alone.

He thought of the things they were doing together sort of like a backwards meal. The activities they'd just indulged in were like eating dessert first, and the part that was coming now, him and her alone together, was the important part, the real meal.

As the cab took off toward his apartment, the old buildings and wrought iron gates and balconies moving past in a blur, she slid up next to him in the backseat. Her hand grazed up his thigh and onto his crotch, where his perpetual hard-on continued to strain against his zipper. Ah, *oui*, he thought as she rubbed his cock. Sweet heaven. But not as sweet as it was going to be soon. He leaned his head back against the vinyl seat and basked in her caress.

Then he returned the favor, slipping his hand under her short purple skirt. He wasted no time finding her crotch, covered by the soft lace he'd gotten to see back at the club. He sensed her parting her legs, heard her release a sigh as he raked his fingertips up, down, up, down, against the sexy lace. Her cunt felt swollen to him, from so much excitement, and even though he hadn't thought he could get any more heated up than he already was, he did.

He could hear her breathing now and wondered if the cab driver heard it, too. *Merde*, they had to have looked like exactly what they were when they'd climbed in the cab—a couple of frantic, sex-crazed lovers racing home to fuck. He leaned over, whispering lower than low in her ear. "Soon. Just me and you."

She answered with another hot sigh, a sexy smile in the dark.

When the cab stopped outside his building, he tossed a couple bills to the driver before following his lady in plum through the archway to the courtyard that led to his place. He liked that she knew the way, that she'd been here before and felt comfortable enough to head toward his door as if she belonged here.

Her heels clicked up old wooden stairs ahead of him, and God help him, his cock throbbed so intently he was tempted to grab her hips, spin her around, and do her right on the steps. Instead, he settled for a few sexy pats on her lovely ass, which was eye level with him as they headed for his second floor apartment.

When she reached his door, she murmured, "Hurry."

"I'm way ahead of you," he said, jabbing his key at the lock.

The door fell open with both of them practically leaning on it. Together, they barreled into the living room, heading straight for the bedroom.

"Take your clothes off," she commanded.

"I'm gettin' there, *chere*, I'm gettin' there." But he was glad she wasn't planning to waste anymore time with titillation, so he yanked off his shirt, letting it drop on the hardwood floor before starting on his belt.

She'd crossed to the other side of his bed and stood smiling at him as she unbuttoned the same suit jacket she'd already had off for her sexy encounter with Felicia, let it slide from her shoulders, then tossed it on a chair in the corner. Her beautiful breasts looked ready to spill from that skimpy bra.

"Keep going," she said when he paused to study her.

He released a short laugh. On her demand, he undid the belt, released the top button of his pants, and carefully unzipped, aware that her attention was focused on his erection. He let the khakis fall to the floor as well, then stepped free. He wore black silk boxers, not his usual underwear of choice, but it had proven a good one this evening because they'd been much less confining and had surely let each of the women he'd come into contact with tonight feel his hard-on better than they would have with briefs.

"You, too," he said when she didn't move.

She unzipped her skirt and let it drop, and there she stood, same as at the club, in that pretty little garter belt and tiny scrap of panty, only this time, it was just for him. "You're a sight to behold, darlin'."

She licked her lips, pointing at his shorts. "Next."

He gave her a devilish grin as he hooked his thumbs in the elastic at his hips. "Waitin' to see somethin' special, *chere*?"

She chuckled and said, "You know I am. Let me see it."

He obliged, ridding himself of the boxers so he stood before her completely naked, his cock at full attention, reaching past his navel. From the look in her eyes, she was well-pleased. "See somethin' you like?" he teased.

"Oh yes," she purred, her eyes still glued to his erection. Then she pointed. "On the bed. Now."

He hadn't quite decided yet if he was going to let her keep bossing him around, but for the moment, he obeyed, lying down atop the comforter so she could keep enjoying the view.

He enjoyed a view of his own as she walked around the bed, heels clicking, to his side. Then she started climbing up onto the mattress, clearly intending to straddle him. That's when he decided. No. He was taking back control of things, right now. There were certain things he wanted to do to her, and he was going to do them, damn it. "Not so fast," he said, raising a knee to stop her progress.

She looked stunned. "What do you mean?"

"We're gonna play things *my* way for a while."

Despite his words, she kept trying to climb on top of him until they were engaged in a small struggle. "Wanna play rough, do ya, *chere*?" he chuckled as they wrestled. But he couldn't get the upper hand while lying down, so he sat up, got to his feet, and tussled with her until he could close his hands on her waist, pushing her back to land in a small easy chair. He dropped to his knees in front of her and thrust his body between her thighs. They were both panting as he looked into her eyes. "I do like your spirit, darlin', but you best not bother fightin' me, since I'm gonna do exactly what I want to you and there isn't a damn thing you can do to stop me."

Her eyes blazed with passion and he felt her struggle against his hold once more.

He only chuckled. "Save your strength. You'll need it."

She sighed and finally relaxed in his grasp.

"That's a good girl," he told her, sliding his hands up, raking his thumbs across her nipples. She shuddered. "That's a real good girl."

Looking into her eyes, he was bitten with the overwhelming urge to kiss her—everywhere. Lips, breasts, sweet little pussy. But he decided to start at the top, leaning in and lowering his mouth onto hers for a long, slow, steamy tongue kiss that had both their hearts racing by the time it was done. "Haven't kissed you enough," he told her, all traces of amusement or triumph gone. "And haven't seen nearly enough of these pretty breasts, either, but I'm gonna remedy that right now." With that, he used his fingertips to lower the lace that barely covered her nipples until her soft flesh spilled out in hot, beautiful abundance.

It was the first time he'd seen her lovely breasts fully revealed. They were beautifully large and round, pale but for the pink crests that looked as hard as two rosy pearls. He ran his tongue over one erect nipple while he took her other breast full in his hand. The feel of that hard bead on his tongue was incredible, made him want to lick her again and again. Above him, she was letting out hot, pretty sighs that fueled him as he moved to the other sweet breast, licking and laving. He soon found himself sucking her nipple, slow and gentle at first, then he drew it deep into his mouth with more abandon. She held his head while he sucked on her, ran her hands through his hair, over his neck and shoulders. Hot little panting breaths escaped her and she arched her back, pushing her breast harder into his mouth. He sucked even deeper, making her cry out, and then he softened his ministrations, releasing her beaded pink flesh to flick his tongue quickly back and forth over the taut peak.

He could have spent hours playing with her perfect breasts, but his cock throbbed almost painfully now, after all the excitement it had endured tonight already, and there was still more he had to do before he came.

So he released her nipple from his mouth and kissed his way gently down her stomach as she watched.

"You have great breasts, *chere*," he purred in between kisses. "Touch 'em for me. Like you did back at the club."

He looked up in time to see her give her lip a provocative little bite as she took them in her hands, rhythmically kneading and caressing their weight, her dark pink nipples peeking between her long, slender fingers.

"Mmm, *oui, ca c'est bon*, just like that."

He didn't stop kissing when he reached the lavender garter belt—he kissed across the lace, down onto her lower tummy, and then onto her tiny panties. Her body was all stretched out for him and she was panting harder, beginning to moan when his kisses passed over her hot, passion-engorged slit. He could smell her sweet, salty juices and knew how soaked those panties had to be.

Part of him wanted to tease her, torture her—God knew, he'd felt tortured enough tonight—but he didn't want to keep them both on the edge forever, and if there was one thing he wanted to do, it was lick her pussy.

He reached for the thin straps at the side of her panties and slid his thumbs underneath. She lifted slightly and he rolled them down, glad she'd thought to put them on over the garter belt. Patiently, he eased them over the lace tops of her stockings, down to her ankles, and over the heels of her shoes.

But he didn't feast on her right away. First, he pushed her legs wide apart and simply looked at her there. Her sweet little cunt was wide open for him, all slick and pink and ready. The sight nearly made him shiver. He traced one finger down the edge of her pussy's outer lip. "You look all swollen down here."

"I feel that way, too," she said breathily. "Tingly. Heavy. Like my pussy weighs more than usual."

He grinned up at her. "Say that again."

She returned a vixen's smile. "Which part?"

"Just the word 'pussy.' I like to hear you say it."

"Pussy," she purred for him.

"What a *bad girl* you are," he teased her in a scolding tone. He still ran one fingertip up and down her fleshy outer lip.

"A few minutes ago you said I was a *good* girl."

"When I'm kneelin' between your pretty thighs, *chere*, it means the same thing."

Jack couldn't wait another minute before finally tasting her. He dipped his head, spread her legs even farther, and dragged his tongue over her clit, which was equally as swollen as the rest of her cunt. A ragged moan escaped her lips. Then he closed his mouth over the pink nub, sucking it just as he had her nipple a few minutes earlier.

"Unh..." she moaned above him.

He released her clit and looked up at her. "Hold yourself open for me."

She bit her lip before doing as he asked, using the fingertips of both hands to spread her pussy so that it was wide open, wet pink flesh exposed.

"Oh yeah, baby," he murmured, bending to drag a long, firm lick from her parted inner lips up to her clit. "*Cher jolie* pussy."

"Oooh."

He did it again, and again, licking up her sweet juice, absorbing her taste and scent until it was all he knew. Then he pulled back, noted how open her little hole was, and pushed two fingers inside. "Oh, oh…mmm, God," she whimpered above him as he moved his fingers in and out, softly fucking her. "Oh, more," she murmured, so he added a third finger and fucked her with them harder as he resumed tonguing her sweet, swollen clit. She moved against his mouth, soft, then more urgently. He laved her as roughly as he could, aware she was growing hotter and hotter beneath his ministrations. "God…oh God…yes, baby…lick my pussy, lick my pussy…oh yes, lick it, lick it."

Jack didn't mind following her commands this time—he happily lapped up all her sweet fluid, wanting to make her come so good that she'd never forget it. He drove his fingers into the sopping wetness of her opening over and over in rhythm with the movements of his tongue on her clit. Harder, harder, harder, and above him she kept whimpering and sighing her hot demands. "Lick me…oh God, yes, lick me more."

He licked her again and again, felt her passion growing, tightening, felt her literally fucking his mouth with the thrusts of her pelvis, and basked in the feeling until finally she said, "Oh yes, now, baby, now—I'm coming for you," and her moans got higher in pitch, her movements more jerky, her pussy convulsing against his tongue in sweet pulsing waves. Her expression stayed wrenched with ecstasy as she rode the orgasm out, whimpering, groaning…until finally she went softer, quieter, and he released her from his mouth and rose up into her arms.

"How was it?" he whispered a moment later.

"Mmm," she moaned. "Incredible."

"Better than with Felicia at the club?"

She laughed. "Jealous?"

"Hardly. I just like to think I can do more to keep you happy than some girl you don't know."

She smiled into his eyes and he realized they'd actually known each other only a few days. And why the hell did he care whether he or Felicia had given her a better orgasm? Ego, he answered himself quickly. Just ego.

"Don't worry," she said. "Because what you did to me just now..."

"*Oui*?"

Her next words came on a pretty sigh. "I've never felt *anything* so good in my life."

He let an arrogant smile unfurl on his face—he couldn't help it. "Well, *chere*, get ready for the next best thing." Then he lifted her legs over the sides of the chair, spreading her wider still, and rose up to join her, planting his knees at either side of her raised thighs. Sliding his shaft over her wet pink flesh just once, he then thrust it deep inside her.

"Oh, God," she whimpered again.

He leaned in close to her face. "You like that, darlin'?"

"Unh," was all she seemed capable of saying.

"Want more?"

"Mmm. Please, baby."

Surprised by the tender begging, he granted her request with pleasure, sliding his hard cock in and out of her tight opening. The position they were in allowed them both to look down to where their bodies joined and watch his length glide in to the hilt, then halfway back out.

"Look how wet you get me," he said.

So wet that each time he moved in her, they could hear it.

"Can you fuck me harder?" she purred.

She sounded so tender now, gentle as a kitten. "I like it when you ask sweet like that, darlin'," he said, "so get ready to take as much as you can handle."

He made good on the promise, increasing the power of his strokes, pounding his cock into her juicy cunt until she was crying out with each hot thrust, screaming so intensely that, if he hadn't seen the ecstasy on her face, he'd have wondered if she were in pleasure or pain. He drove into her relentlessly, never stopping to give either of them a rest, half-amazed that he could keep going this way as close to erupting as he'd been so many times tonight. He fucked and fucked and fucked her, his cock seeming to grow ever more rigid, his balls slapping against her until his pleasure was so deep, so replete, that he finally gave it up. "Damn, baby, here I go," he breathed, and then he felt himself shooting inside her, emptying long and hard as a ferocious moan left him. As his entire pelvis spasmed in climax, he lost himself in the total bliss that overtook his body, and then finally he came back down to earth, feeling so weak he sank into her arms like a baby, both of them lying half in and half out of the chair now.

"*Merde*, you're so damn good," he breathed, letting his head rest on her breast.

Sleep was swallowing him already when he heard her say, through a fog, "Let's get in bed."

Oui, good idea, his sleep-hazed mind thought, although it was a struggle to physically make it happen. When he collapsed on the mattress, he had just enough strength to pull her lush body to his. "I wanna hold you," he heard himself whisper, and then sleep took him away.

* * * * *

Liz woke up the next morning, fully aware that she lay in Jack's bed naked. Waking these last few mornings had been sweeter than ever before, since she'd never felt so alive, never understood until now the depth of pleasure sex could bring.

He lay next to her sleeping peacefully, his hair tousled against a sage-green pillowcase, his jaw covered with dark stubble. She enjoyed just watching him like that, so at rest. She also enjoyed knowing he was just as bare as her beneath the sheets. Seeing his body for the first time last night had nearly taken her breath away. She'd known instinctively he had an attractive physique, but the picture in her imagination hadn't compared with the real thing. His arms, legs, chest, and stomach bore the toned muscles of a man who kept in shape. A light smattering of dark hair covered his chest, narrowing into a thin line that led all the way down to his beautiful cock.

Admittedly, Liz had only seen a handful of penises in her life, but Jack's was the most commanding, the most tremendous. She'd known already that his was the largest she'd ever had—but now that she'd gotten to feast her eyes on it, it confirmed the knowledge that no man had ever filled her so completely, both in width and length. Just lying in bed now, remembering the sight of it, made her pussy tingle.

It was Saturday, so she thought of waking him for a morning quickie, but decided to let him sleep. The last few action-packed days and nights had her much more weary than usual, so she suspected the same was true for her lover.

Instead, she looked around the room, soaking up the man through his possessions and home. High ceilings and hardwood floors dominated the whole apartment, complete with moldings that looked old enough to be original. She could somehow smell the history here, sense the French Quarter all around her. Feeling wanton, she wondered how many couples had fucked in this room over all the years it had been here. She wondered how much pleasure had been experienced in the very place where she lay.

Just then, a large male hand brushed over her inner thigh and glided upward until it cupped her mound, which shuddered with unanticipated delight.

"I thought you were asleep," she said, at once parting her thighs and turning her head on the pillow to look at him.

A lazy grin spread across his handsome face. "Just my way of sayin' good mornin', *chere*."

"Mmm," she purred as he began to lightly stroke her, "what a nice way to start the day."

"We still haven't done it in a bed, ya know. Wanna give it a try?"

She began to move against his touch. "I was actually starting to think about taking you into the shower and having my way with you *there*."

He looked sleepy but aroused. "Want me to wash you?"

A few minutes later they were standing under the warm spray and he was making good on his promise. He had the perfect accessory for shower play—a hand mitt that made lots of suds when soaped. Joyful tremors rippled through Liz's body as she watched him pass the soft mitt over her breasts, leaving running trails of soap, then drew it down between her thighs, where the suds and the mitt and the pressure of his hand behind it all worked together to get her hot and tingly.

When her body was thoroughly soapy, Liz took the mitt from Jack and returned the favor. She ran it over his broad chest and washboard stomach before wrapping it around his beautiful cock, which was once again standing at attention for her. "*Merde*, you'd better be careful, darlin'," he said on a light groan.

"Why?"

"You're playin' with fire down there. Seein' you all wet and sudsy has me just about to blow already."

As much fun as she was having, and as much as she liked his cock all soapy, she stopped immediately—because she didn't want him to come without being inside her first.

He reached out to knead her breasts, the soap suds running between his fingers as she moaned. Her skin was so slick, easy for his hands to glide over—one hand slid down her side to her hip, and then between her legs. When he slipped his middle finger into her slit, she nearly collapsed with the jolt of pleasure he delivered.

"Good," he said with a sly smile. "You're just as hot as I am."

She simply moaned in reply and the next thing she knew, he was kissing her—long, steamy meetings of tongues that she felt all the way to her fingers and toes. "I want you," she heard herself whisper unplanned between kisses. "I want you inside me, Jack, so much."

With that, he turned her around in the shower and placed her hands on the tile wall. "I want you, too, baby," he murmured into her hair. "Damn, how I want you. Now just close your eyes, and feel."

She followed the instructions, clamping her eyes shut, and became aware that he was rubbing his cock up and down in the crack of her ass. Before the last few days, she'd never realized what an erogenous zone that was for her, but she pushed against the pressure he delivered and soaked up the sensations.

Placing his hands on her hips, he guided his hard-on inside her—one long, slow stroke that filled her completely, stretching the boundaries of her pussy.

"Ah, Jack," she breathed. "So big. So good."

"Mmm," he growled. "I love slipping my big hot cock into your tight little cunt, *chere*."

She groaned in response, turned on, as usual, by his dirty talk.

As he began to slide in and out of her, she felt it everywhere, her entire body reacting to each hot thrust. Then Jack's right hand snaked around her, his fingers going straight to her sensitive clit. "Unh," she moaned as the pleasure deepened, rocking her back and forth, back and forth; it was everywhere.

"I wanna make you come," he said low and hot.

"Oooh," she breathed in reply—it was all she could get out. His fingers stroked where she was wet and excited, and his long shaft sent shock wave after shock wave of delight through her body. The heat inside her was rising, rising, seeking that sweet release, when Jack shifted his other hand from her hip slightly back, beginning to stroke the little fissure of her ass with his thumb. Oh God, it sent a whole new flood of heat through her body and she began to whimper, "Oooh, yes, baby, yes."

And then he was more than stroking; he was slowly easing his thumb inside, opening her, entering her through a new little hole. Liz could barely comprehend the added pleasure, the sense of being doubly fucked, of having so many good, hot invasions of her body at one time. As she moved against his cock, she now also moved against his thumb, and the near-ecstasy was electrified by this new intimacy.

Waves of heat radiated out through her clit, the sensations wildly intensified by the sweet pressure in her ass. So powerful, so unstoppable. And then—oh God, yes—his entry in that second hole pushed her over the edge. The climax broke hard and fast and furious, her whole body pulsing with nearly violent spasms that left her so overwhelmed she nearly crumpled to the shower floor. But Jack held her up, held her steady through the consuming pleasure, his arms tight around her waist now as he continued to move his hot column in and out of her wetness in long, deep strokes.

As her orgasm faded to contentment, though, his thrusts grew stronger again, harder, pummeling her pussy with drive after drive of his big cock, filling her, making her scream with each powerful stroke. And then he moaned, deep and low, and she knew he was coming, too—he fucked her faster, even harder, groaning his powerful release near her ear and filling her with satisfaction to know she'd taken him there.

Finally, he went still, just holding her around the waist as they both panted their relief, and Liz murmured, "Thank God Todd has a thing for strippers. Otherwise, I'd never have met you—I'd never have found out exactly how good sex can be."

* * * * *

Once the mind-numbing fun in the shower had ended, Liz had to face an unpleasant task. "I need to call my parents and tell them I broke up with Todd," she explained to Jack over the breakfast of bacon and eggs he'd whipped up. He wore a pair of cotton drawstring pants and she'd donned one of his t-shirts so they could sit out on the balcony and enjoy the morning air.

He looked up after shoveling a forkful of eggs into his mouth. "Haven't done that yet, huh?"

She gave him a chastising look. "When would I have had time? I've been at work every day and with you every night." Then she sighed. "It was nice not to have to think about it, nice to have you to take it off my mind. But today's Saturday and I'm going to use the weekend to get my life back in order."

"Back in order how?"

She took a sip of orange juice and wished uselessly that *this* was her life. This balcony overlooking this historical, legendary street of sin. This man who fucked her so well and then even fed her so well afterward. It was a fleeting, silly thought, so she pushed it from her mind. "Well, besides making that phone call, I need to move some of my stuff out of the house. I called Lynda from work yesterday, and she's offered to let me move in with her, so that's a good solution for now."

Jack nodded. "I agree—I'm glad to see you gettin' outta there. That guy rubs me the wrong way."

Liz shook her head. "He's not a horrible person or anything. He didn't take my decision well the other day, but I guess it was a shock to him. Now that he's had some time to absorb it, things will probably go smoother from here on out."

Jack looked doubtful. "I hope you're right." He finished a strip of bacon, looking at her across the table. "If you need a lift, I can—"

"Not necessary," she said. It was a nice gesture, but she was a big girl and she didn't want to begin depending on Jack too much. The truth was, it was a little scary, the feelings she'd developed for him over the past days. And she certainly didn't need to risk him thinking she was going to be needy, or clingy. Unfortunately, she'd been down that road before, with other guys, and it never ended well. She and Jack had fucked each other's brains out these last couple of nights, but it hadn't come with promises and she thought she'd do well not to expect any. "I'll grab a cab."

As they kissed goodbye at Jack's door a little while later, Liz couldn't help noticing that it was perhaps the most tender kiss they had yet shared. Jack lifted his hands to her face and gently lowered his mouth over hers. "You're sure you don't need any help gettin' your stuff out of the house with that guy there?"

She nodded. "He might not even be home. Sometimes he plays racquetball on Saturday morning."

"All right," Jack replied. "But since your day doesn't sound like much fun, why don't you come back tonight and I'll make dinner for you. We'll try somethin' different and stay in."

She grinned. "You're just afraid that if we hit the streets, you'll get all hot and ready to fuck me and I'll stretch it out again, make you wait."

He answered with a smile. "I thought I proved to you last night that you don't always get to be the one in charge, *chere*."

She acted playfully smug. "We'll see about that."

He kissed her again, then whispered low and sexy in her ear. "*Au revoir* 'til tonight."

* * * * *

An hour later, Liz sat in a claw-footed chair in Lynda's parlor—an old-fashioned name for a fittingly old-fashioned room. The front room of her friend's historic home was done in burgundy and goldenrod, and filled with elegant antique furniture.

"Pardon me for saying," Lynda began with a tentative grin, "but you look like a woman who's seen a lot of action lately."

It wasn't hard to discern why. Glancing down at herself, Liz saw yesterday's suit, marked with more than a few wrinkles, and one of her stockings now sported a long run. She raised her eyebrows. "Caught me in clothes I've been wearing for a while. And...which have also been off of me at several points in between," she added with a naughty grin.

"You were in such a hurry on the phone yesterday," Lynda said, sitting down on the settee across from her, "that I didn't get to ask you how things are with your sexy new man, but I take it this means you've gotten up close and personal."

Liz couldn't help letting out a bark of laughter. Talk about an understatement. "You could say that."

"And *you* could give me some details. Come on, girl, spill."

Liz barely knew where to begin. The last few days had been a whirlwind and felt more like a few weeks. She looked into her friend's eyes. "Lynda, we've done *everything*." Then she shook her head. "Wait, no, that's not true—there's still plenty we haven't done yet—like have sex in a *bed*, for instance. But we've done so many things that are so wild, it feels like we've been around the world and back together."

Lynda looked positively riveted, leaning forward in her seat. "Go on." She made a rolling motion with her hand.

Again, Liz hardly knew how to describe what she and Jack had been sharing. "It's been so...*dirty*," she said, "but so incredibly *good*."

Lynda grinned. "I'm liking the sound of this."

"He turns me into an absolute animal. He's made me want to do things that had never even crossed my mind before."

"Like...?"

Liz let out a sigh; she felt overcome just trying to sort through it all. "Like...be with another woman."

This made her friend smile. "Ah, so you've discovered the joys of feminine flesh."

It still embarrassed Liz a little, even though Lynda, of all people, could understand. "I suppose," she began uncertainly. "Although it's not as if it happened in any sort of...natural way. It was in Club Venus. Let's just say I've had a couple of very intimate lap dances since I last saw you."

Lynda's eyes widened. "Damn, honey—that's impressive. But, uh, just how intimate?"

Liz swallowed. "One of them was with two girls. In a private room. Clothes came off. There was...touching...and rubbing...and coming." Liz felt a familiar heat rise to her cheeks.

Lynda gave an incredulous blink. "My, my, it does sound like you've been a naughty girl indeed."

"But you know what I've discovered?"

"I can't wait to hear."

"That it's mostly about him. Wanting to share these new experiences with Jack. Wanting him to be a part of it, even if that's just watching. The thing that got me hottest with those strippers was knowing he was watching every second of it and that it was exciting him as much as it was me."

Lynda gave her head a thoughtful tilt. "Call me crazy, but something about that almost sounds...romantic."

Liz nodded. "I know. I'm not sure when my lust for Jack turned romantic, but that's how I feel. Attached to him. This fast." Although she preferred not to think about that, since it was scary.

"Then the question is—is he attached to you?"

"Oh, he's very attentive to my needs," she began, laughing, realizing that she meant both in bed and out.

"I'll just bet he is," Lynda said with a chuckle.

"And in his way, he's quite a gentleman. As far as I can tell, he's interested in letting things continue as they are for now...but a guy like Jack wanting something long-term with someone like me, someone who started playing very racy little sex games with him the moment we met...I just don't see it. I think he's a decent man who's happy to have a good time with me, but...I can't imagine him seeing me as anymore than just a wild fling." And it was good she understood that from the start. In past, pre-Todd relationships, it had seemed that every time she fell for someone really hard, it was a death knell. She just had a habit of ending up with men who didn't want to commit, and Todd was another prime example, even if his feelings had come out in a different way.

"Maybe so, maybe not," Lynda said. "Either way, I think you should play it for all it's worth, honey. Clearly, you've got some sexual needs that haven't been getting met, so I say you let Jack Wade meet them for as long as he's willing."

Liz smiled. "I don't think I could resist him if I tried. And by the way," she said, "I have you to thank for most of this."

"Me?" Lynda lifted one hand to her chest.

Liz nodded. "You told me to just let go, to follow my urges, and I took that to heart. Every time I questioned something I wanted to do, I did what you told me, just let go. And because of that, I've had some experiences I never would have if I'd been acting like my normal, conservative self."

Lynda cast a sincere smile. "Glad I could help, honey. Now, tell me about Jack's cock."

Liz let out a cackle. "What?"

"Ever since I met him I've had the notion that that man would have a big, beautiful cock and know exactly how to use it. Was I right?"

"Do fish swim?"

* * * * *

A little while later, Lynda showed Liz to the bedroom that would be hers while she was there. Fortunately, the room had a phone. She took the opportunity to tell her friend she was going to finally break down and call her parents.

Lynda shut the door on her way out to give Liz some privacy.

And although she was dreading the discussion, she discovered as she dialed her parents' number in Maryland that she no longer felt like the namby-pamby pushover she'd always been with them.

Her mother picked up on the second ring. "Hello."

"Hi, Mom, it's me."

"Liz, your father and I were just talking about the wedding. Now that you and Todd have had a chance to get settled in your new jobs, it's really time you two lovebirds pick a date and start making plans."

Great. "Look, Mom, I have something important to tell you about Todd."

Her mother dropped into worry mode. "Is he all right? Nothing's happened, has it?"

Both questions were debatable, but Liz decided to stick to the script she'd created in her mind. "Mom, a few nights ago I discovered Todd has been lying to me for nearly two months. Instead of working late all those nights like he claimed, he was really going to a strip club and...paying to go into private rooms with the strippers."

Saying something like that to her ultraconservative mom had been challenging, and now her mother stayed silent, not responding.

Liz took it as her cue to go on. "I originally thought he was cheating on me, but I think this is just as bad, maybe even worse. When

I confronted him, he told me he's still attracted to other women, and apparently, can't resist acting on it. So...I've broken up with him. The engagement is off."

Finally, after another long pause, her mother found words. "My God, Liz, are you sure this is true?"

She took a deep breath before answering. "Yes, because I saw it with my own eyes."

"Well...perhaps you two can work through this somehow. Maybe counseling? I hear many couples find counseling helpful."

Although one part of Liz had been certain her parents would be horrified by Todd's deception, another part of her had almost expected this. Her mother was in denial, just as Todd had been when she'd broken up with him, so she kept things simple and to the point. "No, Mom, it can't be worked out. Things are completely over between us. I know this will make for an awkward situation with his parents, but you and Dad will just have to deal with that as best you can. I can't be expected to marry a man I don't love, a man who lies to me, just to keep the families happy."

On the other end of the line, her mother let out a long sigh. "Well, this is a lot to swallow, Liz."

"Believe me, I know." *And I can't imagine your reaction if you knew what* I'd *been doing over the last few days.*

When her mother still seemed stuck for words, Liz took the initiative to end the conversation. "Listen, I'll give you some time to fill Dad in, and then we can talk again. Fortunately, we don't yet really have any specific wedding plans to cancel, so that's a blessing. Basically, we can all just go on with our lives. Hopefully, Todd's parents will see the sense in that and it won't cause any business troubles."

"Liz, does this mean you'll be moving back home?"

The question took Liz's breath away. It was a natural one under the circumstances, yet it hadn't once occurred to her to return to Maryland. In fact, she'd enjoyed being in New Orleans more the last few days than she had the prior six months since her arrival. Summoning her voice, she said, "Um, I'm not sure yet, but...I might stay here. I'm starting to like it here."

* * * * *

"Want me to go with you?" Lynda asked when Liz announced she was going next door to pack her things. "He's home, you know. His car's in the driveway. I just checked."

Liz appreciated the offer, but turned it down. "I can do it myself. And I wouldn't want him to think I was the least bit intimidated by him, because I'm not. Besides, maybe he'll be calmer about this now that a little time has passed."

"If you're sure," Lynda said. "But remember, I'm here if you need me for anything."

Liz thanked her, then steeled herself and walked boldly out the door toward the house she'd recently just begun thinking of as home. It was bigger than they needed, and more ostentatious, but Todd had wanted it and Liz couldn't deny its appeal. It was a lovely place. Strange, she thought, approaching the front door, for awhile she'd actually envisioned herself raising children in this house. At the moment, children were as far off the radar screen as Todd himself. It was as if her entire world had somersaulted, but she wasn't sorry. She didn't miss her plans for the future; in fact, she was rather enjoying the unexpected, the thrill each new day suddenly held. Her experiences with Jack were molding her into an almost entirely new person—a person she liked much better than the old, go-along-with-what-everyone-else-wants Liz.

That thought strengthened her resolve as she let herself in.

No sign of Todd yet, but the scents of coffee brewing and bread toasting told her he was likely in the kitchen—that he'd slept late and was just now starting the day even though it was after noon. It occurred to her that if she were quiet enough, she might actually manage to go upstairs and pack what she needed without even running into him. Even if he *was* calmer now, it wasn't as if she really had anything else to say to him. With that thought, she slipped off her heels for quieter travel, heading for the steps.

Once upstairs, she changed into fresh undies, a short, casual skirt and a stretchy pullover top. Then she found a large duffle bag and filled it with clothes—work clothes, casual clothes, shoes, underwear. She made a point of taking every ounce of lacy lingerie she owned, and the few sexy nighties she possessed, as well—thinking they'd come in handy with Jack. Just the thought of him fueled her, made her realize how anxious she was to get out of this house, how anxious she was—already—to see him again tonight.

Moving into the bathroom off the master bedroom, she packed cosmetics and toiletries, everything she'd need to get by until a more official move could be arranged. Returning to the bedroom, she knelt to put the items in her bag, zipping it shut. Turning, she found Todd standing in the bedroom doorway.

His eyes were bloodshot—a hangover, she guessed. He wore old gym shorts and a t-shirt that told her she was right about him just now getting out of bed.

"I wondered when you'd come back," he said, sounding smug and cold.

"Well, as you can see, I'm leaving again already. I just came to get some things. I'll arrange for movers to get my furniture and other belongings soon."

Todd simply shook his head, as if she were a child who just wouldn't behave. "Dear, sweet Elizabeth. I can't believe you're persisting in this charade about leaving. We both know you're not going anywhere." He took a step toward her. "We both know you're going to forgive me and we're going to move on like this never happened."

The strange tone of his voice warned her she should probably be feeling a little frightened of him, but anger was the emotion that filled her at the moment. "I don't know why *you* persist in thinking I would stay with you. The truth is, Todd, this isn't just about the strippers and the lying. The truth is...I don't love you anymore." She shook her head in reflection, then spoke quietly. "I don't know if I *ever* really loved you. And I'm pretty sure you don't love me, either, or there wouldn't *be* any strippers or lying."

His back went rigid and his eyes filled with rage. "Don't say that!" he barked. "Don't say you never loved me! Who's lying now, Elizabeth? We both know you love me, we both *know* that. And I won't tolerate this sort of insubordinance." He'd started moving toward her as he spoke, grabbing her arm. "Tell me you love me. Say it. Now."

My God, he really *was* a madman. How had she not known? He hovered over her as she tried to calculate the smartest way out of this.

"Look, Todd, I don't mean to hurt you," she began, speaking gently, "but—"

"If you value your right hand," a commanding voice suddenly said, "you'll remove it from her arm right now."

She looked past Todd to see Jack a few feet from the doorway, wearing an expression that said he was deadly serious.

Todd looked up, and blessedly, released her from his grasp. "Who the hell are *you*?"

"Not that it's any of your business, but I'm her new boyfriend." He looked past Todd to Liz. "I thought you might need some help gettin' your stuff. I saw your friend Lynda out in her yard and she said I should come over."

Clearly neither Jack nor Lynda thought she could take care of herself with Todd—and maybe they were right. She couldn't have been more relieved to see Jack. "Um, thanks. Yeah, I guess I could."

Jack took a menacing step closer to Todd, who appeared nervous but was trying not to let it show.

"Listen, you shithead. You and Liz are over. Finished. History. And if I find out you do *anything* to bother her, you'll answer to me. And I promise you won't like it."

Todd swallowed visibly, but didn't answer.

Jack looked to Liz, then her duffel bag. "Is this it?"

"For now," she said.

He picked it up and used his other hand to grab hers. "C'mon. *Allons*."

She followed him down the stairs and out the front door.

Only when they'd passed the row of hedges that separated Todd's driveway from Lynda's yard did he stop walking and look at her. "Are you all right?"

She nodded, feeling much calmer now that he was here.

"Are you sure?"

"Yes, I'm fine. But…thank you. What made you come?"

He cast a disparaging glance toward the house she'd shared with Todd until the last few days. "Call it a P.I.'s instinct. Like I told you before, I had a bad feelin' about that guy. My gut just told me maybe I should come over and make sure he wasn't givin' you any trouble. And it looked like I showed up right on time."

Liz let out a sigh and admitted the truth. "I suppose you're right." Still, she struggled to look strong—because she wanted to *be* strong. "But now that I'm out of the house, things will be fine."

Jack continued looking skeptical. "The more I think about it, I don't know that I like you livin' right next door to him. The guy seems a little unhinged to me."

Liz simply shook her head. "He doesn't even know I'm staying with Lynda. Now that you showed up, in fact, he probably thinks I'm staying with you. So even though I'm right next door, that shouldn't be an issue. Todd and I tend to come and go at different hours, and Lynda even has an extra space in her garage where I can park my car, so he won't see it."

Jack didn't look the least bit won over, his expression still stern. "Are you listenin' to yourself, *chere*? Havin' to worry about hidin' your car and makin' sure he doesn't see you comin' or goin'? Maybe you should come stay with me."

Chapter 6

Liz was both touched and stunned at the suggestion. Yet even as wonderful as the invitation sounded, it didn't seem feasible. Despite how intimate they'd gotten so quickly, they'd only known each other a few short days. To move in with him seemed like…trapping him. She didn't want to put him in the awkward position of having to continue their relationship when the time came that he'd rather cool things off.

And it seemed dangerous for *her*, too—for her heart. With each passing hour, she was forced to realize she was developing real feelings for Jack. She'd originally thought—perhaps even hoped—that her new sexual awakening had been *only* about sex, had allowed her *not* to get emotionally involved, but it wasn't true—she cared for him, a lot. She still had no idea how long he'd want their affair to continue, but when the time came for it to end, it would be a hell of a lot easier if she *wasn't* living with him. Having to pack up her things and leave would be much more painful than just saying goodbye—or as Jack would phrase it, *au revoir*.

"Jack, that's very generous of you, but don't worry, I'll be fine at Lynda's." *And this way I'll save myself some awkwardness and heartache in the end.*

Jack struggled for what to say as he peered down into eyes made emerald by the bright March sun overhead. One part of him wanted to persist, get her as far away from her former fiancé as possible, and get her closer to him. But apparently he was the only one of them having those kinds of emotions here, experiencing a real connection, and maybe, all things considered, that was best. After all, he couldn't believe he'd so easily asked her to move in with him. He'd never lived with a woman before. He'd never even wanted to.

He supposed it was time he faced facts: this woman was different.

In the short time he'd known her, he'd witnessed in her so many elements: the ability to be both strong and tender, wild and innocent. At least he had the feeling she'd started out somewhat innocent, even if that had changed over the past few days. She was everything he thought a woman was supposed to be: gentle, provocative, kind, and...hot as hell. All that and they laughed together, too.

Would she control him in the way his father had warned against? Hell, maybe she already was. Didn't she consume his thoughts, night and day? And if she left him now...well, he wouldn't think about that.

"*Mais*, whatever you think is best," he finally replied.

What he *would* think about, he decided, was Todd. He definitely didn't trust the sleazy guy now, and if he found out the jerk so much as *looked* at Liz again, he'd have to take some kind of action.

"I gotta take off," he continued, "but I'll see you tonight. Despite all the fun I've been havin' with you, *chere*, I still got a job to do."

She tilted her head. "On Saturday?"

"My work isn't exactly nine to five."

"Ah, I forgot." She grinned. "I hope I haven't kept you from any late night stakeouts."

"Darlin', *you're* the only thing I want to stake out lately."

* * * * *

Early that evening, Liz stepped out of the shower at Lynda's house, looking at herself in the mirror as she patted her skin dry with a towel. Her cheeks appeared slightly flushed, her lips perhaps more naturally colored than usual. Her breasts felt achy and her nipples stood erect, pink and swollen, above the concave of her waist. Backing up slightly, she studied her pussy, thinking of Felicia's bare, smooth cunt hovering above her, then grinding into her, last night. How incredibly raw and real and sexual it had looked without any hair hiding it. How prettily on display.

Reaching for the bag of toiletries she'd carried into the bathroom, Liz found shaving cream and a pink disposable razor. A sense of arousal gripped her, her cunt almost quivering inside, anticipating what she was about to do.

Spraying a white ball of foam into one palm, she gently smoothed the cream over her pussy in a sort of U-shape, deciding that, like Felicia, she'd leave a thin strip of hair above her slit. The look of Felicia's cunt had pleased and excited her so much that she wanted to do hers exactly the same way.

She'd never have dreamed shaving could be an erotic experience, but the knowledge that she was preparing herself for Jack, along with the sensations spiraling through her sensitive flesh, left her practically dripping by the time she'd carefully shaved herself bare but for a thin triangle of tawny pubic hair extending up from the very top of her cleft. After removing the excess bits of shaving foam, she reached down to let her fingertips glide over the outside of her pussy—she felt smooth, slick, and sexy for Jack. Then she looked at it in the mirror, letting the sight of her freshly shaven mound send a thick bolt of excitement through her.

Returning to her room down the hall, Liz chose a filmy dress with a loose, flowing skirt and thin shoulder straps, the fabric variegated shades of blue. She left off a bra and panties, and as she drove toward Bourbon Street she felt sizzling and sinful thinking about the one other thing that was missing, too. When she shifted in her seat, she could feel the faint sensation of her smooth cunt rubbing against her dress and basked in the feeling of bareness beneath the thin sheath. She even found herself wishing the dress were shorter so she could touch herself as she drove—she'd loved the sensual feel of her nude pussy against her fingertips earlier.

Soon enough, she told herself as she waited at a light, her cunt pulsing madly, Jack would discover her little surprise and give her all the touching and kissing and fucking she could handle.

* * * * *

As promised, Jack had spent the day hard at work on a couple of cases that had recently landed on his desk. He'd gotten a few leads on some stolen jewelry that the police had been unable to recover, but on the other case, an embezzlement, he'd hit nothing but roadblocks. And each time he ran into one of those damn roadblocks, it was all too easy to let his mind drift…to sweet Liz.

It had been satisfying to get some work done, but the hours went too slow. He'd wanted to see her. He'd wanted to peel her clothes off and get more of her. He'd wanted to suck on those luscious nipples and lick that lovely little pussy, all while she moaned and sighed above him.

Yep, looked like he had it bad, all right. The more time that passed, the less he could deny it—she was consuming him. And maybe he was a fool, but he didn't even think about trying to fight it. Even as he thought he'd be smart to slow things down with her, a much bigger part of him, including his cock, knew he couldn't resist his urges where Liz was concerned.

Of course, it wasn't just his dick talking here. It was his heart, too. Damn, his *heart*? The woman had him thinking like a lovesick teenager, but there it was—his heart nearly burst in his chest when she came to mind. When he put that reaction together with what stood so rigidly between his legs, he couldn't do anything but ache to see her again tonight.

Soon she would be here, he thought as he placed two filet mignons in a heated skillet, adding black pepper and a pinch of rosemary. He grinned to himself, hoping they could manage to eat the steaks before they dove on each other.

When he heard her delicate knock a little while later, he opened the door to find her looking beyond lovely in a soft, flowy dress that hugged all her curves deliciously. He let his hungry eyes feast on her luscious cleavage for only a moment before saying, "I best keep my distance from you, darlin', or we'll forget to eat—and you're gonna need a good meal in you to keep your strength up before the night's through."

They dined outside on the balcony, and throughout the meal Liz flashed playful smiles that drove him wild, even when they were talking about things that had nothing to do with sex.

"How did your parents take the news about Todd?" he asked.

"Not particularly well," she said, glancing up from her plate. "I think they're in denial—but I half-expected that, so it's no big deal. As for me, I feel free as a bird for the first time in...forever, maybe."

He couldn't help grinning. "Hmm. If you're tellin' me you *haven't* felt free these last few nights together, I can't *wait* to see how fun you are tonight."

"It so happens," she said, casting another of those provocative little smiles, "I have a surprise for you."

"What is it?"

She tilted her head. "Now, it wouldn't be a surprise if I told you, would it? But it's something you'll find before the night's over."

He raised his eyebrows. "Sendin' me on a treasure hunt, *chere*?"

"You could put it that way."

They shared a bottle of wine over dinner, and Jack opened a second when they were through eating and he'd cleared the plates. She looked positively sumptuous lounging on his balcony, a glass of Chablis in her dainty hand.

And not that he wanted to keep bringing up Todd, but... "So you're tellin' me you're really over your fiancé that fast," he said, snapping his fingers. He grinned lightly and leaned forward. "No lingerin' feelings, no sense of loss, no wantin' to get back at him by havin' fun yourself." When she hesitated slightly, he added, "You can tell *me*, darlin'. I don't mind bein' the way you take your revenge, if that's what any of this is."

Her eyes narrowed slightly and the corners of her mouth curved ever so gently. "*Darlin'*," she said, making him chuckle at her imitation of him, "whether or not you believe me, this is all about me. What I want. What I feel. And I don't feel anything for Todd except glad he's no longer my problem."

Good, he thought, but he didn't say it. Instead, he just looked deep into her sexy eyes and said, "Tell me what you want, *chere*, what you feel. Right this second, what do you want?"

She wore an aloof grin and seemed to be turning the question over in her mind. "Right this second? Mmm, well, right this second, I think I want to sit in your lap."

He flashed a welcoming smile and felt his cock inflate as he opened his arms to her.

Lowering her wine to the table next to his, she settled onto his thighs, and as his arms curled around her, he wondered if she felt his growing erection against her leg. Their position brought her full breasts nearly level with his face, so he leaned down and lowered a small kiss to the ridge of one lovely globe. "What do you want now?" he whispered.

"More of that," she purred, arching her breasts toward his mouth.

At the invitation, he began feasting on them—small, soft kisses rained across her exposed cleavage, making her release a series of small moans and growls until finally he eased one palm up onto her soft, round breast, kneading it as he kissed her chest and neck. The hard nipple jutting against his hand compelled him to reach inside the dress, twirling the hard nub between thumb and forefinger as he raised his kisses to her hot, beautiful lips.

He looked up when she shifted, to find her lowering a shoulder strap and baring one gorgeous pink-crested breast to his eyes, and his mouth. They didn't even talk about the fact that it was barely dusk, that anyone could glance out a window or up from the street and see them—although Jack knew they were both keenly aware of it. "*Jolie,*" he breathed, and sank his mouth over her breast's pretty peak, twirling his tongue over the taut nipple, then closing his lips around her to suck it. She moaned with pleasure and Jack listened as if her sounds were a symphony—hot, sexy background music to his ministrations. He lowered the other shoulder strap so that she sat topless on his lap letting him shift his kisses back and forth between her scrumptious breasts until he was nearly drunk on them.

As he looked down, watching his tongue play over one wet pink nipple in the dusky light, he slid his hand up under her dress, gliding his touch up her outer thigh all the way to her hip. He expected to encounter an elastic band of some kind and when he didn't, he peeked up at her with amusement. "No panties, darlin'?"

She grinned and shook her head.

"Is this my surprise?" He raised his eyebrows.

He didn't expect her giggle. "No."

He smiled anyway. "*Mais,* I still like it."

"Good."

"And I would love to fuck your brains out right here on this balcony, my hot *petite fille,* but I'm thinkin' we should take this party inside. It's not even dark out, and I don't want anyone callin' the cops."

She tilted her head. "On Bourbon Street? You think someone really would?"

He shrugged. "Might sound unlikely, but I don't wanna take any chances on gettin' interrupted. Do you?"

She gave her head a sexy little shake, and then, holding her dress up under her bare breasts, rose from his lap, picked up her wine with her free hand and sashayed through the open French doors into his living room.

He followed, stunned by how utterly erotic she looked leaning against his wall, the blue fabric draping her body from only the ribs downward. She licked her lips and took a sip of wine. "Come here," she said.

He was in no mood to protest. He set his wine on a table and approached her. "There." She pointed to the back of his sofa. "Lean."

He did it, never taking his eyes from her.

After another drink, she lowered the glass next to his and reached up to caress her breasts. The dress dropped to her hips. Watching her—and knowing she was playing with him, just trying to drive him crazy—was sweet agony. Slowly, she began to move toward him, all the while massaging those two pretty mounds of flesh, using her fingers to pinch and tease the hard pink tips under his close scrutiny. She leaned her head back and let out a sexy little moan, hardening his shaft all the more. But like last night, he could be patient. He loved discovering, one by one, what dirty little treats Liz had in store, so he was utterly content to watch her play with her beautiful breasts for him.

When finally she stood directly in front of him, she reached for the bulge in his jeans, cupping it in her palm, massaging him while her other hand still caressed her chest. "*Merde,*" he moaned. Her touch felt so good it almost hurt.

As she lifted her hands to his belt buckle, he reached for her breasts. He felt their delicious weight in his hands, raking his palms over tight, budded nipples, as she undid the button on his jeans and lowered the zipper. Reaching inside, she gently but confidently freed his cock, hooking the underwear down low, under his balls.

Then she reached for his hand. Still patient, he followed, letting her lead him around to the front of the couch, where he sat down. She kneeled between his spread thighs and studied his shaft, but *he* watched *her*—her hungry eyes and full pouty lips, her large lovely breasts hovering just above his rock-hard erection.

Finally, she leaned over, letting her breasts drape around his lengthened cock. Warm, soft; Jack nearly died from the sumptuous pleasure. He lifted himself lightly, pressing himself against the hollow valley between those sweet mounds of flesh, inviting them to close around his hard-on as much as possible. "Ah, beautiful, baby," he murmured, his voice raspy. "Fuckin' beautiful."

She slid her breasts gently upward on his long cock, then back down. Slow, painstaking movements, and he felt every nuance—the soft fleshiness, the hard points of her nipples grazing the skin to either side of his shaft, the deep crevice where his erection was buried. He couldn't help moving a little, fucking her gorgeous breasts—and it made her release a hot little growl as she slid them up and down his length more aggressively.

At last, just when Jack thought he couldn't handle any more pleasure, he felt her tongue flick over the head of his cock.

He looked down to see her lick away the fluid gathered at the tip—watched her lick at the little opening, as if trying to bring out more.

Then her tongue made a circle around the whole head—twice.

"Fuck," he murmured, leaning his head back with nearly unbearable pleasure.

"Want more?" she whispered.

"Oh yeah."

With that, Liz followed her instincts and licked a line from the base of his strong, beautiful cock all the way to the tip, hungrily lowering her mouth over him. Already, she loved sucking Jack's cock more than she ever had with any other man. The very sight of it made her want to kiss and suck and lick it, simply adore it, and now the primal urge was to take as much of that big hard shaft into her mouth as she could. She worked her lips up and down, thrilled by his sounds of pleasure and the knowledge that he was watching her go down on him. He held her hair back as she devoted her full focus on swallowing as much of his length as she could.

When he was good and wet and she needed a break, she pulled away to resume fucking him with her breasts again. Now his cock slid up and down between them with slick ease, and the wetness and friction against her chest got her even hotter. After a moment, she began punctuating each stroke of her breasts with a hungry lick to the tip of his cock. But soon, little licks weren't enough—she wanted to lick away all the wetness gathered there, and then she wanted to suck him, deeper, harder.

"Careful, baby," he warned, "or I'll..."

But Liz didn't care if he came now—she *wanted* to make him come this way, and she wanted to *watch* him come, wanted to see the semen spurt out of his long, thick, beautiful cock, just for her. "Come on my breasts," she breathed. "I want you to come on my breasts." She wasn't sure why, she only knew she wanted to feel that sweet warm white fluid on her oh-so-sensitive mounds, wanted it to cover her, make her even wetter.

She sucked on him a moment longer—hard and wild—until he growled, "Baby, now." Just after she released him from her mouth, his thick seed shot hot and wet in four long bursts, most of it arcing out to land exactly where they both wanted it to. Liz could scarcely comprehend the strange pleasure she gleaned as her breasts became drenched in his fluid, but she felt sexy and dirty and alive, beautifully on display as they both looked down at the sight. Finally, she began to rub it in, moaning at the sensation, and Jack helped, massaging it in while they both watched their hands working over her semen-slick breasts.

Finally, he lifted his eyes to hers. "Was that my surprise, *chere*?"

She couldn't help flashing a vixen's smile. "No, not yet."

"When will I get it?"

"Oh, I think you'll find it soon."

He cast a dubious smile. "*When* soon?"

She couldn't help laughing. "Look, have I disappointed you yet?"

Jack joined in, chuckling, and finally said, "No, *chere*, you certainly haven't. I guess I can try to be a little more patient."

"Something you're not very good at," she teased.

He drew back in mock outrage. "I'm damn patient, but you push me too far."

She cast a coy look. "You want your surprise?"

He nodded, a predatory gleam in his eye.

"Then come and get it." Rising to her feet, she gathered the dress around her and dashed toward the bedroom. Once there, she bound onto Jack's big bed in time to look up and see him barreling in behind her. Trundling onto the mattress, he pinned her to the bed by her wrists and gave her a dangerous look that dissolved as he began kissing her. Her mouth, her cheeks, her neck, shoulders, breasts. Her stomach, her belly button.

Below, he pushed his hands up under her dress and onto her ass, caressing and kneading, until finally one hand grazed over top of her thigh and down into the valley between. The instant his touch sank onto her mons, he raised his eyes to her, his expression filled with fire. "Oh," he said, clearly awestricken. "Oh, baby." His kisses resumed, fast and furious, to her lips, neck. "*Ca c'est bon*," he murmured in between them. "Oh, *ca c'est bon*, baby."

"That's your surprise," she finally whispered.

He smiled. "And what a sweet, delicious, delectable surprise it is."

Only then did he reach down, flip her dress up over her waist, and look at her smooth pussy. He moved farther down, situating himself between her legs to see better, and she felt him studying every bare curve of white flesh, and the slick pink part that divided it. "Beautiful," he finally said. "So damn beautiful."

Then he smiled up at her. "Close your eyes, *chere*."

"Why?"

"Because I have a surprise for you, too."

Liz cast him a curious glance and let her eyes fall shut.

"Don't peek," he warned as he parted her legs.

His gentle kisses across her abdomen didn't surprise her, nor did the skim of his fingertips across the now-smooth skin of her cunt below. When he lowered a gentle kiss to the cleft where her clit was, she shivered in delight and parted her legs for him farther, still deeply pleasured but unsurprised as his tongue laved her, turning her wetter than she already was. She moaned and sighed and seemed to sink deeper into the bed as she relaxed into the growing pleasure, lifting her hands to fondle her breasts, forgetting all about surprises as liquid fire raced through her veins.

And then she felt something new, unexpected, indefinable. Something pushing against her opening with deep, tender thrusts—but not his cock; she knew because his mouth still worked over her there.

"Wh-what is…?"

In response, he held up a long, cylindrical object shaped like a penis, made of some kind of pink rubbery material. Then he smiled. "I bought you a vibrator—one of the ones we looked at in the store last night."

Liz bit her lip, not quite sure what to think, uncertain how she felt. "I've never used one of those…"

His grin deepened. "Really? Never? Not even just for yourself, in between boyfriends?"

She shook her head, and knew her innocence was showing again. And she knew it was okay—that he didn't mind her innocence and maybe even liked it—but she wished she didn't appear so shocked by something as common as a vibrator, something used by women the world over. "I've just never even thought about..."

"*Mais*, I think you'll like it."

"Better than you?" she teased.

"In *addition* to me," he corrected playfully. "As sort of a *supplement* to me."

He redirected his attention to her cunt, and used the end of the pink vibrator to nudge at her opening. "For instance, I can't lick you and fuck you at the same time, but with this, I can."

She couldn't help being intrigued. "Why don't you demonstrate for me?"

"With pleasure," he said, continuing to push the fake cock gently toward her passage again. She tensed slightly, trying to watch, unable to see, and Jack laughed. "Relax, *chere*. Just lie back and enjoy."

She did as he instructed and instead of thinking so much about the vibrator entering her, she concentrated on Jack's hot licks to her cunt. Certainly she was ready for *that*—her whole pussy had been excited and achy since she'd shaved it, so his tongue was a very welcome visitor. And as she watched him lick her, she realized the vibrator was pushing a little deeper into her with each thrust of his hand, and soon it was inside her, filling her the way his cock usually did. Still licking, he moved the shaft in and out with smooth strokes that only hinted at the power he could put behind them if he wanted. And although she thought nothing would feel as wonderful in her pussy as his rock-hard erection, the vibrator felt good, better and better with each passing second.

And then, despite the fact that the toy was a *vibrator*, something happened that she hadn't even thought about. He turned it on. The entire rubber cock pulsated against every part of her pussy—from the outer lips to the deepest inner sanctum.

"How's that?" he stopped licking to ask.

"Unh...good." She found it hard to talk when she got very excited, and she was getting more soaked by the moment.

"There's another little feature on this I think you'll like," he said as he continued thrusting it into her.

"Wh-what?" she thought, thinking, *Lick me*.

"You can't see it right now, but there's a nice little nub on the top of it made to stimulate your clit when you push it in all the way." With that, he inserted it even deeper, shocking her. She'd thought it was in all the way already, but no—at least another inch had just been buried in her, and with it came what he promised—a hot, delightful pressure against her oh-so-excited clitoris.

"Oh..." she said.

Without realizing it, she'd started moving against the vibrator at some point, and now she moved harder, wanting to feel that nub quivering against her most sensitive part. She'd thought for a moment she couldn't survive without him licking her, but the magical vibrator seemed to provide the best of both worlds—stimulation to her inside and out. Time slowed as she got lost in the sweet vibrations that seemed to fill her cunt from front to back, top to bottom. She moved harder, fucking the toy in Jack's hand, and his thrusts came harder, too, as he whispered, "That's right, baby, that's right. Oh *oui, chere, ca c'est bon*. Work that sweet little cunt, *chere*. Work that sweet pussy until you come for me."

And then she was crushing her breasts in her hands and letting out a long, hot moan as some imaginary dam broke inside her and a river of pure pleasure rushed through her limbs, centering between her thighs. "Oh God, I'm coming, I'm coming," she whimpered as her pussy convulsed around the humming tool, her clit pulsing with maddening palpitations that matched her heartbeat. She rode out the orgasm as long as she could, pumping her mound against the vibrator until the hot sweet throbs slowly faded.

Above her, she found Jack wearing a wicked little grin. "I think you like my surprise, darlin', just as much as I like yours."

She gave him a smile. "Very much."

"I'll let you take this home," he said, holding up the big vibrator, "so you can take care of yourself when I'm not around."

To her surprise, that sounded rather pleasant...but also like the words of a man who was trying to prepare her for his absence, a man who intended not to be around for long. She didn't answer, only gave a short nod against the pillow.

"Then I can imagine you doin' it," he said, his voice low and smoky. "I can picture you lyin' in bed, fuckin' your pretty pussy with this."

She decided to go out on a limb. "And thinking of you."

He grinned. "I should hope so." He spoke in so jocular a manner that it gave nothing away about his real feelings toward her.

But that was okay. As she'd promised herself from the beginning, whether this lasted a night or—dare she think—a lifetime...she would bask in the pleasure, enjoy each moment for what it was, soak up all the naughty delights she'd never reveled in before. And she'd just be thankful that she'd found a hot, sweet, sexy man like Jack to indoctrinate her to the true pleasures of the flesh.

* * * * *

An hour later, they lay in Jack's bed in a perfect sixty-nine position. Jack couldn't get enough of her lovely pussy tonight, so smooth and bare and sexy. That smooth skin just seemed to invite his touches and kisses.

Below, she alternated between sucking his cock and nestling it between her breasts, sometimes raking the wet end of his shaft across one sweet, turgid nipple. Sometimes she gave long licks up his length or licked just the tip of him like he was a lollipop—she seemed to know just how to space out her hot little mouth treats so that he didn't get *too* excited and come too fast. He was glad because he was enjoying his pussy play far too much to want it to end.

The bare skin on the outside of her cunt was softer than any he'd ever felt. Even without any stimulation, her hot pink clit and inner lips jutted from the bare cleft, swollen from excitement. He raked his tongue across the knob of her clit and watched her flesh part slightly in response. Then he used his hands to spread her wide and look at how flushed with desire she was. Below, she sucked him a little harder, so he returned the favor, sucking her engorged clit and stroking his fingertips across the damp lips below. Her pussy moved against him, effectively fucking his mouth, so he inserted two fingers. She was so soaked he could hear his fingers moving against her; he entered a third finger and listened to the wet sounds.

A moment later, she released his cock, which was good—damn, much more of that and he'd explode, and he wasn't sure he had the strength to tell her to stop. He looked down in the dimly lit room to see her sweet tongue darting gingerly out against the tip of him, playing, teasing. God, she was good—just watching her made him crazy. He loved how much she enjoyed having his cock in her sumptuous mouth, those berry lips wrapped around him like a soft vise, but the gentle tongue action she was delivering to his cock right now was hot and delicious, too.

Withdrawing his fingers from her wetness, he decided she needed more to fill that hot little cunt, so he reached for the vibrator again. This time it went in easily, buried to the hilt in one thrust. "Oooh," she cried above him.

He released her clit from his mouth. "Good?"

"Unh." She nodded against his groin, before using her mouth to reach for his hard-on again, sliding her lips down over him like a warm, wet sheath.

"Ah, baby, yeah." So good, he thought. So good that he wanted to fuck her pussy as sweetly as she was fucking him with that lovely mouth. He turned on the vibrator and drove it into her with the same rhythm she used to suck him, watching it slide in and out of her slick passage with ease. The sight of her cunt, open and hungry and so accepting of his toy, turned his desire to a heated lust that gathered deep in his gut and made him moan. He lowered his mouth over her pink clit once more, sucking and fucking her, getting lost in the giving and receiving, but keenly aware that she was mouthing his cock more and more passionately. Deeper, deeper, she pulled him in until he thought the tip of his erection must be touching her throat. *God, yes, baby, suck me.* He moved against her, too, fucking her sweet mouth as he worked the tool in her cunt, pushing it farther into her, determined to fill her pussy as well as he was filling her mouth.

Her breath grew heavier; her sounds of passion came with more abandon. Jack tried to hold onto his sanity and not come until she did, but it was hard because she sucked his cock so damn well. Her labored breathing only added to his excitement, increased the tension pulling his entire body taut as a clothesline. He thought for sure he would lose it when finally he heard her coming, moaning against his dick and fucking his mouth and the pink toy hard, hard, hard as she cried out. God, how much longer could he stand it? He worked to concentrate on her orgasm, thrusting the vibrator in time with her passionate cries, watching the way she worked her pelvis, absorbing the heated bliss in her expression.

Only when he was reasonably sure her ecstasy had waned did he give up the fight and let himself go, warning her, "I'm gonna come, darlin', I'm gonna come hard." He thought she might release him from her encircling lips, but she didn't, so his hot seed emptied into her throat as she continued sucking, sucking, through each heated wave of the orgasm, somehow taking him to heaven and back all over again with just that one generous act.

When he'd emptied completely and she finally let loose of him, he looked down into her face, saw the remnants of white fluid at one corner of her mouth, and thought—*God, she's astounding*. He instantly needed to hold her—it wasn't a wish or a desire, but simply a thing he had to do. He reached for her and she came to him, turning in the bed so they were face to face.

He reached up one thumb to wipe her lip, and then held his thumb upright between them so she could see what he'd rubbed away. To his surprise, she wrapped her hand around his, licking the white off, looking just as heated as if she were still licking his cock.

She was killing him.

Of course, she'd been like this—this exciting, this hungry—from nearly the moment they'd met, but he thought all her sensuality was having some sort of cumulative effect on him. The more wild, sexy things she did with him, the more amazed he became.

He leaned his forehead against hers. "Do you know how fuckin' hot you get me, *chere*?"

Her smile was laced with sensuality and her voice came out whispery sexy. "In case you haven't noticed, you get me pretty hot, too."

He smiled back, into her eyes. "A snowball effect, I guess. I get you hot, you get me hot, and it just keeps on growin'."

She nodded, her expression turning almost sheepish. "I love my new vibrator."

He nuzzled her, one hand drifting down to caress the curve of her hip as he let his wicked thought out in a low, raspy voice. "You liked havin' two cocks at once, didn't you?"

To his surprise, she actually blushed. He couldn't help laughing as he ran his fingers through her hair, pushing it back from her face. "Darlin', I can't understand how you can suddenly turn shy with me."

She laughed a little, too, as if realizing how little sense it made. "All this is so new," she explained. "Most of the time it seems as natural as breathing, like something that's been inside me all along, just waiting to get out. But I still have little moments when I can't quite believe this is me."

"It's definitely you, all right, lovely *chere*. 'Cause you're right—it comes to you as easy as breathin' and I love the way you follow your instincts and take every ounce of pleasure you can when we're together. And I loved fillin' you up with two cocks at the same time."

She half-laughed, half-purred at him. "It was...almost overwhelming. But in a very good way."

He flashed a sexy smile. "Ah, where were you back when I was a college boy tryin' to find a girl who wanted it that way?"

Her look was questioning and he realized he'd been thinking out loud and would now have to explain. "You remember my friend, Ty—you met him that first day in my office."

She nodded. "He was...memorable." Then she flinched softly, as if perhaps she'd said something she shouldn't have.

He laughed. "It's all right, darlin', I'm not the jealous type. All the ladies want to get in Ty's blue jeans."

"Well then, all right, yes, I'll admit I found him very attractive."

He grinned, liking that she would be that honest with him, and maybe he was even a little turned on, given the story he was about to tell her. "We met in college, were roommates—became best friends. Anyway, we had this bad habit of goin' for the same girls, and we always joked that we needed to find one who'd let us share her, you know...let us fuck her at the same time. It became a fantasy, somethin' we both wanted to do, at least once, but we never found a girl who was into it."

"Was there a time limit," she began, sounding speculative, "to the fantasy?" She raised her eyebrows flirtatiously.

He rested his head on the pillow, watching her every move, look, wanting to make sure he wasn't misreading her. "No. No time limit."

Then she cast him a playful sideways glance. "Well, that's good. You never know when someone willing will come along."

Down below, his cock perked to life a little. He ran one fingertip down the ridge of her breast, letting it play about the pink nipple, which was slightly erect but quickly got harder, longer, at his touch. "Hmm," he teased, "seems I know a very excitin' woman who hasn't said no to anything I wanted her to do so far."

Liz couldn't help letting a wicked little grin unfurl across her face. She could scarcely believe what she was suggesting, but the very second Jack had relayed the fantasy, she'd envisioned herself as the woman between the two men and her pussy had swollen with a lust she couldn't push down. In a mere instant, she'd decided she wanted to do it, wanted to be with Jack and his friend, together.

"I'm not sure I'd say no," she whispered coquettishly, "to *anything* you asked me to do."

And she meant it. She was so aroused by the very idea of being shared by Jack and Ty that she'd have done anything in that moment, anything at all. The memory of meeting Ty and feeling so instantly attracted to him, so aware of everything that was lean and muscular and hot about him, only added to her heated desire. She wanted to do *everything* with Jack. And at the moment, that meant she wanted to know the joy of two men, two cocks—two real, live, hard, flesh-and-blood cocks—at once.

Chapter 7

The following night Liz walked hand in hand with Jack toward an elegant French Quarter restaurant called Cicero's, on Decatur. She wore a sexy red dress of puckered fabric that clung to every curve. The halter style neckline was low cut, allowing for an exceptional amount of cleavage that made her feel ultra-sexy, and certainly didn't permit wearing a bra. As they walked, her breasts jiggled slightly against the hugging material, making her aroused already—when, she thought, by all rights, she should be nervous.

Jack had driven her home that morning, and later he'd called to say he'd invited Ty to dinner with them. "I…thought you might want to get to know him a little better."

The very idea of being with both of them at the same time had swum vigorously through her mind, a forbidden thought. Whereas, last night, she'd have invited Ty into their bed in a heartbeat, today she was a little more wary—yet still interested, still seriously considering the possibility. God knew the idea was beyond exciting—two hot, sexy men pleasuring her together. But…could she?

"Okay," she'd simply replied.

He'd clearly heard the new doubt in her voice. "But you set the pace, *chere*. If you don't want anything to happen, it won't."

She'd spent most the day after their phone call alternating between—*no, no way, I can't do it*, and priming her body for pleasure. She'd taken a long luxurious bubble bath, again shaving her pussy just to make sure it remained smooth, and then she'd lounged around in a silky robe that rubbed sensuously against her nipples and ass when she moved in it. And when it had come time to get ready for her date, she'd donned one of Lynda's sexiest dresses—and as usual, it was just a little too small in the chest and certainly made the most of Liz's assets. Clearly her body wanted what her mind had grown tentative about.

And even now, as she and Jack stepped into the dimly lit restaurant where she knew Ty awaited them, she wasn't sure what she would do. Would she allow herself this ultimate forbidden liaison? Or would this be the one thing to which she'd say no?

After Jack informed the host that they were meeting a friend, they entered the plush dining room to find Ty in a small half-round booth. He was as ruggedly handsome as Liz remembered, a lock of dark blond hair falling over his forehead, darker stubble on his chin. He waved and smiled when he spotted them.

Jack led her across the big, high-ceilinged room where each table glowed with candlelight and a jazz trio played in one corner. As they approached the table, a little of the nervousness Liz had expected to feel came back to her.

Ty got up to greet them. He wore dark pants and a sports coat, a white shirt underneath with a few buttons undone. "Great to see you again," he said to Liz, holding out his hand. She offered her own and he bestowed a delicate kiss upon it. Despite her nervousness, a tingling awareness skittered through her body.

She sat down between the two men and instantly *felt* them there, surrounding her. That quickly, it was as if sex were a palpable, living thing and as if it were squeezed into the small booth along with them. The sensation reminded Liz vaguely of what she'd felt that very first day, meeting both of them in Jack's office—together, they'd seemed to fill the room with heat and testosterone. Only now did she realize that somehow these two men, together, were truly a sexual force to be reckoned with. No wonder they'd gone after the same women in college; no wonder they wanted to share one. It was almost as if the two of them gave off an accelerated, amped-up sexual energy that was much greater than the sum of its parts.

Somehow, as the day had gone on, as she'd both feared and anticipated this event, she'd envisioned Ty coming on strong, being blatant and blunt, making her uncomfortable. But now, as he drew her easily into conversation, she was instantly reminded he was a pleasant, smooth-talking man. "Have you eaten here before, Liz?"

She shook her head. "No, but Jack tells me it's wonderful."

Ty nodded reassuringly. "This is one of my favorite restaurants in the Quarter. You can't go wrong with anything on the menu. The Italian entrees are especially good, but they make nice Creole dishes, too."

Liz took the initiative to change the conversation to something a little more personal. "You know, I can't help noticing you don't possess the same Cajun accent as Jack, but he hasn't mentioned where you're from."

He smiled. "Unlike Jack, I'm a transplant. I came down on a scholarship to Tulane and never left. I grew up in Lansing, Michigan, but I'm a Cajun at heart." He concluded with a friendly wink. "Jack says you're from Maryland?"

She nodded and wondered if Jack had told his friend *why* she'd moved to the Big Easy, and what he'd investigated for her. She decided to steer clear of that unpleasant topic. "I've been here for six months, but before meeting Jack I really hadn't had the opportunity to get out and enjoy the town very much."

"And do you like it?"

"More and more all the time," she said, again wondering exactly how much Jack had told Ty about their recent string of evenings together.

But that didn't matter, she reminded herself. Because she regretted nothing she'd done with Jack and she wasn't ashamed of it, either. And if she and Jack were going to invite Ty into their bed tonight, it was probably better that he knew a little of her recent sexual history.

She bit her lip, realizing with amazement that she was *truly* considering a threesome with Jack and his best friend. The very thought made her nipples pucker against the gathered fabric of her dress.

After they ordered dinner and a bottle of wine had arrived, Ty excused himself to the restroom, and Jack took the opportunity to place his hand on Liz's thigh. He leaned nearer. "What do you think of Ty?"

She smiled at her sexy lover in the shadowy room. "He's nice. Friendly."

Jack nodded.

"How much did you tell him? About me, I mean. About us."

He shrugged. "Enough for him to know what kind of entertainment we've been enjoyin' together. Not enough that we don't have any secrets."

Secrets. She liked that, the idea of Jack and her having secrets from the rest of the world, the idea that Jack *wanted* them to have things that remained just between them. Somehow the thought put her more at ease with the concept of a three-way.

"Like I told you earlier, though, *chere*, it's all up to you. No pressure. Whatever you want to do. I want to make you happy, want to make you feel good, want to do whatever will leave you the most pleasured in the end." He concluded with a sexy smile and a caress to her thigh that shot straight to her pussy.

He lowered a soft kiss to her lips just as Ty returned from the bathroom.

As Ty scooted back into the booth, Liz thought perhaps he situated himself a little closer to her than he'd been before. It was probably a matter of centimeters, but his knee touched hers now, his thigh brushed against hers on the leather seat. On her other side, Jack sat close, his fingers still gingerly stroking her leg, just above her knee. The thought made her look down, made her see the dress that had risen more than halfway up her thighs upon sitting, so that the lace edges of her stockings were almost visible. She considered pulling it down, but as a ribbon of excitement wove through her cunt, she changed her mind.

That ribbon of excitement and awareness stretched taut over the course of their meal. It was nothing anyone said or did—conversation flowed normally as the men discussed sports, friends they had in common, their work, and Liz talked about her job a bit, too. No, it was how close each man sat on either side of her, the way her legs touched both of them beneath the table, making her sensitive and ultra-aware of each shift or movement anyone made. Adding to that was the way they *did* discuss normal things, acting as if a subtle form of foreplay weren't slowly beginning to take place beneath the tablecloth.

The very act of eating became sensuous, given the sexual tension pulling at Liz from both sides. Her entire body began to feel overly sensitized. Each soft, warm bite she took of the lasagna she'd ordered, each time she closed her lips around one of the garlic sticks that came along with it, made her more aware of her mouth, her tongue, the movements of her hands. Each drink of wine seemed to slither down through her body. Even the smooth stem of the wineglass in her hand turned into something sensual, so that she found herself running her fingers up and down its length. She felt both men watching her throughout the meal, perhaps becoming as aware of these things as she was.

After they'd eaten and their plates were taken away, Jack returned his hand to her inner thigh, higher this time, his fingers delivering a maddeningly soft caress through her stocking. When she attempted to place her napkin on the table and instead accidentally dropped it underneath, Ty reached down to retrieve it. As he rose back up, he let both his hand and the napkin graze her calf all the way past her knee.

"Thank you," she said, sounding a bit breathy as he returned it to the tabletop. At that precise moment, Jack's silky touch rose slightly higher. She parted her legs a little, unwittingly pressing her other thigh more directly against Ty's. The contact made her look up at him—his eyes held a hint of awareness, a hint of fire. But they also reminded her of what Jack kept saying—this was up to her. The men would follow her lead, she supposed. So even as she lowered her gaze, not quite able to maintain the intensely close contact with Ty, she licked her upper lip and made no move to shift her body away, and hoped that told him she was interested in at least a little more of this experience.

"So, what's your pleasure, darlin'?" Jack asked with a hint of raw sensuality that made it impossible not to hear the double meaning of the question.

Let's go back to your place. All three of us. I want this, want both of you on me, in me. But Liz couldn't say those things, not yet. She still wasn't completely sure. "Let's stroll Bourbon Street," she said instead, thinking a little more time with both of them would help her decide.

"Sounds good," Ty said.

"Let's hit Café Du Monde on the way," Jack suggested, "and pick up some beignets for dessert. We can eat 'em on the walk up to Bourbon. Might get some to save for later, too. You know how I like my carbs," he added with a wink in Liz's direction.

Beignets from Café Du Monde were one New Orleans treat Liz had learned to love very soon after her arrival in town. Although she'd never ventured too deep into the French Quarter before meeting Jack, she'd come to the Café Du Monde with girls from work from the start.

As she and her two escorts ate the sweet, sugar-covered confections on the stroll to the party district, they soon found their clothing dusted and streaked with the heavy powdered sugar, and all three of them broke into easy laughter. "As my *grandemaman* used to say, you can dress us up, but you can't take us out," Jack imparted, and Liz found herself loving his easygoing manner. Even as he escorted her to an elegant dinner, he was not as proper and stodgy as Todd, not afraid to eat a messy dessert and laugh about it.

Once the beignets were gone, they dusted themselves off, and Jack kindly licked Liz's fingers clean, sending a lovely little tingle to her already sensitized cunt. A part of her was almost tempted to playfully offer the same service to Ty, but it was still too soon—despite how much fun she was having with both of them, she still wasn't ready to take that next step.

By the time they reached Bourbon Street, it was hopping. Crowds of people roamed the streets, neon lights lit the night, and music of all kinds—Cajun, blues, jazz, and rock—blared from open doors and windows. People wore cheap beads of purple, green, and gold, and held brightly colored drinks or bottles of beer. Mardi Gras had been last month, but Liz thought the place still seemed wild and charged with an invisible sexual energy, an energy which she was beginning to realize was *always* here, part and parcel of the French Quarter.

When the trio stopped at a small, open air daiquiri bar for drinks, Liz's attention was drawn to a group of four or five thirty-something men smoking cigars and whistling when a group of sexy, scantily clad college-aged girls meandered past.

One of the girls looked back with a bold, saucy smile. "I want your beads," she said to the men, who were wearing a variety of them.

"You know what you have to do," one of them replied, laughing.

"Show 'em to us, baby," another guy said.

The girl came back to where the men stood, reaching down to the hem of her skimpy top and pulling it up to reveal a pair of large, pretty breasts with smallish nipples of dark mauve.

"Nice," one of the men said in a lecherous voice.

"Beautiful tits, sweetheart," another offered.

She smiled, obviously pleased to show off her assets, and kept her top raised as each of the men surrendered some of their beads, placing them around her neck.

"A pleasure doing business with you," she said, finally lowering her top and turning to catch up with her friends.

Liz couldn't help watching the scene with a strange, unbidden fascination. Even as intimate as she'd been with Jack and as she might soon be with Ty, she couldn't relate to the desire to flash your breasts for fifty-cent beads. Although she might not have realized it at first, the things she'd done with Jack had always been about more than sex between strangers. Even so, watching the girl lift her top for the men's pleasure had added subtly to her arousal. Clearly, like everything so hedonistic about this city, flashing for beads was not restricted only to Mardi Gras.

"I don't know about you guys," one of the men said to his buddies as Liz continued watching, "but I'm ready to hit a strip joint."

The others laughingly agreed and they wasted no time heading into Club Venus, just across the street.

Just then, Ty approached, handing her a drink, their fingers brushing during the exchange. Jack was still at the bar, paying. "Thanks," she said softly. She met Ty's brown eyes briefly, but again, it was too intense for her, so she shifted her gaze away, back across the street, where a lovely young girl in a micro-mini dress and sexy high heels stood next to the doorman, saying, "Come on in, gentlemen."

"Are you a dancer?" one of them asked, sounding drunker than the rest.

She nodded. "I'll be on the main stage in about twenty minutes, so you'd better get a good seat so you can give me lots of tips." She giggled in conclusion.

"You bet we will, sugar," the drunk guy said. "I want to see your tits."

"What next?"

Liz flinched at Jack's voice in her ear. She'd become entranced by the happenings across the street—by the open sexuality displayed here. No one was shy or reticent; no one was anything but eager and honest about it. Perhaps, Liz reasoned, it had been this erotic atmosphere that had first opened her mind to the things she'd done over the last few days. Perhaps it was so intoxicating that anyone would respond as she had, opening herself up for all these new sexual experiences. But one look at Jack reminded her again—no, this was more than that. He treated her with so much more respect than those guys going into the bar showed the women willing to bare it all for them. He was so good and sweet to her, so committed to pleasuring her as much or more than himself. And she wanted to pleasure him just as much in return.

She knew in that moment she wouldn't say no to his desire for a threesome. In fact, she would embrace it, would love sharing it with him, would dive into it with the same eager honesty about sex that was all around her on naughty Bourbon Street.

"What do you want to do now, *chere*?" Jack asked again when she didn't answer.

She flicked her gaze to Ty, then back to Jack. "Let's stop into Club Venus for a little while."

The fresh heat in Jack's gaze was unmistakable. "Sure thing, darlin'."

Jack placed his hand at the small of her back and the three of them proceeded across the street.

The only seats available were a couple of small plush chairs in front of the main stage. Ty took one, and Liz sat across Jack's lap in the other. On the stage, the Britney Spears look-alike she'd seen here before gyrated around a pole. Her blonde hair hung in two braids and the blouse tied at her waist was sheer enough to provide a good view of her dark nipples.

As the stripper teased the audience by pulling up her short plaid skirt just enough to show the tops of her lace stockings and garter belt, Ty leaned over and spoke softly. "Jack tells me you have excellent taste in women."

Don't blush, she commanded herself. "Yes, he seems to think so."

"So, if I wanted a lap dance, who would you pick for me?"

Liz's pussy went warm beneath her dress.

She scanned the room—the strippers on the various stages, and the girls already naked and giving lap dances. Her eyes were drawn to a girl she hadn't seen there on her previous visits—an exotic-looking brunette with long, dark, straight hair, pert medium-sized breasts, and a sexy dark tan. She currently danced on one of the smaller stages in a black leather miniskirt and high black boots. Tan lines outlined her breasts and drew attention to them.

"Her," Liz said, pointing.

Both guys looked and Ty offered a heated little smile. "Jack was right. Nice choice."

They returned to silence then, all of them watching the schoolgirl shed her blouse and caress her breasts as she shimmied and swayed for them. Jack's cock grew against Liz's thigh, and the combined visual and physical sensations made her wet. Her nipples felt like little bullets against the snug dress and she almost wished she hadn't suggested they come here, that she'd simply had the courage to go back to Jack's place where she could be with them both—now.

Instead, though, she shifted her gaze to the girl she'd selected for Ty, who was sensually wiggling out of her leather skirt, leaving her in another of the flesh-colored g-strings utilized by Club Venus. As the pretty stripper continued her sensual dance, tweaking her nipples, running long, slender fingers around her barely concealed pussy, she noticed Ty was watching, too. Jack's eyes remained on the main stage, and strangely, Liz had the sensation that watching the other girl was something she and Ty were sharing.

The moment the girl's number came to a close, Ty calmly raised a finger, as if he were signaling a waiter, and despite the crowd, the stripper saw him immediately. Still in high-heeled boots and g-string, she made her way over to where they sat.

"How much?" he asked, his eyes sparkling with a slow heat.

Although he'd not specified a lap dance, the girl seemed to know what he meant. "Twenty."

He curled his index finger toward him, as if saying, *Come here.*

The pretty girl smiled, wasting no time straddling Ty in the small chair.

* * * * *

Jack watched as the hot brunette Liz had selected writhed sensually in Ty's lap. His friend leaned back, looking drunk on her, his eyes roaming her face, her breasts, her thighs spread across his with only a miniscule g-string covering her cunt.

Liz watched, too, and he knew all three of them were getting hotter and hotter, primed for what was to come. And even as entranced as Ty appeared to be with the stripper in his lap, Jack knew his friend was anticipating sharing Liz with him in a little while. And Liz would say yes—he knew that, too. He'd seen an anxious little light in her eye when she'd suggested they come into the strip bar.

When he'd told Ty about what might happen between them and Liz, his friend had at first been disbelieving, and then awed. Not only because of the longtime fantasy they'd harbored, but also because Jack was willing to share her.

"Don't deny it, buddy, you've got a serious thing going with sexy Miss Lizzie. So what I don't know is—why are you willing to share the one woman I've ever seen you feel something solid for?"

Jack had considered denying the accusation, but instead had just been honest. "Because I want her to feel *everything*. I want her to know ultimate pleasure."

"And afterward? Will you be okay with it then, knowing I've fucked the woman you love?"

Again, Jack had the urge to deny it—damn, when had the word *love* come into play here? But he didn't. "Look, I'm pretty sure this isn't a serious thing to her. She's in a place where she's explorin' her sexuality, learnin' to lose her inhibitions. No matter what I feel or don't feel, I think sooner or later she'll get her fill of sexual experiments and then we'll probably...go our separate ways. So the after part doesn't really matter. What matters is that I help her have these experiences, that I help her take her sexuality wherever it wants to go."

Ty had flashed an incredulous look. "So you're saying you're going to let her go, that easy?"

Jack had shrugged. "We're in different places in life. She's just broken up with a longtime boyfriend and discovered this new, wild side of herself. I think she's got a lot of livin' to do, probably with a lotta people."

"What if you're wrong and she only wants to do her living with you?"

He shook his head. "For your information, I invited her to move in with me, and she said no. I can take a hint."

Ty rolled his eyes. "Sometimes I think you're a little too laid back for your own good. If I wanted something long-term with a woman, I'd pursue her until she wanted the same thing."

"That's where you and I are different, my *bon ami*," Jack said. Because he wasn't Ty—he had a reason *not* to pursue it. Even if he wanted her, his father's regrets still played through his head—he sure as hell didn't want to end up the emotional mess his dad had been, over a woman. If Liz really wanted to be with him, if he *knew* she wanted something strong and lasting, he wouldn't be able to resist. But if she didn't—*mais*, he was just going to let the chips fall where they would and assume that's how things were supposed to be. He'd done all right with that philosophy in life so far.

And he meant what he'd told Ty about their proposed *ménage à trois*—it was about *her*, and it was about him being *willing* to share her in order to please her, and it was about the two of them *sharing* the experience.

As they both watched the lovely stripper giving Ty a very sexy lap dance, Jack's erection grew more rock solid. The woman swiveled her hips in his friend's lap, arching against his cock in perfect simulated sex. Her breasts shimmied before Ty's glassy eyes, her nipples dark and erect. Ty, of course, couldn't touch her, but his gaze traveled from her delicate face to the swell of her breasts to the pale g-string that hid her crotch.

Jack slid his hand between Liz's knees, gliding it slowly up to the edge of her skirt and underneath, his fingers playing over the lace tops of her stockings. He wanted to do so much more—wanted to reach his hand inside the low opening of her incredible dress, wanted to rake his fingertips across her pussy, which he knew had to be soaked by now. He wanted to press against her naked body from one side while Ty pressed against her from the other, wanted her to know the excitement of being worshipped so decadently. And a part of him even wanted to take her back to his place—alone, no Ty—and lock her up and keep her there forever, his, only his. But that was a little scary, a little like something his father might have thought about his mother—and fortunately for Liz and Ty, he wasn't going to listen to that possessive little voice growing inside him. Instead, he was going to offer all three of them the ultimate thrill.

As the sexy stripper ground her crotch into Ty's, moving in hot little circles, Liz leaned to whisper in Jack's ear. "I think I'm ready to go back to your place."

He looked into her eyes and saw the undeniable passion there. "With Ty, too?"

She nodded solemnly.

"Are you sure?"

"Yes. Are you?"

"*Oui*. Definitely."

Chapter 8

The cab ride, though short, was excruciating. They didn't talk, but Jack caressed Liz's thigh. She sat between the two men, all the while wondering how it would begin, how Ty would become involved in something they'd gotten pretty good at as a twosome, how it would feel, how she would respond. She kept wanting Ty to touch her in the cab along with Jack, but he didn't. The waiting had turned to torture.

Once inside the apartment, Jack said, "Something to drink?"

"Wine," she said.

"For me, too," Ty added.

She took a seat on Jack's couch and Ty joined her. Their eyes met and this time she didn't look away, simply wouldn't let herself. Jack sat down on her other side, lowering three stemmed glasses to the coffee table, along with an uncorked bottle of wine, which he then poured.

He picked up his glass and said, "Maybe we should toast something."

Liz raised her glass and said, a bit breathlessly, but suddenly feeling more daring, "To sharing."

"To sharing," Jack repeated, and the three of them clinked glasses.

Liz took a long sip, then set her glass on the table and turned to Jack. "I'm suddenly…so ready for this," she breathed.

"Ah, lovely *chere,*" he whispered, looking deep into her eyes before slowly leaning in to deliver a long, hot kiss, his tongue swimming in languid circles around hers.

It sent a burst of unquenched desire exploding through Liz's body, leaving her pussy throbbing with maddening intensity. She kissed him back, twining her arms around his neck, leaning over into his embrace.

One kiss turned to another as his hands roamed her back, ass, waist, sliding up to massage one needy breast. And even as she let herself sink into Jack, because Jack was everything in that moment, she remained ultra-aware of Ty's presence, too, knowing he sat on the opposite side of her, watching their passion, waiting to join in. She'd meant it when she'd said she was ready; she desperately wanted to feel his touch along with Jack's, and finally she stretched out her legs beside her, knees bent, until she slid one high-heeled foot onto Ty's warm thigh.

And then it came—his touch, a gentle grazing at her ankle, his fingers playing about the strap of her sexy shoe. Still making out with Jack, she rubbed her foot against Ty's leg to let him know the touch was welcome.

His light caress moved tenderly up her calf, past her knee. Still licking at her responsive tongue, Jack slipped his hand into the top of her dress to take her breast in his hand. She let out a small moan—amazed at the sensation of having two men touch her, and wanting so much more.

Ty's hand slid over her dress up onto her hip, caressing. She wanted both men to touch her freely—everywhere—so she broke from Jack's sensuous kisses and rose up on her knees, still facing Jack, but making herself more available to Ty, as well.

Taking the lead, Jack slid his hands up her thighs, under her dress, gathering the red fabric up past her stockings to her hips, revealing the tiny red mesh thong she wore. Ty joined in, too—mmm, yes—his palms sliding up the backs of her thighs and onto her bare ass, massaging. She arched, pushing her butt into his hands, thrusting her chest forward. Jack took the opportunity to spread the dress's halter top to either side, freeing her breasts. He caressed their softness, twirling her hard nipples between his fingers, all while Ty continued playing with her ass—and then she felt kisses there, light, heavenly kisses that nearly buried her. Her pussy felt electrically charged, so hot, so wet.

Next, Jack lifted his mouth to her breasts. He licked and suckled and caressed while Ty continued his ministrations on her ass—small, light kisses that sent shivery ribbons of heat to her cunt.

Part of her could have let them continue such sweet licks and kisses all night long, but Liz wanted more—of both men. Turning, she lowered herself to sit back on the couch, reaching boldly up to kiss Ty.

He kissed differently than Jack—firmer, more insistent, and she liked the contrast, becoming instantly aware that her two lovers this night would perform together but apart, the same but different.

Jack resumed nibbling one breast, his hand drifting down over her stomach and in between her thighs—not quite to her pussy, purposely teasing her, she knew. Then Ty's mouth left hers, moving down to her neck, shoulder, and finally to her other waiting breast. Whereas Jack suckled her, Ty began with gentle licks over her taut rosy nipple. Together, the sensations were driving her mad, and to look down and see them both pleasuring her breasts was wildly arousing. Soon, Ty's licks turned to sucks—hard, satisfying pulls that shot straight from her nipple to her wet panties. He, too, slid his hand along her thigh and she was sure her pussy would die of agony, but then finally Jack's fingers slid deeper—oh God, yes—stroking her aching little cunt. She instantly spread her legs wide and became aware that both men's hands were at her thong—Ty's fingers slipped beneath the thin elastic at her waist, stroking over the bit of pubic hair she'd left above her slit while Jack rubbed hot circles over her clit through the red mesh.

More, she wanted more. So she pushed Jack back until he half-lay on the couch. She began working at his belt and pants as Ty reached around from behind to cup her breasts in his strong hands. After freeing Jack's beautifully big cock, she couldn't go slow—she bent and lowered her mouth over him, taking in every inch of him that she could. "*Merde*, baby," he breathed. "Your mouth is so fuckin' sweet." She loved the feel of him between her lips, filling her mouth, loved getting him wet as she moved up and down his thick length. She kneeled on the sofa, pulling her knees up beneath her—the position gave her better access to Jack and at the same time offered her backside to Ty.

Ty took the cue and pushed her dress farther up over her ass, caressing as he went. And then—mmm, finally—he pulled the elastic away until she felt the mesh that cupped her cunt being raked aside. She instinctively parted her legs, wanting him to see her bare pussy from the back, all the while enjoying Jack's lovely cock.

Soon Ty's mouth was on her mound from behind. Sweet heaven. Instinct made her push her swollen cunt against him as he spread her ass with his hands so he could lick her better. God yes—she moaned as Ty's tongue sank deep into her slit. She whimpered and groaned around Jack's shaft as the incredible sensation rocked her, bolting through her whole body, making her hips move to better meet each hot stroke of Ty's tongue on her pussy.

It was then that she felt Ty's fingers—he'd reached through her legs to rub her clit. Oh yes, it was just what she'd needed to experience complete, satiating pleasure and she moved her hips a little harder, sucked in Jack's cock a little more deeply. Being pleasured from both ends was incredible enough, but to be receiving that pleasure from two different men was staggering. Yes, yes, yes, she thought each time Ty's long fingers circled over her clit, each time Jack's cock invaded her throat. Yes, yes, soon, soon—she was going to come for them, so hard. Suck, gyrate, suck, gyrate, suck, gyrate—yes, and then...oh!

Sweet waves of ecstasy flooded her, rushing from her cunt outward through her entire body. She released Jack's cock and cried out in all-consuming passion as Ty's fingers and mouth continued working at her, finishing her off.

When finally the waves receded, she opened her eyes to see Jack watching her. His hands cupped her face. "Good, baby?"

She could only nod, too weak for words.

She almost wanted to collapse then—collapse on Jack and sleep. But no. This was her one night to have two men, and she'd barely had them yet. She intended for there to be much more, so she wasted no time, pivoting her body on the couch to face Ty and offer her pussy to her sweet Jack.

Ty's handsome face was as lust-filled as she knew her own must be. And now that she'd sucked Jack's beautiful cock so long and so hard, she wanted to know Ty's in the same way, wanted to show him how good she was, how hungry, how much she was enjoying being with both of them. As she reached for his belt, he shrugged out of his jacket and unbuttoned his shirt, revealing a muscular chest with a sprinkling of pale brown hair. Parting his pants, she reached into black underwear and pulled out his cock. The shaft was not quite as large as Jack's, but it looked strong and capable.

Her bared breasts hovered over him, so she lowered them around his erection for a slow, tantalizing moment, making him release a groan. He felt hot and hard between them, the perfect complement to her lush softness.

From the back, Jack was massaging her ass in his hands, pushing his fingers into her wet opening. They slipped in with ease and he moved them in and out in the same slow rhythm she used to fuck Ty with her breasts. Inside, she felt utterly intoxicated, filled with joy and the new freedom that had brought her to this amazing place.

Raising up, she took Ty into her mouth. He moaned. She felt Jack lean around her slightly and knew he was watching her—he used his free hand to pull back her hair, gathering it in one fist, so he could see her lips wrapped around his friend's hard-on. She kept working at Ty, thrilled by having Jack witness her pleasuring his best friend so intimately.

But finally he released her hair and situated himself more directly behind her. His fingers still glided in and out of her juices and she bucked her hips against them.

Then she felt his cock. It slid between the cheeks of her ass in a pseudo-fucking motion and felt delicious there. Delicious, but within a few seconds, she wanted him inside her, deep, fucking her pussy while Ty fucked her mouth. Two cocks in her—just like Jack had teased her about liking, wanting. She did want it, desperately.

And then finally that sweet, hot cock slipped between her thighs, entering her wetness deep and easy, filling her up so completely that for a brief moment it was overwhelming. She moaned against Ty's shaft at the impact of taking Jack from behind—a position in which she always felt fuller, each stroke more intense.

As Jack fucked her slow and hard, she sucked Ty in the same tempo, so that both shafts filled her in unison. At first she wondered how long she could go on that way—it was so extreme, so overpowering, to take two large, driving cocks into her body at the same time—but soon she realized she never wanted it to end. She'd never felt anything more forcefully pleasurable. Her body felt made for this, made for the hot rhythm they all fell into, made to give and receive such heady pleasure.

When Jack's strokes began to come faster, she sucked Ty faster, too. The sultry air was filled with moans from all three of them as the fucking worked toward a rigid peak. Jack was setting the pace now, deciding how fast or slow or hard they moved against each other, and Liz liked giving him that power, knowing her body and then Ty's in turn would submit to whatever Jack decided. He pounded into her, seeming to give up any control he'd once rendered, and she cried out with each stroke, even as she moved her mouth up and down Ty's mighty erection.

"Fuck, here I come," Jack murmured behind her. And then his strokes crashed hard, hard, hard as he released his hot seed into her just as Ty groaned, "Ah...me, too," and Liz pulled her lips away, immediately aware that she only wanted to give Jack the privilege of coming in her mouth. She aimed Ty's cock at her chest and felt the warm spurts onto her breasts.

Jack eased her back into his arms and he rubbed Ty's milky white sperm into her soft globes of flesh. Below, Ty sat up and did the same with Jack's semen—he cupped her mound and, as the fluid leaked out, massaged it into her pussy. She felt so wet with both of them that she wanted to lie there forever just soaking their come into her sensitized skin.

* * * * *

Jack and Liz stood near the foot of the sofa—Ty lay on it watching them. Jack undid Liz's dress behind her neck to send the halter straps falling down around her waist. Then he pushed the red fabric at her hips until it dropped to her ankles, leaving her in nothing but a miniscule pair of red panties, nude stockings, and sexy-as-hell strappy shoes. She was fucking gorgeous and after what they'd just shared, he knew without doubt that letting her go wouldn't be the easy task he'd made out to Ty earlier today. When his sweet Liz decided it was time for their fun to be over, he would be left with a hole in his heart. But he refused to dwell on that now. This night, this woman, was too phenomenal.

He slid his thumbs into the elastic curving across her hips and pulled the mesh panties down to reveal that lovely, smooth pussy of hers. He dropped to his knees to help her step free of the g-string, bringing his eyes level with her sweet cunt. He couldn't resist delivering one long lick up her naked slit, where her clit and pink lips peeked out for him. She shuddered, turning his cock a little harder.

Rising to his feet, he gazed into her eyes and thought he'd melt from the hot desire lingering there, shining on him like emerald flames. He said nothing because no words seemed adequate to describe the connection he felt with her now. He simply took her hand and led her to the bathroom.

Ty followed, watching as Liz slowly undressed Jack. Jack loved the way she peered into his eyes as she unbuttoned his shirt and pushed it from his shoulders, then dropped to her knees to lower his pants. She delivered one light kiss to his cock—already half-erect again—before turning to undress Ty in the same manner.

Jack reached in the shower, turning on the water, then drew Liz inside, Ty entering behind her. They all remained silent—Jack simply handed Ty a sponge and took for himself the soap mitt Liz had enjoyed during their last shower.

"Lift your arms over your head, *chere*," he instructed her, watching as she leaned against the shower wall, between the two men, arms held sensually above her. She looked like a European statue, only better, because her beauty was real; she was flesh and blood.

After lathering their sponge and mitt, Jack and Ty both began to wash her, running their soapy shower tools over incredibly soft skin. Jack kneeled, concentrating on her round hips, her narrow waist and slender stomach, her lovely pussy. He glanced up to see Ty rake his sponge across her breasts, her taut nipples peeking through the bubbles.

Jack could have taken his time washing her forever, exploring her every curve with quiet fascination, but he could tell from the way she bit her lip that she was getting excited and maybe even a little impatient, and he reminded himself that tonight was about sharing her, and delivering her to ultimate ecstasy. So, reaching for the handheld shower head, he began to rinse the soap from her naked body. "Damn, darlin', you look good wet," he rasped, studying the details of her shape as he washed the suds away. He focused his gaze on little things—her small, sexy navel, the swell of her hip, the curve of her shoulder, the slight sway of her breasts.

"I want to take you both to bed now," she said, her voice low but potent.

He raised his admiring eyes to hers. "Now who's impatient?" he teased.

She smiled playfully, as if acknowledging that she had that coming.

But Jack wasn't inclined to make her suffer—no, this was her night for pleasure. So he reached behind him to turn off the water, and then grabbed the towels.

A few minutes later, she lay in the middle of his bed, Jack and Ty sandwiching her in-between.

His heartbeat took on the rhythm of a freight train just watching her turn to draw Ty into a passionate kiss. There was something indelibly arousing about her knowledge that he was there, watching, just like at Club Venus when she'd gotten those hot, sexy lap dances.

He knew she sought her own sensual delights from it all, and he loved that—but he also knew it was almost like a gift she was giving him, an analogy which certainly fit this particular liaison. He'd told her of his old, never-fulfilled fantasy, and twenty-four hours later, here she was, letting him live it.

Pulling up close behind her, he wrapped one arm around her to caress her lovely breasts while she made out with Ty. He nestled his hard cock in the warm valley of her ass and kissed her shoulders, her back. Ty explored her body, too—his hands roaming her curves, passing over Jack's hands a time or two and bringing home once more the exciting reality that they were sharing a woman. To his surprise, even Ty's touch felt electric in this circumstance—the awareness hardening Jack's shaft still more as he rubbed it against her sweet ass.

After a time, Liz rolled, turning into his arms. "Want to kiss *you* now," she murmured and he lowered his mouth over sweetly swollen rose-colored lips. Her kiss was erotic, curious, seeking—it said she wanted more of this raw, carnal experience.

He kissed her with all the passion inside him as he caressed her large, round breasts in his hands, and again, Ty's fingers passed over his as he explored her. Finally, Jack eased down her body, kissing each pretty nipple and her lovely, soft stomach, working his way to where he could part her legs. She rolled on her back to let him and he shifted his gaze to Ty. "Come down here with me and take a look at this *jolie* pussy."

Ty slid down the bed until they were side by side between Liz's widespread thighs, studying her naked flesh.

"Have you ever seen a sweeter sight?" he asked his *bon ami*.

Ty looked near to drooling. "It's fucking beautiful."

"I know," Jack said, his body aching with the intensity of sharing this most private part of her with Ty. He could barely breathe as he reached out both hands to gently part her flesh, revealing the wet pink center.

"Damn," Ty uttered as a little fluid trickled from her opening.

"Lick it up," Jack said on impulse.

Ty followed the command, bending to rake his tongue thoroughly over the parted lips of her cunt. He paused afterward, as if awaiting further instruction, and when Jack didn't give any, Ty began lapping at her pink expanse with big, wide strokes of his tongue that made her breath come hard. Jack glanced up to see her watching them over her breasts, which she molded and squeezed in her slender hands.

"That's right," Jack murmured. "Lick her pussy. Lick up all that sweet juice."

Ty worked diligently at his task, although he concentrated his efforts on her opening, not her clit—and that was how Jack wanted it. He didn't want her to come again for a while; now that she'd shown him just how good stretching things out could be, he wanted to turn the tables on her.

Yet just the same, that hot clit of hers called to him. It looked practically erect, standing at attention at the top of her cunt. He decided to give her just a little attention there—not enough to get her off, but enough to keep her on edge.

As Ty's busy tongue worked below, Jack raked his own over her stiff little knob. She let out a loud whimper and arched herself toward their mouths. Jack closed his lips over her clit and sucked gently. His beautiful *chere* practically howled with pleasure, reminding him once more that he wanted to stretch this out, prolonging her delights. He drew his mouth back and delivered one more tiny lick across her swollen nub—only this time his tongue met Ty's.

An unexpected ribbon of shock and something more rippled through him. They both went still, their faces close together over her wide open mound. Fuck, what *was* that?

His eyes were closed as he licked her clit again—and once more his tongue collided gently with Ty's as his friend licked upward on her.

This time Jack didn't stop, didn't examine, just resumed licking her. Licking her and letting the tip of his tongue meet up against Ty's at the end of each stroke. Strange, searing pleasure. Something he didn't want to feel, but there it was—the sensation that both Liz and Ty were his lovers in that moment. The biting urge to lift his mouth to Ty's, but he didn't do that—just let the close licking continue, just let Liz's sweet sounds from above intoxicate him, take him away from thought, immerse him entirely into the act of sex.

Finally, he made himself stop, because he still didn't want her to come yet. He wanted her whimpers of pleasure to go on for a very long time. He drew back, but still held her open for Ty, felt her moisture on his fingers—and liked it.

When he suspected his poor, sweet Liz was going crazy from the tongue bath, he pulled his hands away from her cunt and Ty ended his ministrations. When Ty rose up, his face was wet with her. She seemed to notice, too—she looked at him and licked her lips, pinched her nipples. "Want to suck you both," she whispered into the warm night air. "Let me."

She made no move from where she lay, so both men positioned themselves so that their cocks jutted out over her face. She reached up and wrapped one hand around each erection, looking positively ravenous and filled with lust. Her look shot straight to Jack's shaft, making him think he could die of pleasure just watching her like this.

She angled her head first toward him, taking his erection between her pretty lips. Damn, *so good*—he couldn't contain the groan that leaked out when her lips closed firm around him. She sucked him hard and thorough, taking him full in her mouth and moving in slick, rapid rhythm over his length even as she slid her hand up and down Ty's cock, inches away. A moment later, she traded, eagerly sucking Ty's shaft into her mouth in the same fashion and making him growl with heat as she continued working her hand on Jack. Jack had never seen her look so wanton and wild, so unceasingly hungry for what lay between their thighs. Oh, how this woman had abandoned her old self with him. He wasn't sure if it really had to do with him, or if it was as he'd once accused her—a way of getting back at Todd, or if some clock had just been set inside her to make her lose her every inhibition at the precise moment in time they'd met, but his ego liked to think *he'd* done this, *he'd* loosed her sensual side, *he'd* brought her to a place where pleasure knew no bounds.

And he was in love with her, damn it. No fucking denying it now. Looking down on her as she moved her sweet, hot mouth back and forth between his cock and Ty's, he knew he loved her. He loved her when she blushed timidly; he loved her when she sucked his best friend's cock for all she was worth. He loved her when she let go of everything her past had instilled in her, trading it for pure carnal pleasure. He loved her for going for it completely, and for turning him on like no woman had ever come close to turning him on before. No other woman would ever have this effect on him, he knew.

All at once, as if she suddenly could no longer decide whose hard-on she wanted in her mouth, she stopped and pulled on both of them, pulled them in even closer and they had no choice but to let her. She pulled the two cocks together until their heads touched and then she licked at them as if they were one.

Jack couldn't help trembling. So much sensation—physical, visual, visceral. She wrapped her sweet, lovely little mouth around the heads of both shafts then, each of them entering at one corner of her mouth. Watching her was fucking astounding. Feeling the wetness of her mouth on him as she rubbed their cocks together inside was nearly too much to take.

Yet somehow he steeled himself and did take it, because he knew this was a moment that would never come back to him and, like her, he wanted to experience it, every bit of it, even the parts that surprised the hell out of him, like how damn good Ty's hard shaft felt against his own.

Just then she released them from her mouth, but not from her grip—she held their cocks together, rubbed them one against the other like they were sticks of wood and she was trying to start a fire. And still Jack trembled, and Ty was breathing, "God. Oh God," letting his head fall back in ecstasy, and she said in a small but intent voice, "You two are so beautiful together, do you know that? Your cocks are beautiful like this."

He felt the warm rush of delight that came with pleasing her, imagined she must feel something like he felt watching her with Felicia at the strip club the other night.

"And you, *chere*," he managed to say, "are so incredibly hot I almost can't stand it."

"Are you going to come soon?" she asked from below, still scissoring the two hard rods together.

He looked at Ty, who was peering back, and was honest—as honest as being with Liz had somehow taught him to be. "If we keep this up—yeah, any minute."

"Do you *want* to come like this?" she asked, her voice gone breathy.

He managed a sort of strangled laugh. "I think *you* probably want us to, and if that's what you want, darlin', sure...but I really want a hell of a lot more of you first."

At this, she released them both and they leaned back to a more relaxed position. He met her gaze, then Ty's. No point in denying he'd just been aroused as hell by his best friend's cock on his—Ty seemed to know it, too; his *bon ami* just looked at him with the same glassy-eyed passion he'd been wearing on his face the last hour or so.

"All right," she said gently. "Have me."

Chapter 9

She lay between them in the rumpled sheets, her back to Ty, her front to Jack, all of them bare from head to toe. She felt wrung out from all the sex already—not just physically, but in her mind, too. Things had happened that she'd never *decided* to let happen. She'd never made a conscious decision to lie between their big beautiful shafts and suck them so brazenly. She'd never made a conscious decision to bring their cocks together the way she had, to make them move against each other whether they wanted to or not. The reckless wantonness had seemed to spread through her like a disease, taking her over, making her surrender every ounce of the self she knew to make way for the sexual being she had become with them.

And yet, like everything else she'd experienced with Jack, she didn't regret it, *couldn't* regret it. He'd opened so many doors to her, and this, tonight, was simply following her body's lead, succumbing to her darker self. A self that seemed to drive Jack mad with passion, a self that reveled in all she was experiencing, so how could she harbor regrets as she lay sandwiched between two muscular male bodies? She couldn't—that simple. She could only drink it in, experience still more of it and let the freedom of it fill her with hedonistic joy.

She kissed Jack—a series of soft, sexy tongue kisses—as both men ran their strong hands over her receptive body. No curve went untouched, unexplored—and twice the amount of sensation from any normal liaison flooded her sensitive body.

Jack's big, beautiful cock was nestled against her pussy, warm and arousing. Behind her, Ty's rubbed in the center of her ass, creating an indelible friction when she moved against them both. Sweet sensation from the front, from the back, front, back, front, back—*more, I need so much more.*

Her slick movements brought Jack's cock deeper into her slit until finally it lodged just where she wanted it, against her clit. Behind her, Ty's hard shaft eased against her time and again, slowly moving lower, lower, one sweet gentle thrust against the little fissure of her ass, and then lower still, until he was pushing against her opening and finally got inside. She cried out lightly at his entry—that immediate filling-up always caught her off guard with a combination of shock and sheer pleasure.

The way the three of them moved together was just as passionate as either of their earlier encounters, yet slower, more controlled. There was something soft about it, as if they'd grown used to the combination of three now and could settle into a more leisurely sort of fucking.

To kiss Jack as another man fucked her was unbelievably sensuous. She thought he felt it, too—their kisses took on a new life, a new meaning somehow. Whereas once they'd not kissed so much, now a kiss seemed the ultimate form of affection.

Of course, having his cock wedged against her clit so tightly was what really drove her toward orgasm. But no, she thought—it *wasn't* just that. It was *all* of it. It was being filled by Ty, it was having her pussy so gently assaulted from both directions, it was the very act of welcoming two men to her body at once, it was the *sharing*. Between her and Jack. Just as when she'd been with the strippers at Club Venus—so much of her pleasure had been about simply sharing it with Jack, simply experiencing it along with him.

When she came, it was long and somehow gentle yet intense. She leaned her head back, moaned her release, drank in the sensations of each man thrusting at her as the orgasm radiated out through her body. Low, searing pulses echoing through her like sonar. *Yes, yes.*

Ty came next, just after her, pulling out with a hot groan that rippled all through her, murmuring, "Now, now…ah yeah. Yeah." She practically growled when his semen spattered her in three hot bursts, and she relished his labored breath when he finally rolled to his back behind her, spent.

The moment Ty withdrew, she wanted Jack inside her. But she didn't even need to say it—they all three seemed to know the final act of this play would be his. She rolled gently to her back in Ty's arms. He wrapped around her, held her breasts in his hands, as Jack parted her legs. He reached between her thighs, up under, to her ass, and his fingers came away wet with white fluid, which he smeared on one breast. Another swipe and her other breast was wet—he left Ty to rub it in as he pushed his strong cock into her cunt.

Oh God—having Jack inside her felt so immensely right. Being fucked by Ty had been wonderful, but Jack was the man who had freed her, and taken such wonderful care of her. Jack was the man she was in love with. His big, beautiful shaft pumped into her hard and sweet as he kissed her—her mouth, her neck. His hands roamed her hips, sides, finally gripping firmly onto her breasts, still damp with Ty's come.

"This won't take long, *chere*," he breathed close to her ear. "Too much excitement tonight."

"That's all right," she promised. "Just fuck me hard and deep and don't stop until you explode."

At her prodding, Jack's cock pounded into her with even more force. She cried out with each punishing stroke, caught in a place of near pleasure/pain he fucked her so intensely. Above her, his teeth were clenched, his eyes feral slits of darkness. She spread her legs wider, wanting more and more of him inside her—*deep, hard.*

"Oh!" she whimpered when one of Ty's hands dropped from her breast to her pussy. Yes, yes, he rubbed her clit as Jack pummeled her with the most severely pleasurable fuck of her life. "Mmm," she moaned as Ty's fingers moved in brisk, vigorous motions over her clitoris. "God, yes," she breathed, thinking—*soon, soon, oh, she was going to come, so damn hard.*

"Is that good, baby, the way you like it?" Ty asked from behind.

"Mmm, yes!" She fucked his fingers as much as she fucked Jack's cock, and the idea of his hand being so very near to Jack's erection, wondering if there were instances when he was touching Jack, too, was the impetus that pushed her over the edge.

"Ohhhh!" she cried as the short but brutal climax broke, echoing fiercely through her whole body.

"That's right, honey, come for us," Ty urged.

She drove her cunt harder against both means of stimulation—*Yes! Yes! Yes!*—until, when she least expected it, Jack yelled, too.

"Ah, me, too, baby! Here I go!" He drove himself even deeper into her, his eyes shut in ecstasy, grunting a release that seemed as powerful as hers had been. "I'm comin' in you, darlin', I'm comin' so fuckin' hard for you!" His powerful strokes continued to pummel her, bury her, making her close her eyes and see new colors…until finally they eased, stopped, and the only sound was that of heavy breathing; hers, his, Ty's.

Jack bracketed her face with his hands and kissed her, firm and long, and then finally he withdrew as, together, they all collapsed in an exhausted heap.

* * * * *

The next day was Monday—which brought a rather rude awakening to an utterly astounding weekend for Liz. Ty was gone when they woke and she would have loved to snuggle with Jack for awhile, but Monday, of course, meant work, and she knew she'd never make it on time.

"You could just wear your sexy red dress," Jack teased her from bed as she washed up in the bathroom. "I'm sure the men in your office would enjoy it as much as I did."

Coming back into the room naked, she grinned at him. "Not *quite* as much as you did."

He laughed. "Well, I hope not, but I'm sure they'd enjoy the view from the *outside*."

She did don the dress again in order for Jack to drive her home, and even as rumpled from sleep as she was, she thought he seemed aroused by the sight of her in it.

"So," he said, pulling into the driveway of Lynda's opulent home, "tonight? Or...do you need an evening to rest?"

The truth was—she did need an evening to rest. She needed an evening to look for a new place to live, to maybe figure out how to get the rest of her things from Todd's house, to get her life reorganized a little since the shock of having it turned upside down. But she couldn't pass up the opportunity to be with Jack—he was beginning to seem as essential to her as air or water. "Tell you what," she said with a hopeful smile. "Maybe we could...tone things down a little. Maybe you could come over here for a change, we'll order a pizza or something simple, and just have a quiet evening."

"All right." He nodded, but she couldn't tell if he was disappointed by the suggestion. She had no idea if Lynda would be home tonight, or if they'd have any chance for sex; surely he was wondering the same thing.

As she kissed him goodbye, she said, "Last night, Jack, was...the most extraordinary experience I've ever had."

"Me, too," he told her. "*Merci, chere*. Thank you for giving me that. Fulfilling my fantasy."

She gazed into his dark, hypnotic eyes. "It was truly my pleasure."

* * * * *

It had been a long day and by the end of it, Liz was glad she'd opted for a quieter-than-usual night with Jack. She still wasn't sure if such an evening would satisfy a man with such a zest for life and sex, but her odyssey of the past few days had left her exhausted.

Walking in the front door, she found the house quiet—and a note from Lynda on the refrigerator: *Barhopping tonight on Bourbon with some old friends. If you and Jack are in the neighborhood, keep an eye out for me—I'll probably be the drunk one pretending it's still Mardi Gras and flashing her tits at young boys for beads :) Hope you had a nice night with Jack, honey—and hope the red dress wowed him.*

What an understatement, she thought with a chuckle. Both the part about the dress wowing him *and* the part about having a nice night with Jack.

Although she adored Lynda, she couldn't be sorry her friend had other plans tonight, so she and Jack could be alone. Climbing the stairs to her room, she contemplated what to wear for this evening's get-together and decided to play it simple yet a little bit naughty with a pair of denim shorts and a fitted t-shirt—a sexy bra and panty set underneath.

Shedding the day's suit, blouse, and pantyhose onto her bed, she moved to the dresser and opened the drawer where she'd placed her lingerie. She selected a demi-bra and matching thong made of sky blue lace.

Padding down the hall in the white bra and panties she'd worn to work, she entered the bathroom and washed up with a cool cloth—the grueling heat and humidity she'd been warned to expect in New Orleans' summer months was coming on full force already and she wanted to freshen up before seeing her lover this evening.

Upon returning to her room, she shed her bra, adding it to the pile on the bed, and had just reached for the sexy blue one when she heard a noise and looked up to see the closet door opening.

Fright assailed her, freezing her in place.

A second later, Todd appeared, his eyes filled with venom.

Damn it, damn it, damn it—she'd been so typically naïve to think he wouldn't realize where she'd gone. She'd just thought...oh hell, she'd *wanted* to think he wouldn't realize she was there because it had been a simple, easy answer when she'd needed one, and she'd honestly never thought Todd was crazy enough to sneak into someone else's home—but clearly she'd underestimated him again.

"You look lovely, my dear," he said, a wry smile reshaping his face.

She felt more truly naked before him than ever before—felt his eyes assaulting her, turning her into more of an object than a person. She instinctively reached for the blouse she'd recently discarded, holding it up over her breasts.

"Come now, you don't think you can keep me from what's rightfully mine, do you, Elizabeth?"

Oh God, he really was off the deep end! Her only choice, though, was to act tough, *be* tough. "Look, Todd, I don't know what you think you're doing, sneaking into Lynda's house and hiding in my closet, but I suggest you get out of here before I call the police."

He glanced at the room's phone—unfortunately located on the side of the bed where he currently stood. He looked smug, still wearing a menacing smile. "I don't think you'll be able to make that call, my love. And I don't think you really want to, either."

She blinked, nonplussed by his bizarre demeanor. For the first time, he was actually scaring her—a lot. Before now, she'd taken these episodes as aberrant behavior based on his shock over the breakup, but finally she was seeing—*believing*—that *this* was the real Todd.

She had to figure a way out of this situation, and that meant she had to keep herself from panicking.

He began slowly rounding the bed, heading toward her. She refused to cower, though—and only hoped her fear didn't show on her face.

"Elizabeth, my dear, I can only presume you were planning to put on that hot little bra and panties for the Neanderthal who came to your rescue a few days ago, but I forgive you. You're just a little confused right now." He stood directly in front of her, only a foot away. "You're angry with me and I understand that. But you don't really want anyone else, you only want me. And I'm fully prepared to remind you just how much."

She shook her head. "Todd, you're delusional. I *don't* want you. We are *over*, okay? Listen to me. We're done. And I don't know why you want me so much—now you're free to have *whoever* you want in your lap *whenever* you want. So go home and leave me alone."

"My dear little Elizabeth," he said, as if berating an unruly child. "I want you because you'll be the perfect wife. We belong together—you know that as much as I do. So I might get a little extracurricular entertainment on the side now and then. What does it matter? You've had your fun with your big caveman, but that's over now. From now on, you're only going to be with me."

A sense of self-preservation forced her to finally take a step back from him, but he reached out and grabbed her wrist, using the other hand to rip the blouse away from her chest. "You have such great tits, my love—just seeing them right now has me turned on." He tightened his grip so much it hurt. "You're going to fuck me now, Elizabeth. You're going to fuck me just like you've been fucking that other guy. Only you're going to like it better with me, do you hear me? Then when we're done, you're going to tell me how much you missed it, and how good I was. And we're going to go home together where we belong, where all this nonsense can come to an end."

Up to now, Liz had kept her head about her. She'd been frightened, but able to act brave, still not quite believing Todd would really do something like hurt her or—God forbid—rape her. Before a week ago, she'd never seen him behave this way. He might have been sneaking off to Club Venus every night for weeks, but when he'd been with her, he'd remained his steady, reliable, respectful self. Today, though, his eyes were different than she ever remembered them being. Maybe she just hadn't really looked at them all that much before. Or maybe she just hadn't wanted to *see,* because back then, good conservative Liz always played the role she was given without protest or doubt. Now, a true sense of panic began to bite into her, seeming to gnaw at her from the inside out.

Still, she had to try to reason with him, even if he was out of his mind. She was here alone, Jack wasn't due for another hour, and she certainly couldn't overpower Todd. Reasoning with him was her only hope.

"Todd, I'm not having sex with you. You need to go. Now." She'd sounded forceful, but her voice had come out shaky, damn it.

"I can't go without making love to you, darling. Once I do, you'll realize we belong together. You won't want anyone else. You'll just want to put this whole silly breakup behind us, like I do, and get on with our life together."

He continued squeezing her arm so tight it hurt. "Let go of me, Todd. Let go of me right now."

"Are you going to make love to me the way a good wife should?"

She let out a nervous breath. "Of course not."

"Then I can't let you go yet."

As panic began to consume her, she reacted with her gut and tried to jerk her arm away. His grip was too tight and she only succeeded in pulling him off balance, making him crash into her—his other arm came around her nearly naked body, tight.

"Fuck me, Elizabeth," he growled as if they were sharing mutual passion. "Fuck me now."

Chapter 10

She couldn't take this—having his arms around her, being naked with him, *against* him. Following her instincts, she began to struggle, and when that didn't work, she drove her knee upward into his crotch as hard as she could.

Thank God—a direct hit. It made him release her entirely as he yelped and curled into himself, backing away. "You bitch!"

Just then the doorbell rang and, even in her state of near-nakedness, Liz ran out the door, down the hall, down the steps, thinking of nothing but getting help before Todd got his strength back. She ripped open the door to find Jack on the other side.

"*Chere*," he said with a wicked little smile, taking in her nakedness but not her panic, "I thought we were gonna have a quiet evenin', but–"

She shook her head furiously. "Todd's upstairs. He was waiting in my closet. He came out when I was changing clothes."

Jack's eyes turned instantly hard and black as he absorbed her words. His stance grew rigid and his hands curled into fists. "Did he hurt you?"

She thought vaguely about her sore arm, but knew she'd gotten off lucky. "No. Not quite. I mean...I think he was going to...but then I..." She couldn't get anything sensible out of her mouth.

Yet it didn't matter because Jack stepped inside, shut the door and headed to the stairs. By the time he reached the top, Todd was yelling, "Come back here, you bitch! I'm not done with you yet!"

Jack headed straight toward the voice and Liz frantically followed.

When she stepped in the room, Jack was hovering over Todd's crumpled form. He looked back at her. "What happened to him, *chere*?"

"I kneed him in the balls."

Even through his anger, she saw the admiration in his eyes. "Nice job. But it's not half as bad as the little shit deserves."

Jack reached for a robe on a nearby hook and tossed it to Liz, reminding her she wore nothing but a pair of white undies. She slid the silky beige robe on, cinching the tie tight in front.

"Get the hell out of here," Todd suddenly spat at Jack from his place on the floor. "She's mine and we don't need an outsider interfering in our business."

Jack looked from Todd to Liz and said in a surprisingly calm tone, "Darlin', why don't you give me just a few minutes alone with Todd here?"

Liz had no idea what Jack intended to do to Todd, but she hardly cared. This had been the scare of her life and she was more than ready to exit the room and leave the decisions in Jack's hands.

* * * * *

Once she was gone, Jack looked down on the little creep and thought about what to do. He wanted to beat the shit out of him, wanted to pound him to an unrecognizable pulp. Given the adrenaline pumping through his veins, he thought he could do it with ease.

But he had to play this smart. Todd was the sort of "upstanding" guy who could sic the police on him, all the while seeming totally aboveboard with his suit and tie life of high finance. And even though a lot of the New Orleans police knew Jack—by reputation if not personally—some of them didn't like him. They didn't like a guy who could solve the cases they couldn't, who could make them look bad at their profession.

He wanted to teach Todd a hard lesson, but he also didn't want to go to jail for assault—not the least of which reason was that if he was in jail, who would keep Todd away from Liz?

Even so, as he stood there watching Todd slowly rise to his feet, he just couldn't help himself—he pulled back his fist and slammed it squarely into Todd's jaw. The blow knocked him back to the floor and again Jack thought of all the things he'd like to do to a guy who attacks women—*his* woman especially. When Todd once again stumbled to his feet, muttering, "You better back off, buddy, or you'll be sorry," Jack said, "No, Todd, you're the sorry one," and belted him in the gut.

Todd doubled over and Jack felt damn good as his fist began to ache from the contact with Todd's jaw. It was satisfying to inflict pain on the asshole.

But he had to stop before he got carried away. So he simply dropped to one knee, hovering over Todd, and lifted him by his shirt collar. "Listen to me, you shithead. You're gonna stop botherin' Liz right now. In fact, you're gonna do more than that. You're gonna stay as far away from her as you physically can. 'Cause if I find out you've so much as looked at her, let alone talked to her or touched her, I promise you're gonna hurt a lot worse than you do right now. Got it?"

The man on the floor looked as if he might break into tears, but then he seemed to regain a bit of his usual pompous air. "Are you threatening me?"

Releasing Todd's collar, Jack shrugged. "No, not me. You must have misunderstood. And if you bother tellin' anyone about this, I guarantee that's how it'll come out. I'm pretty convincin' when I need to be." Jack leaned a little closer to Todd, tried to look a little more dangerous. "Now, do you get the message here? Do you understand that you're gonna leave her alone?"

Todd still looked defiant, and Jack mentally dared him to disagree—it would be all the incentive he needed to rip the man to shreds, jail or no jail. But Todd finally said, "Yeah, sure, I got the message."

"Good. 'Cause you know those balls Liz just kicked? Give me a reason and I'll tear 'em off and feed 'em to you with a spoon."

With that, he yanked Todd to his feet, handily bending one of the dickhead's arms behind his back so he couldn't break free of the hold. Without wasting any more words on the little shit, Jack escorted him from the room. Liz stood by the stairs, eyes wide.

"This asshole won't be botherin' you anymore. *Right*?" He jerked hard on Todd's arm.

"Yeah. Right."

Accompanying Todd down the stairs, his arm still locked behind his back, Jack opened the big front door and gave the creep a shove. Todd stumbled down the front steps, landing on the walk. "Get the fuck outta here," Jack said, "and don't even think about comin' back." He slammed the door and locked it, looking up to see his sweet Liz padding down the steps on bare feet, the satiny robe hugging her curves.

He met her at the bottom and swept her into his arms in a huge, protective bear hug.

"Thank God you showed up when you did," she whispered against his chest.

He smiled lightly to himself. "Oh, I don't know—looked to me like you did a pretty good job of takin' care of him all by yourself."

"Wh-what are you even doing here?" She looked up into his eyes. "I wasn't expecting you for another hour or so, and I was so sure I was alone and on my own with him."

He shrugged, still holding her. "I just had a feelin' maybe I should come early." Part wanting to see her so bad it hurt, but also part P.I.'s instinct—like before, something had indeed nagged at him, urging him to check on her and make sure she was okay. He said a silent prayer of thanks to have been blessed with such gut feelings.

Gazing down at her, he lifted one hand to push the hair from her face. "It's time you move in with me, *chere*. I can't stand knowin' this guy is right next door to you."

He thought she looked tempted, almost heard the "yes" leaving her lips, but instead she gently pulled free of his embrace and walked into the living room to sit down on the couch, her back to him. "We'll see, Jack. We'll see."

He sighed, glad she couldn't take in his face at the moment. He could read the writing on the wall clearly enough—she still had no interest in turning this into a serious relationship. Which he'd known already, but somehow, in these last few minutes, he'd hoped against hope that maybe things would have changed.

Whenever she left him, it was going to wound him in a way he might never really recover from. It wasn't a choice, or a circumstance that might change—he knew as surely as he knew alligators lived in the bayou that it's just how things were.

"How about I order that pizza?" he said, now just wanting to comfort her in whatever little ways he might be capable of. He walked around the couch to face her. Her expression looked a little more peaceful than a moment ago, which made the fist squeezing his heart loosen a little.

"That would be nice." She pointed toward the kitchen. "Phone book's in the drawer by the fridge. Anything but anchovies and onions." She got to her feet. "I'm going to go get dressed now. I just...kind of want to have clothes on right now—you know?"

He nodded, and for the first time, he thought he understood how close she'd come to being raped by her ex-fiancé. The knowledge sent a cold chill slithering down his spine. "Sure, darlin', I understand. Go get dressed."

As Jack thumbed through the phone book looking for a pizza place, he made a decision. Just threatening Todd wasn't good enough. As he'd contemplated a few days back, he was going to have to do something about the jerk, take some measures to keep Liz safe—without her knowledge, of course.

What she didn't know wouldn't hurt her.

* * * * *

The world seemed almost normal and sane as they lounged on the couch, an open pizza box on the coffee table, an old movie on the TV. Liz nibbled at the crust of the slice she'd just eaten, feeling full. She wore the tee and shorts she'd intended; Jack, too, was casual in blue jeans and a t-shirt.

Seeing she was done, Jack took the plate from her hand and lowered it to the table, then gently pulled her into his arms. He didn't say anything for a long time, just held her, and it felt so good, perfect, like nothing could ever hurt her as long as she was with him.

"You doin' okay? You've been quiet since..."

Yes, she had been quiet for awhile. For so many reasons. Certainly the scene with Todd had been terrifying, but there was something else on her mind, too—her love for Jack. It was tearing her apart, yet she'd still kept herself from agreeing to move in with him. She couldn't accept that much kindness from a man who'd unwittingly been drawn deeper into her problems than she'd ever intended—nor could she let herself risk falling any harder for him than she already had. The pain when it was over would be excruciating, already, but to live with him would be to love him even more, and it wasn't something she was willing to put herself through. Being with Jack had made her realize she'd never known real love before, and now that she did—damn it, it was scary.

"I was...really frightened earlier," she admitted softly.

"You wouldn't have to be afraid if you just came to stay with me."

So sweet, this man, so protective. In the beginning, she'd thought him gruff and unemotional—now she knew better, knew his emotions came through in actions or touches more than mere words, and she knew he was too good of a man to let a woman live in danger if he could help it. She didn't reply.

"Either way, here or there, I won't let him bother you again, *chere*." He pulled her close and kissed her forehead.

Hours later, they awoke in each other's arms on the couch. The TV was still on, the clock on the mantel said it was close to midnight.

"Guess Lynda isn't home yet," she thought aloud.

"I'm stayin' the night," he told her.

"You don't have to do that, Jack. I'm sure she'll be home soon."

"I don't care. I'm not lettin' you out of my sight tonight. It's non-negotiable."

* * * * *

She dreamed of Jack that night, slightly nonsensical but pleasant dreams of making love to him on the lawn of a castle, of dancing with him in a large, ornate ballroom, of sweet kisses beneath a maple tree turned October gold. Echoes of old, romantic fantasies from her girlhood made new. So apparently *that* part of her still existed, too.

Waking up in his arms the next morning was like leaving a good dream for an even better one. She'd awakened with him on several successive mornings, of course, but somehow having him in *her* bed was different, even more comforting. Perhaps the truth was, despite her bravado, she was feeling less and less confident about living right next door to Todd, so she'd have to change that situation very soon. In the meantime, though, just feeling Jack's warm body next to her in her own bed was like a little slice of heaven.

They hadn't made love last night—she supposed they both knew she needed a little time to recover from her encounter with Todd. Still, she'd felt the need to bring it up—it was such a change of pace for them. "No sex tonight?" she'd asked with a half-playful smile when Jack suggested they go up to bed, to sleep.

"*Rest* tonight," he'd replied, his hand at the small of her back as she climbed the stairs ahead of him.

She'd peeked over her shoulder. "You're missing a beautiful bra and panty set under these clothes."

He'd grinned, although he'd looked tired. "Time for that another night, *chere*."

His simple reply had, oddly, put a new bit of hope in Liz's heart when she'd not expected it. Those uncomplicated words had planted a seed, something she'd never really even considered before—that maybe this would go on, not be a short-lived thing. Maybe her affair with Jack, in spite of—or maybe even because of—all its hedonism, meant something to him. Who knew, maybe falling asleep with that idea in her head had been part of why waking up next to him this morning had felt so new, so special.

Throughout the day at work, though, Liz decided that she wanted to get back to normal with Jack tonight. Normal meaning "normal for them." Meaning new sexual adventures. Last night she'd felt so vulnerable, and feeling that way with Jack was still dangerous. When she thought of having something serious with Jack, all she could see was the way all her past relationships had turned out—leaving her heartbroken. Strangely, her relationship with Todd was the only instance where she'd come out emotionally strong and unscathed. Maybe that was why she'd been able to trust in him and say yes when he'd proposed. Maybe deep down she'd known she didn't feel the deep emotions for him that she'd felt for other men, known he didn't have the power to hurt her. Jack, however, was a different story. And the truth was, maybe she was in too deep with him already, but she just kept telling herself that so long as she knew this was temporary, so long as she kept her head about her, that she could handle it when it was over. So getting away from emotions and back to hot sex seemed like a very good idea.

Besides, she wanted to get last night's terrorizing meeting with her ex-fiancé out of her mind, and she knew from experience that sex with Jack definitely had the power to rid her of all other thoughts.

She called him from work at his office to tell him she wanted to hit the Quarter tonight. "Let's do something fun, exciting," she said.

She heard him chuckle on the other end of the line. "Still lookin' for adventure, huh, *chere*?"

She was glad he couldn't see what she suspected was a sheepish smile. "I suppose you could say that. It just seems like...there's still more out there to do, more I haven't experienced."

She felt his sexy grin without even being able to see it. "Well, darlin', whatever you want to experience, I'm real happy to experience it with you."

Just hearing his voice curl around the words made her hot. And going to work every day in her professional suit, knowing what she'd been doing at night, made her feel like she harbored a delicious secret, that she lived a shocking double life. "Jack?" she whispered into the phone, feeling oh-so-daring even as co-workers buzzed about the office around her.

"*Oui, chere*?"

She lowered her voice even further. "I'm wet just thinking about you."

The little growl he emitted sent another surge of moisture into her panties. "You just made me hard."

"Mmm, that gives me something to look forward to."

"Me, too," he laughed.

"Until tonight."

"*Au revoir*."

* * * * *

That afternoon after work, Liz went shopping at a store on Canal Street that she'd passed several hundred times without ever a thought of going in. The shop windows at The Leather Lair housed mannequins wearing all forms of sexy leather—from motorcycle gear to lingerie that looked designed for some serious S&M. She told the salesclerk she was looking for a sexy dress, and twenty minutes later, she walked out with a shopping bag of items that would transform her into a different sort of woman than she'd ever been with Jack before.

As she drove home, she was filled with anticipation, wanting to don her new ensemble and show Jack—but first, she needed to talk to Lynda, so she was glad to find her friend's car in the garage when she pulled in.

"Long time, no see," Lynda said when Liz walked in the door. She sat on the couch watching the evening news, but she turned the volume down at Liz's arrival.

Liz joined her on the sofa. "I'm glad you're home."

Lynda wrinkled her brow, realizing immediately something was amiss. "What's wrong, honey? You look worried."

"It's about Todd," she began on a sigh. "Lynda, you need to know that Todd let himself into your house yesterday. He was waiting in my room when I got home. I checked the locks and he doesn't seem to have broken in, so he must've found the key you keep under the planter on the back porch. I'm so sorry to have brought that kind of trouble upon you."

Lynda reached out for her hands. "Don't be silly, honey! The only thing I'm concerned about here is your safety. Now, what the hell happened? Did he try to hurt you? What did you do? I'll kill the son of a bitch if he hurt you."

Liz let out a breath she hadn't realized she was holding. Lynda was such a good friend to her. "Well, long story short, I kneed him in the balls and, fortunately, Jack showed up right then, so he got rid of him for me. I think he roughed Todd up a little, too, but I still can't guarantee Todd won't come back."

"Well, thank God for Jack! Now, the first thing we'll do is get rid of the key under the planter. And even though I've never been fond of Todd, I don't think he'd actually break in, do you?"

Liz gave her head a skeptical tilt. "Before yesterday, I would have agreed with you. But now, I'm not sure. He seemed to be off the deep end, and I think I've underestimated how nuts he is over this breakup. He just can't seem to accept it."

Lynda looked pensive, thoughtful. She rubbed her thumb over the back of Liz's hand. "Honey, I truly love having you here and I want you to stay as long as you want, okay? But I just have to ask—do you think it's wise for you to be living so close to him if he's acting as crazy as you say?"

Liz sighed, tired of worrying about Todd, wishing he would just go away. But it wasn't that simple. "Well, since yesterday, I'm not sure it's wise at all. So I'm going to be actively looking for a new place, and until then, well...I guess I just have to hope for the best."

"I'm glad you have someone like Jack looking out for you."

"So am I, Lynda, but..."

"But what?"

She let out a sigh. "But it's hard not to feel like a burden to him. He's very protective and I'm so thankful he cares, but I also don't want to depend on him to look out for me with Todd forever, you know? When the time comes that he wants to end the relationship, I don't want worries about Todd to make him stay with me if his heart isn't in it."

Lynda gave a solemn nod. "I understand what you mean. But from where I sit, Jack doesn't seem to be going anywhere. Maybe he's...here to stay."

Another kernel of hope—but Liz just couldn't let herself believe that Jack cared for her in a deep, lasting way. If she did, she'd end up feeling stupid as well as hurt in the end. She'd been there before and she didn't want to go there again. She wanted desperately to come out of this thankful for the passion they'd shared, not sorry. "Maybe, but I don't want the situation with Todd hanging over our relationship. So the sooner I can get my own place, somewhere away from Todd, the better I'll feel on all counts."

"Well, you know I'll help any way I can. And I'll miss you when you go."

Liz summoned a small smile for her friend. "Thanks, Lynda. You're the best." Then she gave her head a curious tilt. "So, how was *your* night? Did you come home with any beads?"

"Oh, honey," she laughed, "you wouldn't *believe* my night." She placed her hand on Liz's nylon-covered knee.

"Try me."

Lynda's eyes widened slightly. "Well, let's just say I ended up in the arms of a very handsome and well-hung college boy before the night was through."

Liz blinked. "Going for the young ones now, huh?"

Lynda shrugged. "What they lack in finesse they make up for with enthusiasm. And how about you? Any new adventures with your hot P.I.?"

Liz regretted the blush, but couldn't stop it. One of these days she'd get past her old shyness, but for now, it kept rearing its head from time to time. "Actually, we've been doing *lots* of naughty things together, but I suppose the most noteworthy is..."

"Yes?" Lynda prodded, wide-eyed.

"We had a three-way with his best friend."

Lynda's mouth dropped open and Liz was actually pleased to have shocked someone generally so unshockable.

"A very sexy blond named Ty," she went on. "You'd love him. We had a very...memorable time together at Jack's place and..."

"And?"

"And...having two men at once was the most amazing experience of my life. I would definitely recommend it."

Lynda broke into a broad smile. "You, my friend, have come a long way in a very short time. And maybe I'll just take that recommendation, coming from such a trusted source." She winked. "I'm proud of you, honey, for loosening up so much, for learning to enjoy your sexuality. And I bet Jack is just in heaven."

* * * * *

Liz suspected the French Quarter was the only place in the world she could get out of her car in a leather mini-dress and black leather boots and walk up the street without feeling out of place or self-conscious.

Even so, though, she felt changed in this outfit, as if she were someone different than she'd been a few days before. The sleeveless dress stopped high on her thighs and closed in front with a two-way zipper that could be adjusted from the top or the bottom. So she'd lowered the top to show considerable cleavage, and she'd raised the bottom as high as she dared without getting arrested. The supple leather hugged her every curve—her breasts felt heavy and big pressing against the tight fit. Her pussy tingled in the warm breeze, only a few short inches from being exposed.

The boots looked downright sinful with pointed toes and silver stiletto heels. They rose up over her knees, yet the short dress still showed plenty of thigh. She'd accessorized with large silver hoop earrings and a black choker, as well as more eye makeup than usual. As she approached the bar where she'd planned to meet Jack, she felt like walking sin.

She quickly felt all the eyes upon her—men who wanted to see what a woman like her would do to them in bed, and women who were perhaps curious of the same thing. A week ago she couldn't have worn this outfit. Even when she'd walked into Jack's office that first day, dressed so sexy and acting so brazen—that was nothing compared to this. The heat of knowing she was *worthy* to wear such a sex-promising outfit ran through her veins and made her cunt pulse against the barstool she climbed up on. Her breasts strained against the leather; her whole body felt super-sensitized in a way that only anticipating Jack could make it.

Strange, she thought, that she felt so much better upon leaving home and reaching the French Quarter. Much of the Quarter was considered very dangerous after dark, yet she felt much safer here in Jack's world than back in the Garden District of Todd's. Most people would think she was crazy, but being in Jack's little part of the universe made her feel at once content and adventurous; safe, yet in another way more willing to take risks. The thought—and her daring new dominatrix look—made her want to do something even riskier tonight, made her want to keep living life to the fullest with her hot, sexy lover.

Could anything be more intense than being in bed with two men at once? She wasn't sure, but she wanted to try, both for herself, and also to reward Jack's noble sweetness. He took such good care of her; she was going to take good care of him, in a different way, for as long as he wanted her to.

"What are you drinking, sweetheart?" She looked up to find the bartender, an attractive mid-thirties man with dark hair and a strong jawline. "The guys at the end of the bar want to buy you a drink."

She glanced down to see several handsome suit and tie types. A couple of them smiled, one lifted a hand to wave. She smiled back, then returned her attention to the bartender. "I'll have a hurricane, but I hope they won't be too disappointed to find out I'm meeting my boyfriend here."

My boyfriend. It had just come out. And it had felt wonderful to call Jack that.

The bartender offered a shrug and a grin. "Hey, you take your chances when you send a drink across the room." After placing the tall red concoction in front of her a moment later, he moved to the end of the bar to fill the guys in on her "taken" status.

"Gettin' started on the fun without me?" Jack asked, suddenly next to her. She looked up to find him wearing a teasing grin.

"I have admirers at the end of the bar," she informed him coquettishly.

He glanced down to the suits, then back at her. "Can't blame 'em—look at you, *chere*." He gave her a long once-over from head to toe. "Almost didn't recognize you. You look...dangerous."

She smiled. "Is that a good thing?"

"If you're askin' me if I'm turned on, oh yeah. Those boots are killer and I already wanna feel 'em wrapped around my back."

When the bartender returned, Jack ordered a hurricane of his own. "So," he went on, "are we into whips and chains tonight?"

She laughed, considering her answer. "I'm...not sure exactly *what* we're into tonight, not yet. I'm hoping it will just sort of reveal itself to us—know what I mean?"

His grin was typically wicked. "What I know is that you're gonna be fightin' guys off tonight, so maybe we'd best stop somewhere and buy ourselves that whip anyway, darlin'. Then again," he glanced down to her feet, "I suppose those heels could qualify as weapons on their own, huh?"

After they finished their drinks, they left the bar to roam Bourbon Street. Darkness was descending on the thoroughfare of sin and debauchery, another night coming to life in the French Quarter. As Jack had predicted, Liz garnered even more stares than usual. Going from merely "sexy" to "sexy and dangerous" was making her feel as alive as the night itself. She wouldn't want this sort of attention every day or even every night of her life—she might not ever even want it again after tonight—but in this moment, each glance cast her way registered inside her, seeming to raise her temperature, making her cunt even more tingly and wanting.

Jack kept his arm around her as if to make sure every man on the street knew she was with him. And while it had been wildly thrilling to be shared with Ty the other night, it was equally as exciting to see Jack acting a little possessive.

As usual, the mood on the street was intoxicating and infectious. One didn't have to venture into the sex shops and strip joints to feel their aura in the air, and as on past nights, the decadence that was Bourbon Street was seeping into Liz's veins. As she and Jack passed by one sex club in particular, called the Pussycat's Claw, she urged him to slow down so she could take a closer look. Beneath the neon signs touting the "Live Sex Show" was a display of photos. Like the club she and Lynda had stopped to look at during her "reconnaissance mission" to the Quarter before meeting Jack at Club Venus that first time, these pictures showed a wide mixture of people actually fucking on a stage. Most pictures showed a man and woman having sex in a variety of skimpy costumes and settings, but one showed three girls in the remains of harem costumes touching each other, and one photo featured a guy with two girls.

"Maybe this is it," she said to Jack.

"Maybe this is what?"

"The exciting thing we're going to do tonight."

He smiled. "My hot *petite fille*, you never cease to amaze me."

She fluttered her eyelashes, feeling playful. "I'd think by now you'd be getting used to my wild side."

He gave a knowing nod. "Oh yes, indeed, darlin', you've proven yourself to be one hell of a wild woman, and yet..." He looked thoughtful, a small smile gracing his face.

"And yet what?"

"Like I just said, you still amaze me. Every single time you do somethin' new, I'm fuckin' astonished. Because I can't believe you're the same woman who still blushes sometimes when we talk about sex."

Liz bit her lip. "Blushing is an old habit, one I'm trying to break. But I like having the ability to surprise you."

"*Mais*, you've sure as hell succeeded at that," he said on a laugh. Then he looked toward the door of the establishment, open but revealing only darkness inside. "So, you wanna go in?"

She nodded, her skin tingling with anticipation. It was truly like a drug to her, having the power to keep shocking her lover, and now she was excited to see what exactly was taking place inside this building and how she would respond to it.

Stepping up to the door, she waited as Jack paid the doorman, then took her hand and led her into the dark interior.

They stepped into a small lobby area, where a cute but scruffy-looking guy stood behind a counter selling glasses and t-shirts with the Pussycat's Claw logo. Hard rock music filled the air, along with the smells of alcohol and...undeniably, sex.

The guy silently pointed the way and Jack led her through a curtained entrance to another room, dark but for the brightly lit stage where, as expected, a man and a woman were fucking. The woman lay on her back on a small bed covered with a girlish pink bedspread—she wore white stockings with a pink garter belt and pink high-heeled shoes. Her hair was in two blonde ponytails, tied with pink ribbons. The man wore a suit, with only his cock exposed. It was so raw; unlike the strip club, it held no teasing, no slow sensuality. It was real—a very hot fuck between what was portrayed to be a businessman and a young girl. He drove into her slow but hard, making her cry out with each thrust, and her face looked as impassioned as any Liz had ever seen. "Yes! Yes! Give me that cock!" the woman cried out, sensually pinching and toying with her nipples as she met his rough strokes.

Liz felt a bit frozen in place by the bluntness of the act before them, but Jack led her through the room until they reached two plush chairs. The chairs reminded her of the ones at Club Venus, except they were clearly older and well-used. They were sprinkled around the room, which, to her surprise, was somewhat full, with quite a few other women in the crowd. Although the room was kept very dark, likely to protect the patrons from being seen, Liz could make out enough to know the spectators crossed the spectrum from t-shirts and baggy jeans to guys in suits just like the one on the stage. The women were more like Liz—dressed sexy and looking ready. They all appeared entranced by what was taking place before them, and indeed, it was captivating to Liz, as well.

She was not as comfortable as at Club Venus—as evidenced by the chairs and other small details, the Pussycat's Claw was less lush and sophisticated, and the very rawness of the show gave her the sense she was witnessing something she should not be. Something intimate and forbidden, much more so than even the many lap dances she'd seen performed at the other club.

Yet the woman on stage appeared to be enjoying herself as much as Liz did when Jack was buried in her. She was beautiful with large, firm breasts and long, lovely legs which were now upright, her ankles resting on the man's shoulders as he thrust in and out of her. Every so often, the girl cried out, "Yes, baby," or "More, more," and as her initial shock wore off, Liz's pussy resumed the same hot throbbing she'd felt earlier—only now it was stronger, aching, needful.

After a while, the girl turned over, onto her hands and knees. The man reinserted his big cock and she let out a sexy moan. "Fuck me," she begged. "Please fuck me." The suited man pounded into her, picking up speed, making her whimper and moan. When he slapped her on the ass, she emitted a low growl. "Oooh, yeah, spank me! I've been a bad little girl!" Liz spotted beads of sweat trickling down the man's face as his slick shaft drove in and out of the blonde, who clenched her teeth now, saying, "Yeah, baby, give it to me! Let me have it!" They fucked much more frantically now than when Liz and Jack had first arrived and Liz was beginning to feel intoxicated by watching, drawn into the heat and roughness of their performance. As if reading her needs, Jack reached over and eased his hand high onto her thigh, caressing.

The man's groans grew deeper, louder, more intense, until he finally pulled out and shot his seed onto the blonde's pretty round ass, rubbing it in while she moaned. Liz's breasts felt so heavy she wished she could unzip her dress and reach inside to fondle them. This blunt, dirty live sex had aroused her wildly—*with* its bluntness, its very *realness*.

As curtains closed on the two "performers," Jack leaned over and, despite the room's darkness, she saw the wicked glimmer in his eye. "Wanna sit on my lap, little girl?"

She couldn't help smiling—and leaving her chair for his. Snuggling up on him and feeling the warmth of his arms close around her, she leaned to whisper in his ear. "Would you like that? Would you like me to dress up like a little girl for you?"

His grin was filled with heat. "I like *all* your surprises, *chere*. Don't tell me, just do it sometime."

His low whisper and the sexy possibilities his words implied made her cunt surge with moisture. She drew him into a slow, sexy tongue kiss and he ran his hands over her curves. "Just like the way you look tonight," he went on. "I love that you didn't tell me, that I just found you in a bar lookin' like you're gonna tie me up and make me obey you."

She smiled down at him. "Would you like *that*? Being tied up?"

"Didn't you hear me? I like *all* your surprises, and I like that you never seem to *stop* surprisin' me."

Just then, new music started and they looked up to see the curtains reopen on a new setting—a row of gym lockers and a long wooden bench. Onto the stage came three bouncy, pretty girls in cheerleading uniforms and more ponytails, and within a minute or so, two of them were sitting on the bench kissing each other—slow, soft

French kisses that looked undeniably delicate and sensuous taking place between only feminine mouths, feminine faces. Then the third cheerleader kneeled before one of the girls, parting her legs and pushing up her skirt.

After that, Liz only half-watched the staged seduction, thinking of her *own* seduction. Thinking of surprising Jack, shocking him, thrilling them both in a whole new way. That first night on Jack's balcony, Liz had discovered that when she was deeply impassioned, she hardly cared whether anyone was watching them or not—and that was how she felt now.

And the room was so blessedly dark, and they were in the back, almost in a corner—and she wanted to fuck him so badly she could taste it.

He was wonderfully hard against her leg, and his fingers already toyed with her zipper, easing it down slightly, then brushing his bent knuckles across her soft cleavage as he watched one cheerleader eat another's pussy. The third girl had taken her tight cheerleading sweater off and was kneading her small, high breasts. Liz almost leaned in to ask him if he'd like it if she dressed up as a cheerleader sometime, but then remembered—he liked all her surprises. So she'd just do it sometime.

Right now, though, tonight, she was not a cheerleader, or a little girl—she was a dominatrix in black leather, and she was going to remind him of that.

She turned in his lap until she could bring her leather-clad knees down on either side of him. Meeting his eyes, she saw the shock there.

"What are you doin', darlin'?"

She spoke low but with firm potency. "Fucking you."

Chapter 11

He raised his eyebrows. "Here?"

"Yes." With that, she unzipped her dress from the bottom, up to her crotch—just enough for him to see she wasn't wearing any panties, enough to see her freshly shaven pussy, and also enough that she'd be able to spread her legs wide enough to ride him.

He glanced down at what she'd revealed. "*Merde*." Then he lifted his eyes back to hers. "Do you really think this is a good idea? I mean, we're in a crowded room."

Where no one is looking, where everyone's eyes are glued to the cheerleaders. But in true dom form, she resisted pointing that out and instead said, "Shut up and do what I say or you'll be punished."

The light of understanding dawned on his face. "Oh. I see. Mistress Liz." He smiled. "Damn, darlin', I should've bought you that whip, after all."

She ignored his playfulness, wanting to stay in character and see how it felt to play the dominatrix. "Unzip the top of my dress more," she commanded.

He glanced around the room, still looking a little doubtful, but also excited—which was exactly what Liz had wanted. Finally, he did as she asked, unzipping it nearly down to her navel.

"Now spread it open until my nipples are out."

He looked dubious, met her gaze. "Are you sure you wanna do this? Here?"

"Do it," she snapped lowly.

So he did, baring her breasts and making her feel ever-so-naughty to think about how many people were in the same room with them, part of her hedonistically even wishing someone would see, watch them, watch her fuck her man.

"What now?" he asked, suddenly seeming to acquiesce, which pleased her.

"Lick them."

Jack raked his tongue over one of her stiffened nipples and pleasure ricocheted through her body, all the way to her cunt. Moving his mouth to the tip of her other breast, he touched his tongue to the distended nipple, flicking it up and down. Despite herself, she let out a small sound of delight.

Without further instruction, he took the same nipple into his mouth, suckling her, soft at first, then harder.

"Yes, suck them," she whispered, "suck them."

He shifted back to her other breast, drawing the peak tight between his strong lips, and his hard sucking reverberated through her.

"Now open your pants and show me that hot cock."

Below the music and the excited moans of the cheerleaders onstage, she heard Jack's breath grow labored, and as he undid his belt, she thought his hands were actually trembling with excitement. A moment later, his beautifully erect shaft was freed, jutting up out of his underwear. He shoved the fabric down so she could see it pointing rigidly up his abdomen.

"So big, baby," she murmured without thought. "Such a big, perfect cock." She ran one palm up his length, used her fingertip to wipe the pre-come from the end, and then inserted her finger in her mouth.

"God," he breathed, and now even his voice sounded quivery, making her relish the power she had over him. "What now, *chere*?"

"Rub it against my pussy," she demanded.

Without delay, he reached down, took his erection in hand, and grazed the head up and down at the center of her mound. She couldn't help moving against it, she was too excited to stay still, especially when it passed over her ever-sensitive clit.

"Oh..." she moaned. "Just like that."

He continued raking it up and down, and Liz wanted to feel more of him, so she shifted closer to his body and took the cock from his hand, pressing the whole length of it into her slit, still moving, still rubbing against him. "How does that feel?" she asked.

He was moving his hips now, too, sliding his big column against her. "So fuckin' good, baby," he rasped.

"Now hold it up," she said, her own breath labored now, "so I can ride you."

Following her command, he steadied his cock as Liz rose onto her knees, impaling herself on him. "Oh yes," she breathed. It was almost as if he'd driven his shaft nearly up to her navel, the entry sending shockwaves out to her fingers and toes. He was so incredibly large inside her; lowering her whole weight onto his cock brought home to her just how deep within her pussy he was, how well he filled her. As she began to fuck him, she twined her arms around his neck and drew him into a sensual kiss, unable to keep herself from it. She needed his mouth on hers, needed to consume him in any and every way she could.

As she gyrated on her lover, moving in hot, tight circles that brought her clit into sweet contact with the base of his shaft, she almost forgot where they were; it didn't matter. All that mattered was having Jack's enormous cock inside her, and riding him all the way to hot ecstasy. He held her hips, helping her move; he leaned in to suck her breasts, hard, harder. "Yes, so good, baby," she whispered. "Suck them." He did, more and more intensely, and it pushed her toward the orgasm that felt only heartbeats away.

Her cunt was filling with heat, and her tight circles grew smaller, giving her clit more and more strokes against him. Both of them were breathing hard, nearly panting, but it was drowned out by the music and all the moaning and cries on the stage.

Was anyone watching them? She didn't look around to see because she really didn't want to know, yet at the same time, she hoped *desperately* that someone in the room was watching her fuck him, witnessing the heat that passed between them as she drove her pussy down on his hot cock.

Finally, it hit—like a hot summer storm that gathered tremendous power before crashing down. Fierce sensations vibrated from her pussy outward until she was lost to them, replete in spasms of blinding pleasure. She bit her lip in order not to scream, but small, driving moans escaped her anyway as the staggering climax shuddered through her.

"Ah *merde*, me, too," she heard Jack moan just as she finished, so she kept riding, riding him hard, and loved watching the agony of pleasure etch itself on his face as he pumped harder, deeper, gritting his teeth as he spilled himself inside her.

Then his arms closed warm around her and she lay her forehead over on his shoulder—trying to recover from the exhaustion of coming.

Slowly, she gathered her strength and rose up off of him, choosing to stay that way, up on her knees, until she felt his semen leaking down onto her thigh. One last command. "Rub your come into me," she whispered.

He looked in her eyes, his own gaze dark and as filled with smoldering lust as she suspected her own had become. Then he shifted his attention to her pussy, lifting both hands to slowly smear the fluid onto her inner thighs as she straddled him. Finally, he drew his wet hands to her breasts, moving his palms in slick circles on her welcoming mounds. She closed her eyes and basked in the raw sensation of taking him into her in an entirely different, oh-so-sensuous way.

When he'd finished, she glanced over her shoulder to see the three cheerleaders still on the stage—all of them were naked now but for the ribbons in their hair. The room was awash in their moans as they slid colored vibrators in and out of each other's pussies.

"Is Mistress Liz ready to get the hell outta here and go back to my place where I can fuck her some more?"

She turned back to Jack's dark, hypnotizing gaze. "Mmm, yes, I think Mistress Liz is retired for the evening." She let a small smile make its way to her lips. "But she hopes she surprised you. Excited you."

He simply shook his head, as if in disbelief. "You have to ask?" he said as he zipped her dress back into place.

"I just want to hear it."

She climbed off him, still feeling sexy in her leather and boots. He zipped himself up, too, then took her hand and led her to the door. Once they were outside, back in the wild hustle and bustle and neon of Bourbon Street, he turned to her. "I *loved* what you just did back there. I love *everything* you do to me, baby. I love helpin' you explore this hot, dirty part of you. And I can't get enough of you."

Another arrow of hope pierced Liz's heart. A man who couldn't get enough of her might stick around for a while. But she tried not to dwell on a hope that seemed so dangerous, so thin—other lovers had professed devotion to her in the heat of the moment only to regret it later. So she just concentrated on the moment, since that had been working for her well enough so far. She concentrated on the sights and sounds and smells of the Quarter as they walked hand in hand through the party district, and then she focused on the quiet, the dark, the sultry night air, as they traversed the opposite end of Bourbon where Jack's apartment was located.

Of course, all of that was about *him*. She might like to think she was taking in other things, but all of those sights, sounds, tastes, smells—they were Jack's life, Jack's world. And she couldn't wait to get to his place, where she intended to give him all the pleasure he could handle.

* * * * *

"Move in with me."

She opened her eyes the next morning to find Jack lying next to her, propped on one elbow. Both of them were naked and Liz could scarcely recall a time when she'd slept more peacefully than these last few nights with Jack. But his words shook her from sleep, startling her.

He kept making this request—a request she would surely dream about if it wasn't being made only because she had a madman stalking her. What to say? She simply shook her head. "You're sweet to ask, but..."

"But nothing, damn it. I want you here. Want you with me."

His dark eyes shone so sincere. *He wanted her with him*. Didn't that say it all, wasn't it what she wanted so desperately to hear? She was still so afraid of getting hurt, and moving in with him had somehow come to represent that total surrender, the final act of putting herself out there, at risk, but in that early morning moment of weakness, she could no longer turn him down. "Okay," she said, letting out a breath, realizing she was really doing this, really accepting his invitation. "Yes, okay."

Lifting one hand to her cheek, he lowered his mouth on hers, kissing her long and hard and passionately. Then he whispered, "I never want you to be afraid of anything again."

* * * * *

As Jack ate a sandwich at his desk that day, working through lunch, he felt more at ease than he had in a week. He couldn't deny the reason why, which was twofold. Liz was going to move in with him, which meant Todd could no longer bother her. And it also meant that this woman he'd fallen for so quickly and completely was coming into his life in a whole new way. Dare he think a permanent way? That was probably too far ahead to be thinking, so for now he'd just be happy with what he had—Liz in his apartment, his bed, full time. He'd wake up with her in the morning and go to sleep with her at night. They'd eat together, shower together...hell, just *be* together.

Wadding the deli wrappings and tossing them to the garbage can beside his desk, he turned his attention back to his work. He had some surveillance videos to look through, and even fast forwarding through them when nothing important was happening still took a lot of time—and he wanted to get through them all as quickly as possible and get home early today. He intended to show up at Lynda's house with a bunch of empty boxes and get Liz out of there and into his bed tonight.

* * * * *

Liz called in sick for work. She'd driven home in a pair of Jack's gym shorts and one of his t-shirts with every intention of changing into a suit and making her way to the ad agency, but by the time she'd showered, she realized that if she was really going to move in with Jack, she needed to just do it, today.

For one thing, if she had all day at work to dwell on her decision, she might talk herself out of it. And even if it was scary as hell, she didn't want to change her mind. She realized now that she wanted desperately, madly, to live with her lover, to give him a chance to fall as deeply in love with her as she was with him. Maybe, despite all her fears, she had a chance at real happiness with a man who truly understood her and accepted her and encouraged her to be her own woman.

The very idea of living with him filled her with crazy naïve schoolgirl wishes. She wanted to see him all the time, wanted to cook for him, wanted even to do inane things like fold his socks and underwear for him. She just wanted to delve as deeply into him as he would allow her to, and if she was going to do this, she had to do it the way she'd done everything else the last week or so—she had to go for it completely.

That led to the other reason for skipping work today. She could go to Todd's while he was at the office, gather more of her things, and start moving stuff into Jack's place before he even got home tonight. He'd already given her a key, and he always said he loved her surprises, so she hoped he'd love this one, too. She wanted to be there waiting for him when he walked in the door after a long day of investigating. She thought she'd greet him in a baby doll nightie with a glass of wine. As exciting as last night had been, now the idea of just making love to him at home, alone, sounded perfect to her.

Dressed in shorts and a tank top suitable to the hot day of hard work that lay ahead, she'd gathered a few boxes from Lynda's garage, then ate an early lunch before getting to work, since she didn't want to be interrupted once she started the business of moving.

Now she made her way around the hedges to the house she used to share with Todd. She still had her key, so she only needed to gather her stuff and go. There would still be big things, like furniture, but she could take the smaller things she'd contributed to their household: her CDs, her books, some new sheets she'd bought but not yet opened, the small painting she'd bought in Paris when she'd vacationed there with girlfriends during college. They weren't things she needed this very minute, but they were things she *wanted*. Things which, once she had them back in her possession, would help her feel less and less connected with Todd and the farce of a life they'd shared.

Stepping in the front door, she noticed how things had been let go in her absence. The floors hadn't been swept or vacuumed, fast food wrappers and white napkins lay strewn across the coffee table. Even the couch cushions seemed in disarray.

But none of that was her problem—it only made her even more eager to get her belongings out of there.

Taking one of the boxes to the bookshelves in the corner, she began methodically scanning the shelves and retrieving the volumes that were hers. The stereo set next to the bookcase, so after closing up a box of books, she reached behind her for another box and repeated the process, finding the CDs she'd brought into the relationship, and loading them neatly inside. After kneeling over it to close it up, she got to her feet, ready to head upstairs. That's when she saw Todd sitting in a wingback chair by the window.

She flinched—damn it! He was just sitting there watching her. For how long? "What the hell are you doing here?" she snapped.

He tilted his head smugly. "I live here."

"Why aren't you at work?"

"I called in sick."

She let out a sigh. What were the chances? "You look fine to me."

"Well, I'm not. In case you've forgotten, I'm heartbroken."

She drew a deep breath, then let it back out. *Be calm.* He seemed a little more normal today. Snotty, but not crazy. "I'm sorry about that, and sorry to have burst in on you. I'll just take my things and go."

He glanced at the boxes she'd filled. "Really, Elizabeth, you could have called. I'm not going to hold your books for ransom or anything."

She pursed her lips. "Well, given the way you've reacted to this whole thing, I wasn't sure."

He actually smiled. "Need help carrying them over to Lynda's? Books are heavy. I'm happy to help."

She didn't know quite what to think. Was it possible Jack had actually gotten through to him the other night, that he was really going to leave her alone now? Was it possible he was being sincere, trying to end things on a civil note? She wanted to believe that, but in her heart, she couldn't quite take that step. "Thanks anyway," she said, "but I can carry them." She picked up the CD box and headed for the door. She'd half-expected him to follow her or detain her somehow, but when she stopped to look back, he still sat comfortably in the chair. "And just so you know, I won't be next door anymore." She wanted to make sure he wouldn't bother Lynda--the last thing she wanted was to heap trouble or danger on her friend.

"Where are you moving?"

She sighed. "What difference does it make?"

He pierced her with his suspicious gaze. "I bet I know. I bet you're moving in with that Neanderthal of yours." When she didn't reply, he lifted his hand to his chin, stroking an imaginary beard. "Now that troubles me."

She simply turned back to the door, murmured, "Sorry to hear that," shifted the box to one hip, and reached down for the knob.

"I don't want you living with that guy."

The smart thing would be to ignore him, just keep going. Yet somehow she couldn't. She was so tired of letting him push her around. He'd been doing it since they'd met and now that she'd started fighting back, she couldn't seem *not* to. "Well, where I live is really none of your business anymore."

He shrugged. "Maybe not, but I'd advise against moving in with him."

She blinked, wondering what the hell he had up his sleeve. "Oh?"

"I know some things about your Neanderthal man."

She didn't reply, simply stood there by the door, waiting for him to go on.

"I know things like where he works, where he lives."

She let out a disgusted sigh. She had no idea whether he was telling the truth or not, whether it was even possible for him to know, but… "What are you getting at?"

"Do you know, Elizabeth, that a guy can learn how to do practically anything these days on the Internet?"

What on earth was he talking about? She was about to give up finding out and had just reached for the doorknob once more when he said, "Do you know that a person can find out how to make a simple bomb with just a few clicks of the mouse?"

Liz felt all the blood drain from her cheeks. She finally lowered the heavy box to the hardwood floor. She put her hands on her hips and tried to sound stronger than she felt. "What the fuck are you talking about, Todd? Spit it out. Exactly what are you trying to say?"

He made a *tsk*ing sound. "Such language. Maybe you aren't my perfect little wife, after all."

"About time you got that message."

He simply chuckled. "I didn't mean that. I can forgive the occasional slip, darling, unlike you. But either way, whether or not you and I get back together right now, I don't want you living with that guy. And if you do move in with him, Elizabeth, I promise you'll regret it. Or, I should say, *he* will. And I'll know if you do it—trust me, I'll know."

Liz simply stared at him. To think she'd been foolish enough to believe he'd been acting reasonable there for a few minutes. God, he was truly psychotic. As that and his threat against Jack began to sink thoroughly into her skin, she knew she had to get out of there—now.

She couldn't stand being in Todd's presence for one more minute. She opened the door and stepped out onto the porch, then hurried across the yard toward Lynda's with the box in her arms, no longer caring if she got the rest of her stuff back, ever. She just wanted Todd out of her life.

Letting herself into Lynda's, she dropped the box just inside the door and turned the lock, then plopped onto the couch. She'd been so close, so close to really having him out of her life. She'd thought by day's end she'd be moved into Jack's, where a wonderful new existence of happiness and acceptance and freedom could begin. *Now* what was she supposed to do?

Leaning her head back against the sofa, she took a deep breath and tried to think.

Gathering her courage, she went to the phone and called the police.

"NOPD," a woman answered on the second ring.

Liz's stomach churned. "I...need help with a problem."

"Gonna have to be a little more specific than that, honey."

Liz rolled her eyes at own idiocy. *Pull yourself together and make some sense.* "My ex-fiancé is...making threats against me, and also against my new boyfriend."

The woman on the other end took on a kinder, slower tone. "What kind of threats?"

"Well, he implied that he knew how to make a bomb and said if I moved in with my boyfriend, I'd regret it."

"Is that all?"

All? Wasn't that enough? "He's sort of been stalking me, too, but...yeah, the part about the bomb is what's really scaring me."

The policewoman paused. "Does this ex-fiancé of yours have any kind of a record, a history of arrests or tangles with the law?"

Liz closed her eyes as a rush disappointment swept down through her chest. "No."

"Look," the woman said softly, "if it were up to me, I'd slap this whack job in handcuffs in a New York minute. But, honey, unless you have some proof that this guy's dangerous, there's not a lot we can do for you. At best, you might be able to get a restraining order against him."

Liz had always heard restraining orders did no good. "What would that do exactly?"

The policewoman let out a sigh. "It would state that he couldn't come within so many feet of you, and it *should* protect you." Yet then she hesitated, lowered her voice, and spoke in a woman-to-woman tone. "But just between me and you, it's only a piece of paper. It only counts for something if the jerk violates it, but by then it's often too late, if you know what I mean."

Liz hung up the phone a few minutes later, totally dejected. Weren't police supposed to keep you safe from bad people? Then again, maybe she shouldn't be surprised. How many stories had she heard over the years on the news or in the papers about wives and girlfriends who *weren't* protected from men who claimed to love them?

Settling back on the couch, she hugged a throw pillow to her chest and tried to devise her next move.

But what moves were left her, really? She'd tried to get help from the authorities and had failed.

And she'd ignored Todd's lunacy too many times already. She had no idea if he could really make a bomb or if he even knew where Jack lived and worked, for that matter, but any way she looked at it, she couldn't take the chance that Todd was for real, that he'd make good on the threat. She or Jack or both of them could *die*, for God's sake, if Todd was telling the truth.

And Jack's safety was simply something she couldn't risk.

Which meant she couldn't move in with him.

Of course, if she told Jack about Todd's crazy threat, he'd be all the more determined to get her away from Lynda's house and into his—to protect her.

And yet, how could anyone really protect anyone else in this world? Jack might be the strongest, surest man she'd ever known, but how could he really keep either one of them safe if Todd decided to do something crazy? You just couldn't protect against crazy. She sat shaking her head at the hopelessness of the situation, and thinking how one little conversation with Todd had shattered all her hopes for happiness with Jack.

* * * * *

Two hours later, Liz had unpacked her CDs next to Lynda's stereo, figuring she'd be staying put for at least a little while longer. Maybe even a *lot* longer. After all, if she moved out of Lynda's to *anyplace* else, Todd would likely assume she'd gone to Jack's. And she certainly couldn't tell Todd wherever she *was* going. The whole situation seemed impossible, and while part of her just kept thinking she should ignore it and move in with Jack as planned, another very frightened part kept remembering how each and every time she'd met with Todd since their breakup, he'd seemed more and more out of his mind. No matter how she twisted it, she felt she was at his mercy now and for some time to come.

Letting out a deep sigh, she put the empty box back in the basement and walked back upstairs, feeling trapped.

She didn't even know how she could face Jack, how she could tell him she wasn't moving in with him, without being prodded into explaining why. And other than her little act in the beginning, she'd always been so honest with him—she wasn't sure she could lie now.

Pouring herself a glass of iced tea, she sat down at Lynda's kitchen table, trying to think through the problem.

She couldn't see Jack tonight—that was that. If she did, she'd probably tell him everything and put him at risk. In fact, she couldn't tell him she wasn't moving in with him—not in person. She'd crack, she just knew it.

After draining her glass, she went upstairs to her room and got out her laptop. She and Jack hadn't had much occasion to e-mail each other, usually opting for the phone when making plans, but she knew his e-mail address and she knew he checked it often, as much of his business communication was accomplished that way.

Opening the laptop on the dressing table in her room, she keyed in Jack's e-mail address and began to type.

* * * * *

Jack used the remote to turn off the TV he used for scanning videos in his office. He still hadn't gotten current on them, but he wanted to close up shop and help Liz move her things—and he wanted to leave time for some romance before the evening was through, too. He intended to show her exactly how happy he was to have her moving in with him.

One last check of e-mail and he'd be out the door.

He clicked on the appropriate button, surprised to see a message from Liz in his inbox. He double-clicked to open it, more than a little curious.

Jack,

I've decided I can't move in with you, after all. It's kind of you to be concerned for my safety, but I'm confident I can take care of myself. This morning you caught me off guard, and later, I realized it was a bad idea.

I'm also breaking our date tonight. Sorry, but my boss asked me to work late on an overdue pitch for a big client.

Liz

Jack read the message over twice, then simply sat staring at the screen.

He'd been so damn happy this morning when she'd agreed to move in with him and he'd been on top of the world all day. Now, as his heart constricted in his chest, his father's age-old warning came back to him: Don't fall for a woman—she'll only hurt you in the end. Her message was polite—something he thought the old Liz would send—but equally as brisk and short, and he could read between the lines. He'd pushed too far by pressing her to move in with him. She'd realized she didn't want to be tied down to him that way, didn't want to go from one committed relationship to another so quickly. She hadn't even mentioned the future, when they would see each other again, which—as far as Jack knew—might mean she was ready for this to be over, her and him. She was ready to move on.

Fuck. Talk about hurt. He hadn't even known hurt like this existed. He'd been right all along—she was having way too much fun to settle down now. If only he'd stuck to his guns and not ever let himself believe anything differently.

As for the safety issue, he couldn't help feeling angry at her. Hadn't Todd proven over and over again what he was capable of? Why was she so thickheaded about this? Didn't she realize a guy like that was dangerous and that if she didn't change her situation he was probably going to do her real harm?

Jack closed his eyes against the vague but ugly picture in his head—Liz, and Todd, and rape. He couldn't help thinking how horrible it would be to have her burgeoning sexuality crushed by an ugly, violent act—somehow he feared it would affect Liz even more than the average woman; she'd decide it was punishment for the wild things she'd done with Jack and that she should have kept on letting other people dictate her life. The very idea nearly took the breath from his lungs.

"Damn it, Liz," he said, and banged his fist on his desk. "What do I have to do to get through to you?" If she wasn't scared of Todd after their encounter two mornings ago, what would it take? She'd told Jack she'd been afraid, so what had happened to change that? It wasn't that he wanted her to live in fear—just the opposite. He wanted her to live in freedom, and safety, and love.

Love. He rolled his eyes, hating the word, hating that he'd let himself feel it for a woman who couldn't return it.

When it came to the Todd issue, well, he could at least keep an eye on the guy, something he'd already put into play. But as for Liz and building a real relationship, he had no choice but to abandon that idea. He just didn't think he could be with her anymore, knowing it was only sex to her, only fun, that it would lead nowhere in the end. Funny, only a week ago that had been just fine with him, but not anymore. He couldn't be with her and not have her completely.

Chapter 12

Liz waited to hear from Jack, at work, or at Lynda's, or even by e-mail—since she'd used that method of contacting him, but no matter where she waited or checked, he didn't get in touch with her.

Three days later, she was strung as tightly as a violin—she still hadn't heard from him and she felt herself growing more and more anxious. Her body was on edge, almost painfully. She missed his hands roaming her curves; she missed his incredible cock buried deep inside her, fulfilling her in a way nothing else ever had. But it was more than sexual frustration eating at her. She missed *him*—his voice, his sexy smile, his sweet indulgences of her newfound sexuality, his concern over her safety. She missed simply kissing him, seeing his face, his eyes. She missed the warmth of his embrace.

Each time the phone rang at Lynda's, and even at work, where the phone rang all day, she tensed—hoping desperately it would be him.

But his call never came. And she began to wonder if she'd been foolish to let Todd's threat interfere with her plans for Jack.

Fortunately, Todd didn't attempt to contact her, either, but whereas *his* absence in her life was a tremendous relief, being without Jack made her feel like she was missing some part of her *self*.

One day when she came home from work, Todd appeared to have pulled in just before her. He did no more than lift his hand in a small wave as he went to the mailbox, but something in his gaze was sharp and cutting, reminding her again exactly why she'd let him talk her out of moving in with Jack. He was clearly watching her—and as long as she stayed put, it kept Jack safe and seemed to be keeping her out of harm's way, as well.

Of course, if she'd known her message to Jack would result in driving him away from her, she'd definitely have found another way to deliver it. She'd have gone out with him that night as planned, despite how hard it would have been. Somehow, unwittingly, she seemed to have closed the lines of communication between them.

When Liz got home from work the following Friday, she kicked off her shoes, pulled her pantyhose off under her skirt, and plopped on the bed, far too tired from the work week. She knew it was really just missing Jack that was tearing her up, breaking her down. Even now, as exhausted as she felt, she ached for him. She wished he were there to push up her skirt, unbutton her blouse, tell her how beautiful her breasts were, then fuck her long and hard and deep. Mmm, a nice fantasy, she thought, closing her eyes. But after the sexual odyssey she'd been on with Jack, fantasies weren't very fulfilling—she needed the real thing, the real man.

Taking a deep breath, Liz slowly picked up the phone. She'd been considering calling him for days, but had kept holding out hope that he would call her first. She'd kept remembering all the sweet things he'd said that had slowly made her begin to think he cared for her in more than a physical way. Exhaling, she dialed his number. By the third ring, her stomach was in knots. Then came the nerve-wracking sound of the receiver being picked up.

"Hello?"

Courage, Liz. Have courage. "Hi Jack, it's me."

His slight hesitation served to deplete what little bravery she'd mustered. "Liz?"

Her heart nearly shattered at his non-receptive tone. "Yeah."

He said nothing.

"I just wanted to apologize," she rushed, nervous now, "about my e-mail. I should have called. But I knew you checked your e-mail a lot, so...anyway, I just wanted to...see how you are."

More of that damned hesitation. "I'm fine," he finally said. "And you?"

Aching and needy. I need you in my bed, taking me away from everything bad. She swallowed nervously. His chilly tone made it impossible to be honest—it was suddenly as if the lies about why she couldn't move in with him and why she couldn't see him that night had ripped to shreds her ability to tell him anything true. "I'm...fine, too."

"Has Todd bothered you anymore?"

Tell him. Just tell him the truth about Todd's threat.

But no—that might only create trouble. Jack might confront Todd and endanger himself.

"He's kept his distance the last few days," she said, glad it wasn't exactly a lie.

"Good." Even that sounded strangely cold.

Liz was out of things to say. She'd really believed that if she called him, he'd suggest getting together. She'd been sure he'd tell her he'd been meaning to call, was just busy with some important case, but missed her and wanted to meet her someplace on Bourbon Street tonight. Yet that wasn't happening, and the dead air between them was as stifling as the humid heat outside.

"Well," she finally said out of desperation to fill the silence, "maybe I'll...see you sometime soon."

Another hint of hesitation. *Say yes,* she begged silently. *Ask me to see you.* "Maybe," he slowly replied, still as distant-sounding as he'd been since picking up the phone.

She swallowed again, this time having to work past the lump in her throat. "Well then, bye."

"Bye, Liz."

The line went dead and Liz fought back the tears behind her eyes. Damn it, she wasn't going to cry over him. She'd known from the start she was playing a game that shouldn't—*couldn't*—involve her heart, and it had been a fatal mistake to let herself even *begin* to fall for him. She'd known *that* even before it had happened. All this meant, she told herself, was that as she'd predicted from the start, the time had come when he was ready to end things. He'd had fun with her until the newness had worn off their heady, sexy relationship. Clearly, finding out she'd decided not to move in with him had been a relief, and a convenient time to call it quits.

She couldn't even be angry. He'd certainly never promised her anything, and she'd never asked him to. Despite not wanting their affair to end, she'd known it would, and probably sooner rather than later.

Still, it hurt. It felt like someone had just dropped a ton of bricks on her chest, like her heart and lungs were going to burst apart any second. Damn her for letting herself fall in love—damn her weakness.

Just then, a small knock came on her door. "Honey, you in there?" It was Lynda.

"Yeah," she managed, hoping she didn't sound as crushed as she felt.

Lynda opened the door. "Listen, I was thinking you and I should go out tonight." As she approached the bed, it was clear she could read Liz's sorrow. "Are you okay?"

She'd kept Lynda filled in on her predicament, so there seemed no reason to lie. "I just called Jack."

Lynda seemed to tense slightly on her behalf. "And?"

"And...my fears came true. He wasn't interested in talking to me. He was so...cold." She'd never heard Jack sound that way before—ever. Even in that very first confrontational moment when they'd met, he'd been warmer to her than he'd been on the phone just now.

Lynda sat down on the bed and placed one hand warmly on Liz's thigh through her skirt. "Oh, honey. I'm so sorry."

Liz nodded slightly against the pillow sham.

"But you know," Lynda said with a tilt of her head, "this is all the more reason for you and me to paint Bourbon Street red tonight."

Liz let out a sigh. Without Jack, Bourbon Street sounded...boring. "Thanks for the invitation, Lynda, but I don't think so. I'm not exactly in the mood for fun."

"Precisely my point." Lynda gave her thigh a light squeeze. "I think the best thing in the world for you would be to go out and get your mind on something else. Even if you don't totally enjoy it, it's a distraction—which you need. You've been moping around here all week, and I hate to see you so sad. It's time to start getting over Jack."

"I only just now officially discovered I *have* to get over Jack," she complained.

"Even so, it wasn't a long relationship, so you need to bounce back and move on."

True enough—it had only *felt* like a long relationship. She'd done more living with Jack in a week than she had with anyone else in her whole life.

"Come on now," Lynda said, taking her by the wrists and pulling her to a sitting position. "I'm not taking no for an answer. You and I are going to get totally dolled up, then we'll have dinner at Pat O's, drink a hurricane or two, and find someplace fun to party."

* * * * *

Liz and Lynda sat at a small round table at a sexy new dance club in the Quarter called Jade. Lynda had heard the atmosphere was wild, and the place definitely lived up to its reputation. The large dance floor was filled with people dirty dancing—girls with guys, girls with other girls, touching, caressing, kissing, grinding. In a small dancer's cage at one corner of the floor, two girls in skimpy halter tops and short skirts danced while sensually pumping their crotches together and French kissing, much to the crowd's delight. Across the room at the opposite corner, a pretty girl danced in another cage, wowing the crowd by flashing her tits every few minutes. Liz watched, as finally—the girl took off her top and let it drop at her feet. The dance floor cheered the loss of her top and a guy joined her from below, starting a slow bump and grind with her.

Despite herself, Liz's pussy throbbed. Yet she still felt sad, empty. She knew if Jack were here she might be inspired to join in the crowd's debauchery, to excite herself, and moreover, to excite him. When she analyzed any and everything she'd done in Jack's presence, exciting him *was* what excited her. Oh, certainly she'd enjoyed the lush indulgence of having two men lavish sexual attention on her, just as she'd enjoyed playing naughty little games with the girls at Club Venus, but Jack was the necessary ingredient. Without him, the recipe simply didn't work—she simply didn't want to be a bad girl if he wasn't there to encourage it or enjoy it.

"Which one of you lovely ladies wants to get down and dirty with me on the dance floor?"

She and Lynda both looked up to see a guy in his early twenties with a sexy twinkle in his eye and a hot, muscular body visible beneath his simple t-shirt and jeans.

Lynda winked at her. "My friend, Liz, would love to dance with you."

He flashed a killer smile designed to seduce, and held out a hand to Liz.

But despite how gorgeous he was, and how clearly interested in her he appeared to be, the idea of being with anyone other than Jack simply didn't appeal, not even for a *normal* sort of dance, let alone a "down and dirty" one. "I'm sorry," she said, trying to sound gracious, "but I don't really feel like dancing."

He put on a persuasive look. "Come on, you'll have fun. I promise."

She had to be an idiot to pass this up. After all, wasn't this what sexual freedom was about? In theory, she should be using the freedom she'd gained through Jack's guidance to expand her horizons now with this new, very hot young guy—yet she just couldn't. Something about it felt terribly wrong.

Ironic, she thought, given all the things she'd done recently that *hadn't* felt wrong. But she knew it all came back to Jack. Fucking Ty had simply been fucking Jack in another way. Rubbing her pussy against Felicia had simply been rubbing her pussy against Jack in a different manner. It was Jack who made her want to be sexy and decadent, Jack who loosed all her inhibitions.

"I'm sorry," she said again, "but Lynda here is *always* up for a good time. Aren't you, Lynda?" She looked pointedly to her friend.

"Are you sure?" Lynda asked. "I have a feeling you're missing out on something good."

Liz forced a smile at both of them. "If I know you, you'll enjoy it enough for both of us. Now go dance," she finished, nudging Lynda's thigh with her stocking-covered knee.

Finally, Lynda eased down off the barstool and let young Mr. Hottie usher her onto the floor. Liz watched them disappear into the crowd, and then, for lack of anything better to do, she returned her attention to the topless chick and her new boy toy. The girl now gripped the cage's vertical bars, arching her ass while the boy toy—now shirtless, too—pumped at her short skirt with the bulge in his blue jeans; simulated sex in time with the driving beat of the music.

"Hey there, sweet thing."

The feminine voice came with a light touch on Liz's arm. She looked up to find the lovely Felicia. Think of the devil and here she was, looking like sin itself in a tight, skimpy red dress that just barely covered her nipples.

"Don't tell me you don't remember me," Felicia said, fists stabbing playfully at her hips.

Liz smiled politely. "Oh yes, don't worry, I know who you are."

Felicia's grin turned hot, predatory, as she leaned to whisper in Liz's ear. "The last time I saw you our sweet little pussies were pounding at each other."

Liz's cunt flinched, reluctantly excited at the memory. Her breasts turned achy and she knew her nipples had just hardened into buds against the bodice of her dress, a low cut pink confection that draped her body in all the right places.

Felicia flashed a seductive smile. Stepping closer, she tossed her long, dark mane over her shoulder, lowering her hand to a spot high on Liz's thigh. Again, Liz's pussy tingled against her will, even more when Felicia eased her fingers under the hem of Liz's dress to play with the lace top of her stocking. "You want to dance with me?" she asked.

To her surprise, Liz was almost tempted. Her first foray into discovering her true sexual self had been with Felicia and the memories of how thrilling it had been to have Felicia's lovely body move against hers remained fresh and strong. Images of Felicia's big, beautiful breasts and her shaved pussy, all smooth and pouty, entered Liz's head. The strong hurricanes she'd consumed tonight had her just intoxicated enough that maybe she could let go of her depression for a little while and indulge in what sexy Felicia had to offer. Maybe she could actually enjoy a little girl play without Jack. And maybe if she could make herself get down off this barstool and grind against this hot woman on the dance floor, it would be a good first step to doing exactly what Lynda had wanted her to do tonight—find a distraction, start getting over Jack.

"I'm…not sure," she finally heard herself say.

Felicia tilted her head. "You look sad, sweet thing. What happened? Did that man break your heart?"

Liz slowly nodded.

Felicia's smile took on a new warmth, a woman-to-woman camaraderie. "Why don't you let me take your mind off him?" She leaned closer, her arm closing intimately around Liz's waist, her breasts brushing against Liz's to send a warm skittering sensation all through them. She whispered again in Liz's ear. "We don't even have to dance. I only live a couple of blocks from here. We can go to my place and I'll make you forget you ever thought you needed a man. I'll kiss your pretty lips, lick your pretty breasts, and eat your pretty pink pussy all night long."

A shiver ran the length of Liz's body. Part of her was tempted to see if Felicia *could* make her forget how lonely she felt without Jack, and she was flattered that a woman who made a living pleasuring countless men and sometimes women wanted so badly to pleasure her now for free. Yet even as her hungry cunt throbbed at Felicia's promises, deep inside she knew it wasn't the answer, and even feared she'd regret it in the morning if she fooled around with Felicia tonight.

The physical pleasure would be there, yes—she still felt as attracted to the stripper as when she'd gotten her hot lap dances at Club Venus—but what she'd discovered with Jack was that she felt *more* than physical pleasure anytime he was with her. And she understood now that purely physical wasn't enough. The joy she'd experienced on her wild sexual adventures was as wrapped up in her emotions for Jack as in the satisfaction to her body.

"What do you say, baby?" Felicia whispered, her voice so sexy that Liz went wet.

Liz leaned to Felicia's ear to whisper back. "You're incredibly beautiful, incredibly hot, but I'm afraid I can't."

Felicia looked disappointed. "Why not?"

Liz offered a wry smile. "I'm just not over him. I'm sorry."

Felicia tilted her head. "Maybe another time, sweet thing." With that, she eased their curves apart, but placed her hand on Liz's cheek, giving her a short, sweet kiss on the lips. "If you ever change your mind, look me up at the club."

Liz nodded, then watched as Felicia walked away, her ass looking delectably touchable wrapped in a tight sheath of red. But words like delectable and touchable didn't matter to Liz very much if Jack wasn't there.

A moment later, Lynda appeared beside her, leading her muscular young stud by the hand. She eased her arm around Liz's waist and Liz became aware that, just like with Felicia a few minutes earlier, their breasts were pressing together. Despite herself, in her current state of unwanted arousal, her crotch went warm. Also like Felicia, Lynda was leaning in to whisper in her ear. "Honey, Mike and I were thinking of leaving and going back to his place, just down on Bienville. We were hoping you might want to come."

At first, Liz assumed the invitation was an obligation, that Lynda simply didn't want to leave her in the midst of her depression, especially since she'd practically dragged Liz out against her will. But when Lynda eased back and Liz could look in her eyes, she understood what Lynda was really asking—she and Mike wanted Liz to join them for a *ménage à trois*.

Yet another rush of unbidden excitement raced through her pussy at the notion, but she already knew the answer, which she delivered softly. "I don't think so, Lynda."

Lynda's expression turned coquettish. "Are you sure? It would be fun, I promise."

Liz nearly laughed, suddenly feeling a bit overwhelmed by all these sexual invitations coming at her right and left. The funny part, she supposed, was the irony. A week ago, she might have thought she'd be up for *anything*, but now she wasn't. She smiled indulgently. "I...appreciate the invitation, but...no, Lynda—I'm not into it."

Lynda tilted her head, looking drunk and honest and sweet. "Jack's an idiot to give you up. How he can resist you, I'll never know." With that, she ran her fingertips lightly down Liz's arm. "Will you be all right if I go? If you want me to stay, I will."

"Actually, I think I'd rather head home. I'm just...not really ready to be out on the social scene yet."

Acceptant, Lynda nodded, taking Liz's hand to help her down from the stool. "Come on. Mike and I will make sure you get a cab before we go."

* * * * *

Liz thought she'd feel better by the time she got home. She thought she'd relish the privacy, knowing Lynda would be out late, figuring Todd, too, was probably out at Club Venus or some other similar establishment on a Friday night. She'd thought she'd climb into a comfy pair of pajamas, watch a little TV, and go to bed. But when she got home, she felt so lonely that it was like a physical thing, a gnawing in her stomach that wouldn't let up.

Despite the late hour, she picked up the phone and called her sister, Diana. The middle Marsh sister always made Liz laugh, and even though she hadn't talked to Diana in a few weeks, her recent sexual awakening had made her feel a new bond with her younger sis, who had always been a free spirit.

"What time is it?" Diana asked groggily.

"It's late, but I need to talk."

Liz could picture her sister trying to sit up in bed, shoving her long hair out of her face. "Okay. What's up? It's not like you to burn the midnight oil."

Liz sighed. "You wouldn't *believe* all that's up here."

Diana suddenly sounded more awake. "Well, fill me in."

Liz spent the next fifteen minutes catching Diana up on her life. Diana, of course, had heard from their parents that Liz's engagement was off, but was utterly stunned to hear Liz's tales of Jack, not to mention tales of Ty and Felicia and sex clubs. In one way, Liz was amazed she could tell her sister everything so openly, but it was so freeing, and she'd known Diana would understand. And once Diana got past her shock, she seemed thrilled at the change in Liz. She laughed, saying "Now, if only we could get Carrie to loosen up a little, all three of us could know the joys of good sex."

"Well, the sex isn't good anymore, remember," Liz said. "Now that he's gone, I don't want to be with anyone but him."

She heard her sister sigh. "Believe it or not, I'm kind of in the same boat."

Liz started. This didn't sound like Diana. "Oh?"

"Remember I told you about Bradley, the guy mom fixed me up with? Well, turns out he's, um…not into sex, or at least not until well into the relationship, so I'm sort of frustrated these days myself."

Liz barely knew how to reply. The Diana she knew wouldn't date a guy who wasn't into sex, early and often. But then again, maybe this meant Bradley was someone special, someone who was changing Diana's wild ways. "Are things serious between you two?" she asked.

"Maybe. Kind of. I'm not sure. But back to you…"

"Yeah?"

"I'm sorry you're sad, Lizzie. This P.I. guy sounds like he was a keeper."

Liz didn't reply, simply bit her lip to hold back her emotion.

"Maybe you should just go ahead and tell him about Todd's threats," Diana suggested.

"Easy for you to say. You haven't been here watching Todd self-destruct. He's an entirely different guy than he was back in Maryland."

"Hmm, seems that city you're in has strange powers over everyone, doesn't it?"

Indeed, Liz thought. The French Quarter had certainly changed *her*.

When she hung up with Diana a little while later, nothing was particularly changed or resolved, but she was still glad to have filled her sister in on the happenings in her life—and she hoped she'd be good and sleepy now, ready to doze off.

But despite herself, her body was still humming with sexual need.

She'd have been far better off if she'd stayed home tonight. Seeing all the sensuality on the dance floor, then getting unwittingly aroused by Felicia's touches and dirty talk, and then Lynda's invitation...it was all too much. Add to that giving Diana all the details of her relationship with Jack, and her poor pussy wouldn't quit pulsing no matter what she did. If Felicia walked in her door right now, she thought she might invite her upstairs.

As it was, she simply ascended the stairs to her room alone, walked to the chest, and opened her lingerie drawer. Digging down under the lace and silk, she pulled out the vibrator—Jack's gift to her. She ran her hand over the head, the veined shaft, missing Jack's cock so much it hurt.

Walking to the bed, she lay down without even taking off her strappy, heeled shoes. Lifting her ass, she pulled her dress up to her hips, then hooked her thumbs into the white thong panties she wore, pushing them down until they were off, finally flinging them away with her toes.

Keeping her knees bent, she parted her legs and looked down at her pussy. Even without seeing Jack every night, she'd kept it shaven but for the trim tuft of hair extending up from the top of her slit. Now she ran her hand over the outside of her cunt to feel the soft, smooth skin there, before placing the shaft of the vibrator flush against herself and twisting the end to turn it on. Sweet, electric tremors echoed through her hot flesh. She felt her pussy lips spread, inviting the shaft to nuzzle closer, where she was wet. She rubbed it up and down her slit, letting the buzzing vibrations fill her.

But it wasn't enough, she soon discovered—she wanted a cock inside her. She wanted *Jack's* cock inside her. She closed her eyes and imagined it, all hard and lovely, the dark pink head with just a dot of pre-come resting there, the blood-filled shaft—silk over steel in her hand. Raising her ass just slightly, she slid the vibrator into her passage—an easy entry. It filled her, but...it so clearly wasn't Jack and she wanted to keep pretending it was. She turned it off, killing the vibrations but making it feel more like a real phallus. She moved it in and out, gentle at first, then harder, harder. And it felt good, something like what she needed...but damn it, still so far from *exactly* what she needed. The pretend cock was a little smaller than Jack's, and fucking herself with it simply didn't hold the power, or pleasure, that Jack's hot fucking delivered.

She sighed. God, how sad. She missed him so badly she couldn't even get herself off.

But then she let a new fantasy grow in her mind. Instead of imagining the vibrator was Jack, she imagined that Jack could see her, that he was watching her pleasure herself with it. Yes, he would like that—he'd once even said something to that effect. So she turned it back on, sending the hot, fast, quivering vibrations back through her cunt once again, and she slid it in and out, pretending Jack was watching every move, listening to her labored breath and watching as she sensuously licked her upper lip, hearing her low moans as she began to fuck herself harder, deeper.

Then she felt—remembered—the little nub Jack had pointed out to her. Each time she pushed the shaft in all the way, the raised knob rubbed against her clit. Mmm, yes. Very nice. The sensation made her slow the thrusts, got her lost in the pleasure—and also the fantasy. Jack watched the slow, deep fuck. He watched her reach up with her available hand to pull down her dress, freeing her breasts and then massaging one of them, enjoying the feel of her stiffened nipple jutting into her palm. He watched her quit thrusting the cock altogether, instead inserting it all the way, as deep as possible in her pussy, then writhing against that sweet little nub with a rhythm she knew would make her come.

Watch me, Jack. Watch me fuck my sweet pussy for you. Watch me.

She felt Jack's eyes, permeating her, consuming her, and that's all it took—a hot, blissful orgasm rushed over her like a tidal wave, the consuming pulsations echoing through her body and swallowing her in mindless pleasure, until finally the tide inside her calmed...and left her sad and heartbroken once more.

* * * * *

Jack's life felt like a fucking disaster. A week ago, he'd been in heaven—in love with a beautiful, sensual woman who fulfilled his every sexual fantasy like a dream come true. At the same time, work had been good, steady and manageable, fulfilling without being overwhelming.

Now he felt like a man trapped in a snow globe—like someone had picked up his fragile little world and given it a hard shake, and he was still waiting for the dust to settle.

His days now, without Liz, felt like one devastation after another. He kept forgetting—waking up in the morning expecting to find her there, or having her absence in his life strike him like a blow with a baseball bat at moments when he least expected it: turning his key in the lock to go home at night, ordering take out for one, finding—and then subsequently tearing up—the computer-generated bill for her case.

It was Friday night—he didn't bother turning to check the clock, but he knew it was late. The last hours had been a blur and as he sat in his office, fast-forwarding through surveillance tapes looking for the relevant stuff, he thought back over the long evening.

Earlier, when a glimpse of the time revealed it was after nine, he'd decided to take a break and walk around the corner to Pat O's for a helping of jambalaya and a side of catfish strips to go.

His cell phone had trilled nearly as soon as he'd walked out the door; he'd reached in his pocket and flipped it open. "Jack Wade."

"Dude, where are you?" It was Ty.

"On my way to Pat O's."

"Cool—I'll meet you there. We can grab some drinks, then maybe hit some clubs."

"No, *ami*, I'm workin'. Just takin' a break to get somethin' to eat."

"It's Friday night, buddy."

"And I'm busy," he'd replied shortly. He didn't mean to be gruff with Ty, but he was in no mood for partying.

He'd listened as Ty released a huge sigh. "Have you called her yet?"

Ty, of course, knew exactly why he was in such a pissy mood, and had been giving him unwanted counseling on it for days. He rolled his eyes as he kept moving, dodging a pair of ready-looking women who were giving him the eye on the sidewalk. "The truth is, I've considered callin' her probably a hundred times since that day I practically hung up on her...but no, I still haven't."

"Why not?"

Ty *knew* why not, yet he'd made Jack say it again. "Because she taught me a valuable lesson, which I'm not gonna forget this time. And the lesson is that my old man was right—fallin' for somebody only gets you kicked in the teeth in the end."

He still didn't know what had prompted her to change her mind about moving in with him, but he could only conclude the same thing over and over—that she didn't want to let the relationship go that far, get that serious or committed. As for her phone call, well, he supposed she missed the sex, but he'd learned the hard way from her that he was more than just a sex toy—he had feelings, and she'd fucking trampled them. A lonely sounding phone call didn't change that. There were a thousand guys in this city she could fuck, and quite a few girls, too, if she wanted—he wasn't playing stud to her anymore. He missed sex with her so much he sometimes felt like he couldn't breathe, but he couldn't fuck her and not love her, and not having her love him back hurt too damn bad to even contemplate.

Ty had sounded put out with him. "If you ask me, you're screwing up big time."

"And for the twentieth time, I didn't ask you."

"Okay, okay." Finally, his friend changed the subject. "So why the hell are you working this late on a Friday night?"

"It's like I told you a couple days ago—the job's suddenly runnin' me ragged." Lately, it seemed that if he wasn't chasing down leads on a missing person's case the police had given up on, he was trying to track down a bundle of laundered money or looking for a jewelry thief who'd managed to heist an expensive diamond necklace from a private collection. Of course, it got like this sometimes—cases got stacked up, one upon another, for no particular reason. But now, added to all that was the task of trying to keep tabs on Todd.

"Still spyin' on the nutjob?" Ty had asked, seeming to read Jack's mind.

"Yep," he answered shortly.

Despite how much Liz had hurt him, he still intended to keep her out of danger, at least to the degree he could control the situation—something she'd made a lot harder by deciding to stay put next door to her psycho ex. That decision still boggled his mind, and he knew from his caller I.D. system that she was still at Lynda's, or at least she had been when she'd called him.

In fact, that was what really had him stuck in the office long after dark on a Friday night. He was off the clock, no longer billing anyone for his hours, but he had a shitload of surveillance tapes to catch up on—surveillance on Todd.

The very day after he'd had to escort the little bastard out Lynda's front door, he'd let himself inside Todd's back door with the help of a simple credit card, and he'd placed a few tiny cameras and mikes throughout the house—one in the kitchen, one in the living room, one in the master bedroom. He'd also placed one strategically on the corners of both the front porch and the back stoop—if Todd set out for Lynda's, those cams should catch it. And Jack monitored those particular cameras in real time as much as possible, keeping one or the other on the little TV in his office while he made phone calls, handled e-mail, or worked on billing. He had it set up to monitor at home, too—so when he came home each evening, a little television that perched on top of his big screen stayed tuned to the space between Todd's yard and Lynda's. He couldn't watch it constantly, but he tried to keep an eye on it as much as possible.

"Find anything interesting yet?" Ty had asked.

"Nope, but I've got a huge backlog of video and audio to scan." There was no way to monitor both the outdoor camera and the others, inside the house, at the same time, and inspecting the hours of videotape from inside took a long while, but anytime the cameras caught Todd at home, Jack stopped the fast forward and listened to what the little dickhead had to say. He wasn't even sure what he was waiting to see or hear, but the guy seemed like such a nutcase, Jack figured he might start talking to himself—or even someone else—about any plans he had that included Liz. So far, that, too, had turned up nothing, but as he'd told Ty, he was way behind in viewing the tapes, hence his decision to spend Friday night in the office.

"Well, dude, I'm gonna hit the streets and look for some fun. You want to try to hook up later?"

Fun was the last thing on Jack's mind these days. "No, I'll still be workin'."

"You know what they say about all work and no play."

Jack couldn't help a short, wry chuckle. "*Oui*. They make me a dull boy. But that's too fuckin' bad right now, *ami*."

"Have it your way," Ty said. "And hey, get some rest. You're testy as hell."

"I know. Gotta go now."

Jack had put his phone away just as he walked through the brick archway leading to Pat O's courtyard, and he'd no sooner made his way to the outdoor bar than he'd seen Liz, dressed to kill. Speak of the devil. She sat with Lynda at a table in the courtyard looking as sweet and edible as cotton candy in a little pink number that hugged her breasts and showed lots of cleavage. She was drinking a tall hurricane and laughing with her friend.

Seeing her hurt worse than he could have imagined. He'd immediately looked away and that's when someone had arrived to take his order. While he waited for the food, he was sorely tempted to go over and say hi, to see if maybe, by chance, he saw any sort of emotional spark in her eye, anything that meant she gave a damn about him, but he resisted. Her confection-covered breasts beckoned to him, but that dress also told him she was out to party, and seemed to be getting by just fine without him.

After his order came up and he got his change, he took one last look in her direction, whispered, *"Au revoir, chere,"* then headed back out onto St. Peter and down to Royal.

And as he'd eaten his dinner and gotten back to scanning video, he felt like a fucking idiot. Because only a fucking idiot would waste every free second of his time trying to protect a woman who didn't care about him.

It had almost been enough to make him turn off the tape, lock up the office, head up to Club Venus, and do a little partying himself, after all. But, he'd thought cynically, he was as likely to bump into Liz there as anyplace else on Bourbon, so that was a no-go. The deeper truth was—if trying to protect her made him an idiot, then he would just have to be an idiot. Because he wouldn't stop monitoring Todd until something happened to make him certain Liz was out of harm's way. Being hurt, even angry, didn't kill the love inside him. He might wish it did, but it didn't—sadly, he understood his father's undying heartache a little better with each passing day.

Now, he still sat there, hours later, remote in hand, slowing the tape when Todd appeared in the picture, speeding it up when he didn't. Fast forwarding through the days when Todd was at work took a damn long time, but he kept his eye on the screen anyway, and much to his surprise, he suddenly saw Liz come in the front door of the house. He stopped the fast forward, watching as she crossed the room and began loading books in a box.

It made him stop and check the date on the tape. Curiously, it was the day he'd expected to be moving her in with him. And it was just after noon, so she must not have gone to work. He watched in silence for five minutes, ten, and then…Todd walked into the room behind her. But rather than approach her, he sat down in a chair and watched her pack. His silent observation of her sent a chill creeping up Jack's spine.

When Liz turned and saw Todd, it was clear, even from the odd angle of the camera, that she was startled. And then it happened…Todd started talking to her—and before Jack knew it, Todd was threatening…*him.*

Jack sat up a little straighter in his chair and watched Liz, the rigid stance she took, the nervousness in her voice, until finally she left—but Jack understood immediately. She hadn't moved in with him in order to protect him.

Let me get this straight. She's been trying to protect me *while I've been trying to protect* her? It boggled his mind.

So was *that* the real reason for her abrupt message about not moving in with him? To Jack, it seemed incomprehensible, but maybe he was forgetting just how afraid of Todd she was. *He* wasn't afraid of the little shit, and a threat against *him* didn't bother Jack in the slightest. But maybe to Liz, it was something to be taken seriously. In fact, the more Jack thought about it, the more it slowly dawned on him that Liz must have taken the threat against him more seriously than she'd taken the threat against herself. Just as Jack naturally did—except in reverse, worrying only when the danger affected Liz.

He stopped the tape and pulled up her e-mail, which he'd never deleted, and read it again. If he hadn't been so consumed with his own emotions, maybe he wouldn't have jumped to conclusions and imagined things that weren't there. Maybe he wouldn't have been such a self-absorbed jerk.

Merde, this explained everything. It all made sense. She'd thought it would be safer for her to just keep living at Lynda's—and she'd probably known Jack would give her a hard time about that, so she'd decided to deliver the news by e-mail. He suddenly suspected she'd never intended to dump him, just to put him off for a day while she figured out how to deal with Todd's threat.

Damn, clearly he'd taken his father's warning too much to heart, let himself base his worries and insecurities too much on the marriage that had failed and left him without a mother.

And if he hadn't been so stubborn, just waiting for the ax to fall and jumping to conclusions when he'd thought he'd seen it happening, he might be buried deep inside her right now.

A rush of heat enveloped him at the thought and made his cock perk to life. He missed her so much.

He had half a mind to go find her right now, and pushed up out of his chair with that thought in mind.

But shit, she was likely somewhere on Bourbon partying, and trying to look for her among that many people in that many bars and clubs would be futile.

Besides which, there was something else he needed to do first, before he talked to her. He needed to take this tape to the police. The Big Easy's finest weren't always his greatest fans—and Jack's video of Todd was actually illegal, and therefore, inadmissible as evidence—but plenty of the men in blue were decent guys, and he didn't think any of them could refute what he'd caught on tape here. If there was one thing cops didn't like, it was nutballs who talked about making bombs and blowing up places and people. And threats weren't generally against the law, but once the cops found out a little recent history on this guy, like that he was a stalker who *had* illegally entered a neighbor's house and likely attempted to rape Liz, Jack suspected they'd either dig up a reason to arrest him, or they'd put the fear of God in him and just dare him to trip up.

* * * * *

Five o'clock on Saturday afternoon and Liz felt like a lifeless blob. Despite a late night that had turned to morning, Lynda had pulled Liz's old trick of rushing home just long enough to shower and change before heading back to her shop in the Quarter. Liz had stayed indoors all day, never bothering to change out of the silky shorts set she'd slept in, just lying on the couch, watching movies on cable and drifting in and out of a sad sleep.

Last night had been eye-opening for her. Maybe a tiny little part of her had thought a night on the Vieux Carre with Lynda *would* be healing. Maybe she'd *hoped* she could shed her sorrow with some handsome hunk or lovely lady who wanted to play with her. But she'd been dreadfully wrong. Just as she'd known all along, Jack was the only person who made her want to play, who made her want to be a perfect bad girl. And she had a frightening feeling it might stay that way. After all, no one *before* Jack had ever awakened the hot, daring woman inside her. Why should she think anyone would do it *after* him? *He's the one,* she thought, *the man who releases everything inside me, every doubt, every worry, every inhibition, the man who makes my heart—and my body—want to run wild.*

When the phone rang, she didn't answer it, didn't even budge. Let the machine get it, she thought. No one would be calling her anyway. Six months after moving to New Orleans, her only real friend was Lynda. A fleeting thought raced through her mind—why on earth had she told her mother she wanted to stay here? She should go home to Maryland and forget the past two weeks had ever happened. Because none of what she'd learned about herself in those two weeks even mattered without Jack. She wasn't sure what it was about him that had opened up the box of secret desires inside her, but he was the man with the key. Without him, she'd begun to feel the box slowly closing back up. She didn't want to share such hot, brazen intimacies with anyone else—ever.

"You've reached Lynda. Wait for the beep, then tell me what you need."

"Liz? *Chere*, are you there?"

Liz gasped at the sound of Jack's voice. Then she bolted off the couch and got her feet tangled in an afghan as she tripped her way across the carpet to the phone. She yanked it up just as he'd started to speak again. "Jack, I'm here."

"I'm so glad," he said, his tone familiar, wonderfully warm. "I've missed your voice, darlin'."

"You have?"

"I've got so much to explain to you, *chere*. But I don't wanna do it on the phone—I wanna see your face. That is, if you'll see me."

Liz nearly couldn't answer, too pent-up with emotion. Finally, she managed to say, "Yes. I will, Jack. I will."

"Tonight?"

"Yes."

"Can I make dinner for you, here at my place?"

Liz had missed the cozy privacy of his apartment and couldn't think of anywhere else she'd rather see him. "That...would be nice," she struggled to get out.

"Seven?"

She glanced at the clock, then down at herself. She had a lot of grooming to do. "Seven-thirty."

"I can't wait, *chere*."

"I'll...be there," she said. Hanging up the phone, she fell back into the nearest easy chair.

What had just happened here? Was she feeling too happy too fast? This didn't mean he loved her—it didn't even mean he wanted to get back together. But he'd sounded so sexy, so seductive. And the important thing was that she would see him in only a couple of hours. And that the night, like every night in the French Quarter, was full of possibilities.

* * * * *

She showed up in a long, pretty, flowing dress that bloomed with tiny blue and purple flowers and made her look like some kind of beautiful storybook fairy princess. Well, a *sexy* storybook fairy princess, because the dress clung to her curves and possessed a low v-neck that instantly made Jack want to kiss the shadowy valley between her breasts and run his hands over her lush curves. He checked the urge and hoped he'd have the chance later. "It's good to see you," he said, standing back to let her in.

Her smile—the sweet, timid one he'd seen on more than a few occasions—seemed to radiate through him. "You, too."

He took her hand—*merde*, just to touch her again was so damn good—and led her out onto the balcony. He held out her chair as she sat down at the table he'd set with good dishes and linen napkins, and even a small vase of fresh flowers.

She bit her lip and gazed up at him. "This looks so nice."

"It's all for you, *chere*. I hope you like it."

Her smile said yes, and he couldn't help smiling back.

After reaching into the ice bucket he'd brought out earlier, then pouring wine in two stemmed glasses, he returned to the kitchen where he'd prepared a Cajun feast. He hoped he'd made a good decision, but deep inside he wasn't worried—something told him he had.

"I never asked if you like Cajun food, darlin,' but if this doesn't suit you, just say so and we'll order somethin' in." With that, he set down a large plate for each of them, both heaping with piles of his homemade jambalaya, red beans and rice, Cajun shrimp, and crawfish cakes.

She cast a tentative smile as she lifted her gaze from the plate to his eyes. "To tell you the truth, in all the time I've been here, I've never really tried any Cajun food."

Taking a seat across from her, he raised playful eyebrows. "An adventurous girl like you?"

She laughed lightly. "As you well know, I didn't used to be so adventurous. And I suppose my taste in food was a lot like me—I've always played it safe. When I go to a restaurant, I order something tried and true."

He tilted his head. "*Mais*, are you willin' to try this, or should we get somethin' else? I don't mind if you'd rather go for a steak and baked potato."

She reached for her fork. "As you said, I'm much more adventurous now, so I'll give this a try."

Jack watched as she lifted a bite of his jambalaya to her lovely berry lips. A moment later, she gave him another smile. "Spicy, but I like it."

He couldn't help laughing. In one simple sentence, she'd summed up his feelings for her.

One by one, she tried each of the other dishes, and one by one, she gave her approval, finally thanking him for introducing her to so many Cajun delicacies all at once. "I didn't really know how much I liked hot things before."

Again, he grinned at her unintended double entendre. This time he couldn't help himself from saying, "I did, *chere*."

She blushed and he laughed. "Darlin', there you go again."

"Old habit," she said, swallowing, looking nervous. "And...I haven't seen you in a while. I suppose my comfort level has...faded a little."

"My fault," he supplied. "And I need to tell you why."

She blinked, looking interested in what he had to say, and reached for her wine. "I'd like to know...what happened. I mean, I know it was me who changed my mind about moving in with you, but I never wanted to stop seeing you."

He tilted his head, wanting to get the truth on the table right now. He wanted her honesty back, every blunt, lovely, raw part of it. "You didn't change your mind about movin' in with me, *chere*. Todd changed it for you."

Her mouth dropped open.

"Darlin', I hid some surveillance cameras in Todd's house, but then I fell behind on my work, so it took me this long to get around to lookin' at 'em all. Late last night I watched the tape from that day after you said you'd come live with me. I saw his threats, Liz. I know why you sent that message now."

He shook his head, continuing. "But back then...I didn't understand. I was just hurt, and angry. I thought you didn't want to be with me...be with me in a way that means somethin', a way that lasts. I fucked up. I should've called you. I was an idiot to go runnin' in the opposite direction, but I was afraid of exactly that—of gettin' hurt, and I didn't want to get hurt any worse than I already was. I was so wrapped up in my own feelings that I didn't spend enough time tryin' to figure out yours." And the truth, of course, was that he *still* didn't know her feelings, not really. He hoped she cared for him, hoped she wanted the same thing he did from their relationship. But he wasn't going to push that right now. There was more to tell her.

"I took that tape to the police this mornin', *chere*. They were real interested, especially when I filled 'em in on his threats and his attack on you. He hasn't really done anything they can arrest him for without you or Lynda pressin' charges, and they said they wouldn't even recommend that, Todd bein' a pretty slick guy in terms of credentials and corporate backing, and the incidents bein' unprovable other than the one on tape, which is inadmissible. But you don't have to worry anymore because a couple guys down at the precinct are gonna make enough trouble for him that you won't hear from him again."

She looked astonished. "How can you be sure? What are they going to do?"

"First they're gonna have a little talk with old Todd, tell him what they know, then suggest he clear outta New Orleans, ask his bosses for a transfer somewhere else. If he's too stupid to do that, they'll do it for him—they'll let his company know exactly what sorta shit he's been up to and explain that it's in everyone's best interest for Todd to relocate." He gave her a knowing grin. "And trust me, darlin'—these guys can be pretty persuasive."

In that very moment, Liz felt a huge weight lift from her shoulders. It was as if she'd been holding her breath for a very long time and now could suddenly breathe again. Perhaps she'd managed to keep Todd out of her thoughts, but she supposed he'd never really been out of her mind completely—except for those wonderful, wild nights she'd spent with Jack. Now, suddenly, it was as if Todd and his ugly threats had been banished from her head and her heart for good. Jack had, amazingly, just succeeded in wiping them all away.

"Jack, I can't thank you enough for this. I can't tell you what a burden you've just taken away from me."

He shook his head. "Don't thank me, darlin'. I didn't have any other choice. I couldn't rest easy until that guy was outta your life for good. I only hope maybe it makes up just a little for my shitty behavior."

"Jack, I—"

"Shh, wait." He reached across the table for her hand. "I have to say somethin', right now. I can't let another minute pass." He paused, took a deep breath, and Liz got lost in the depths of his dark, consuming gaze. "I'm so sorry, *chere*. Is there any way you can forgive me?"

A rush of pure joy invaded Liz's lungs, her whole body, her whole being. "Yes," she said. Then more emphatically, "*Yes*."

For a long moment, only silence stretched between them as they gazed into each other's eyes across the table. Night was falling in the Quarter; in the distance, someone played a saxophone, and bits of neon began to light yet another evening of excitement and decadence on the other end of Bourbon Street. But Liz was barely aware of anything else but the man before her, the man whose eyes at once seemed to cherish her and ravish her, the man who embraced every part of her, from the shy to the wanton.

Finally, Jack spoke, his voice low and filled with seduction. "I've missed bein' inside you, *chere*. I've missed it so bad it's like I can't breathe."

She glanced down at her breasts, felt the warm familiar stirrings between her legs, thought of something she wanted to tell him and almost didn't, too shy, but then remembered—with Jack, she didn't *have* to be shy. Jack would want to know. "Last night," she began, lifting her eyes, "I fucked myself with the vibrator you gave me and I pretended you were watching me."

His eyes fell closed for a moment, his jaw dropping slightly—she loved how taken aback and breathless he appeared. His voice was no more than a rasp. "Did you make yourself come?"

She nodded, feeling nearly as weak now as he looked.

"Was it good, baby?"

Another nod. "But afterward...I was so sad. I missed you. I wanted it to be *you* inside me."

He rose from his chair and took her hands, guiding her to her feet, as well. His palms rose gently to her cheeks and his mouth descended on hers—strong, sweet, firm, his kiss filled with a desperation she'd never felt before. She kissed him back without reserve—the sexy honesty she'd just dished out had filled her with heat and readiness and the sense that with Jack, she didn't need to hold anything back, nothing at all. He got to have all of her. And tonight there wouldn't be anyone but the two of them making each other's bodies echo with pleasure.

His hands eased down to her shoulders, onto her breasts, where they tenderly squeezed, and then his fingertips closed around her nipples through the dress and bra, and she was moaning without thought, and whispering up to him the words that kept playing in her brain. "Fuck me, Jack. Please fuck me. Now."

He took both her hands and silently drew her in through the open French doors.

Her body ached for him. She wanted him to devour her.

Without ever letting his eyes leave hers, he reached around behind her, found the zipper at her back, and slowly lowered it, each painstaking inch seeming like a mile. Then his strong hands were on her back, roaming in a hot, lingering caress, until they came to her shoulders to peel the dress down, letting it fall to her hips. Not wanting to stretch anything out this time, she wiggled slightly and the fabric dropped at her feet.

Jack's gaze traveled the length of her, taking in the blue lace bra and thong, and the strappy heels the color of warm cream. "Mmm, *chere*, you look good enough to eat."

She pinned him with a wicked look. "This is what I wore for you on the night you threw Todd out. This is what you never got to see."

Jack gave his head a short shake. "Don't mention his name. I don't wanna think about anything bad here—just me and you and all this pretty blue lace."

His words burned through her, again reminding her how anxious she was. It wasn't like her, this urge to rush, but having Jack's hands on her again—even just his eyes—was getting her hot to the point of combustion. She'd been missing him too long. Her pussy throbbed and her thighs ached. Her breasts seared with need, as well, her nipples hard and pointed just inside the low scalloped edge of her bra. She whispered again. "Fuck me, Jack. Fuck me so hard I scream."

To her surprise, he tilted his head, letting his heated expression be replaced with one of amusement. "Now, now, *chere*—what happened to stretchin' things out?"

"That's when we were seeing each other every night. It's been too long, Jack."

"I agree. I've been sufferin' through life with a perpetual hard-on lately. But I can only guess you rubbed off on me somewhere along the way, 'cause as much as I want to nail you to the bed with my cock right now, I also want to take it slow, make it steamy, make it...special."

Liz let out a breath and felt guilty for the times she'd tortured him with hours of foreplay. Now she found herself wondering how he'd stood it. "It *will* be special. Whether it's fast or slow, hard or soft, it'll be special. I don't want to wait."

A slow, confident smile unfurled on his stubbled face. "Well, Mistress Liz, I'm sorry, but I'm the one takin' control tonight, so you'll just have to play it my way."

Chapter 13

The words made her cunt swell even more. She was so wet for him, needed his big, hot shaft inside her so bad. How was she going to survive it?

"Go in the bedroom and lie down," he instructed.

She thought of protesting, but decided it was futile. Just like her when she got her mind set on controlling their sex, she knew Jack wouldn't give in until he was good and ready.

Once she'd reclined, she realized he hadn't followed her. "Jack? Are you coming?"

She heard him chuckle. "My impatient *petite fille,*" he murmured from the other room. She thought it a vast understatement.

When he still hadn't appeared a few seconds later, she couldn't help touching herself. With one hand she began caressing her breast through her bra, with the other she delivered light strokes to her clit through the lace, thinking—*please, Jack, please.*

Finally, he appeared in the doorway, but to her utter surprise, he'd been...transformed. He stood naked, his big, lovely cock at full attention, stretched up past his navel, his broad chest draped with purple and gold Mardi Gras beads, his handsome face covered with a shiny Mardi Gras mask so that only his eyes, mouth, and dark-stubbled chin were visible. He looked as mysterious and dangerous as she'd ever thought him and her pussy seemed to clench, her nipples tightening as she studied him, this Bacchanalian man who looked ready to perform primitive sexual rituals on her.

Only as he approached did she realize he held more Mardi Gras paraphernalia in his hands. Leaning over the bed, he tenderly lifted her head and draped strands of the colored beads around her neck, across her chest. Around her shoulders he arranged a long purple feather boa. Finally, he placed a mask of purple glitter and sequins over her eyes. Suddenly, she felt as enigmatic as she thought him just now; something about hiding themselves behind the masks was almost as erotic as if they were two strangers at Mardi Gras who'd rendezvoused in this apartment for a primal sexual encounter.

"Get up," he said softly.

The beads jangled together as she rose to her feet, gathering the boa around her. Following his lead, she took a few steps until, together, they stood before the long mirror on his closet door. "Look at you," he breathed, his voice a barely audible wisp, coming even lower than that distant saxophone still playing somewhere beyond the windows and doors of Jack's apartment. "The perfect Mardi Gras queen, looking for her king at a Bacchanal. Looking for the man worthy of fucking her."

"You look very worthy," she whispered, letting her gaze drop to his dick in the mirror.

A small grin formed below his mask. "Do you remember, *chere,* when you told me your fantasy about havin' sex on a float in a Mardi Gras parade?"

Up to now, it hadn't crossed her mind, but the question made her smile.

"Well, darlin', it's a long time 'til Mardi Gras rolls back around. But come next February, maybe I can arrange such an erotic little treat for you. And until then, we can just consider this practice."

With that, he stepped behind her and reached around to cup her breasts. As they both watched themselves in the mirror, he gently massaged them, causing the beads to click softly together, making her breath come heavy from the long-awaited pleasure. Dipping his thumbs into the lace, he first raked them over ultra-hard nipples, forcing a whimper from her, and then he pulled the lace edges down just far enough that her stiffened buds jutted out. "Such pretty breasts," he whispered in her ear, twirling the sensitive pink tips between his thumbs and forefingers.

"Suck them," she said.

To her shock, he responded with a laugh, then whispered, "Only when I'm good and ready, darlin'."

The man was maddening.

His hands left her breasts then, slowly making their way down over the curve of her waist, the thin strap of blue lace at her hip, her thighs. She knew the tender touches were purposeful teases, and she endured them not only because he was giving her no choice, but also because she was starting to accept that she would do what he wanted, when he wanted, how he wanted, on this particular night.

He turned her from the mirror to face him then, and slowly backed her into a wall. He pinned her wrists at either side of her head, his grip like a vise as he delivered a long, slow kiss, his tongue licking at hers. His hold never loosened as he rained kisses down over her shoulder, chest, the ridge of her breasts—finally his mouth closed over one straining nipple and she cried out. He sucked hard, just like she wanted, and she felt the sensation shoot straight from her breast to her cunt. Finally, he released her wrists, dropped to his knees, and lowered an exasperatingly chaste little kiss to the front of her panties, just above her needy clit.

"Your bra," he said, still kneeling before her. "Take it off, slowly."

Biting her lip, Liz reached behind her to undo the hook, loosening the tight lace. Then she reached up, hooking her thumbs beneath the straps, and leisurely extracted it from her Mardi Gras accessories, leaving her breasts draped only in the colorful beads.

Now, she thought, tossing the bra away, now he would lick her pussy, kiss her breasts—*something*!

And then—damn him—he backed away to look up at her.

"More, baby, please," she begged. Maybe that was what he wanted, for her to beg. She'd beg and plead all night if it would get her what she needed.

He smiled. "Sorry, *chere*, but don't waste your breath. I'm callin' the shots here."

Infuriating man! She pulled in her breath, leaned back her head in frustration.

And then he was suddenly on his feet again and reaching for her breasts—but no, no, damn it, not her breasts at all; he was only reaching for the beads she wore. Yet then—sweet bliss—he rolled the strings of beads outward over the curves of her breasts until they met both turgid nipples, stopping them in place. But only for a brief moment—he kept dragging the beads until they flicked hard past the pink peaks impeding them, creating a tense echo of pleasure throughout her body. She bit her lip and moaned.

She sensed his grin of arousal as he next dragged the beads back from the outer curves of her breasts until once again the stiff buds halted them. Delicious pressure weighed on her nipple as Jack slowly continued pulling the strings inward, finally snapping the beads across the little rock-hard crests and sending another tremor of heat through her. "Unh," she breathed.

He continued playing with the beads, pulling them this way and that over her ever-sensitive breasts, doing it faster, raking the hard beads back and forth over her nipples until she thought she'd die from the rough little jolts of pleasure. And then his tongue entered the fray—he dropped to lick at her taut nipples, making her pussy surge with wetness below, making her grunt and moan and grip his head in her hands, making her wild and wanton for more. *More, more*. She wanted to beg him, but resisted, because he was so single-minded tonight, so driven to do it his way, and she suspected begging would only make him stretch it out further, so she only whimpered and groaned and let him know how hot he was getting her.

Finally, he let go of the beads, released her nipples from his sweet wet mouth, and the absence of all touching made her realize exactly how roughly her cunt throbbed. She didn't think it had ever felt this hot and swollen.

And maybe he read her mind, because that's when he took the lush feather boa from her shoulders and slipped it between her legs. He held it taut against her pussy, one hand behind her, the other in front so that it was like riding a feathery rope. He never said a word, just looked into her eyes. She knew she was meant to move against it, relieve a little of her ache that way, and she couldn't have resisted rubbing herself on it if she'd tried. At that moment, having *anything* offer a little sweet pressure against her mound would have made her respond, but she couldn't deny the thick feather boa was particularly soft and sensuous, especially where the feathers brushed against her ass in back, where her panties were just a tiny strip of fabric.

As always, she relished his intent gaze on her as she rode the boa for him, and grew even hotter inside when she glanced up at her lover and remembered their masks. The sight made her imagine for a short moment that they were perched high on a Mardi Gras float, spectators all around them. He'd called her the perfect Mardi Gras queen, and she felt just as sexy and sensual and daring as such a title would demand.

Finally, Jack withdrew the boa from between her thighs and led her to the bed. Mmm, he would finally fuck her here, she knew it—and she could barely stand the wait. "Lie down," he commanded.

She followed the order willingly, watching him, waiting for what would come next. Kneeling between her legs, her Bacchanalian god of all that was carnal slid his massive cock lengthwise against her pussy through the lace, playing her like a violin. So good to finally get that sweet hot tool against her cunt—she reached down, planning to pull the lace to one side, but he stopped her, grabbing her hands, again pinning them to her sides while he sawed his cock against her aching slit.

More, baby, please, she silently begged, but instead she got it someplace she hadn't expected at that very moment—he shifted on the bed to straddle her face, his cock looking even more majestic than usual towering over her like a column of steel. Mmm, she wanted it in her mouth, as deep as she could take it, so she reached up, wrapped her hand around the thick shaft, and drew it down to her lips. Yet instead of sucking him just yet, at the last second she decided to tease *him* a little—two could play at that game.

Smiling up at him, she raked a tiny lick across the tip. He shuddered visibly, closed his eyes. She licked again, this time dragging her tongue in a circle around the head, French-kissing his cock.

Above her, he moaned and she continued the teasing treatment, thoroughly enjoying each little lick and lave. Her pussy still yearned to have his hot shaft inside her, but the mouthplay was wildly fulfilling, too. As her licks grew broader, longer, she needed to feel his length, so she began licking upward from the base of his cock, long, languid strokes that had him groaning with each movement, until finally she had to swallow him—she closed her lips around him and drew him as deep toward her throat as she could. Mmm, yes, having her mouth filled with him was the next best thing to having her cunt filled with him. She sucked up and down, breathed hot air over and around him, listened to him moan and murmur, "That's right, baby. So fuckin' good when you suck me."

Finally, he groaned and drew his dick from her mouth, breathing, "No more, *chere*. I don't wanna come yet."

She didn't want that, either. If she was tortured, so should he be.

"What now?" she asked, unable to go even a second without wanting him to touch her or kiss her, desperately needing their bodies to connect in some way.

His grin was as wicked and sensual as ever. "Now you get a surprise."

Despite herself, she returned the smile. "Another vibrator?"

He shrugged behind his mask. "*Mais,* yes and no. But I promise that my adventurous Mardi Gras queen will like how it makes her feel."

Curiosity bit at her, making her anxious to see what he had in store for her.

Kneeling beside her in bed, he reached to remove her panties, and she lifted her ass, letting him. "Spread for me," he said. "I've missed seein' this sweet little pussy."

Pleased, she did as he asked and basked in the sexy joy of having him just look at her. She knew she was wet and wide open by now, knew his eyes were feasting on her tender pink flesh.

"So fuckin' pretty, *chere*," he said, eyes intent on her cunt.

Maybe he would fuck her now. *Please, baby, give me that beautiful cock where I need it.*

"Roll over."

She did.

And then she felt the most peculiar sensation—something smooth and cool and wet sliding down the crack of her ass. "What…?"

"Shh."

She quieted, intrigued and aroused enough not to argue.

The cool pressure continued until it reached her anus and there it played around the sensitive opening, making her sigh with a pleasure that radiated through her body. She'd assumed he would keep going then, with whatever this new tool was, that he would glide it down to her waiting pussy, but to her surprise, the unknown object continued to gently poke and prod and rub the little fissure.

Without planning it, she found herself lifting her ass off the bed toward the mystery tool, wanting this sweet, slow teasing to persist. Only she wasn't really thinking about what might lay ahead, was only drinking in the pleasure of the moment, so it surprised her when she realized this new object was beginning to ease inside the tight, tiny opening. "Oh God," she moaned.

"Feel good?"

She couldn't deny it. "Mmm, yes. Strange…but good." Like that day in the shower when he'd put his thumb inside her there, but different, because this was harder, more probing, than his thumb.

"Strange how?"

"That hole has never been opened before. Not like this. *Oh!*" she cried out when the object sank suddenly deeper into this unexplored part of her body.

"Still good?"

She tried to analyze the feeling. So different than having something in her pussy, yet...oddly satisfying. A whole new sensation, just when she'd thought there was nothing more completely new to experience. "Um, yes."

"Good," he said, and then—mmm—he began to gently slide the object in and out, in and out, and the hot sensations in her ass echoed through her cunt, making her clit ache for stimulation. "*Merde*, I wish you could see this, *chere*. Wish you could see your tight *jolie* little ass right now."

She pulled in her breath at his words, the excitement in his voice.

"Tell me how it feels," he said.

She bit her lip, thinking. "Different than anything I've ever known. Even more sensitive than my pussy, but in an entirely different way. And, oh, my poor clit. This is making it so hot, so needy."

She'd been sure he'd enjoy hearing how tortured she was, but to her surprise, he gently rolled her over, careful not to let his special tool leave her snug asshole, then he spread her legs and, still fucking her ass with the toy, began to lick her swollen cunt.

"Oh God, yes," she moaned as his sweet tongue worked over her. The pressure in her ass magnified the effects of his licking. He started low in her pussy, but quickly moved up to her aching clit, delivering hard tongue strokes in the same rhythm he fucked her ass. Liz had never felt anything so blindingly pleasurable. She forgot where she was, who she was—she seemed to sink into the bed, through the floor, and into some dark, sweet blanket of black velvet sky, into a place where the only things that existed were her body and the man who set her wild soul free.

"God, yes, baby, lick me," she moaned. "Make me come." She was so ready, her body so primed—every inch of flesh on her bones needed that hot, furious release that she knew was only heartbeats away. "Yes, baby, lick my clit. Lick it. Lick it. Lick it." She said it in time with his sweet tonguing, and thought her pussy and ass would burst apart with all the pleasure rushing through them. She whimpered as the orgasm got nearer, nearer, just within reach, and then—oh God, she came so hard it almost hurt. Each hot, staggering burst of heat and pleasure wracked her body with spasms that left her weak. "Oh..." she murmured as the rough orgasm slowly began to fade, leaving her limp and feeling unbelievably well-fucked, considering that his cock hadn't even been involved.

She opened her eyes to find him kneeling between her legs, gazing down at her from behind that sexy mask that turned him into her secret Mardi Gras king. "How was that?" he asked, but his tone said he already knew it had been overpowering.

She could barely speak, still weak. "A-amazing. *What* was that?" she countered.

He held the toy up for her to see—a small, thin, gold vibrator, slick and smooth. "It's made just for your tight little ass."

"It felt…wet."

"I oiled it up, wanted to make sure it didn't hurt."

"I…didn't feel any vibrations."

He grinned. "We'll work up to that. This first time, I figured just fucking you there with it was enough."

She nodded, knowing he was right. "It was *more* than enough." Almost more stimulation than her body could handle. And yet, at the same time, she still wanted…"Will you fuck me now? Please." She didn't smile, hoping her expression told him how much she needed his cock inside her.

His eyes went dark behind the mask, and his voice came low. "Yeah, *chere*, I'll fuck you. I'll fuck you so good, so long, so hot, better than ever before."

Reaching down, he parted her legs and again studied her bare pussy. Then he parted the pink lips and bent down to blow on it. A little shiver snaked through her and then his cock was there, pushing inside her, filling her like nothing else could. It was like reclaiming a lost treasure and she wrapped her legs around his back to pull him in deep.

The following hour was filled with tumultuous fucking, just as he'd promised. He fucked her on the bed; he fucked her standing up, bracing her hands on his dresser; he fucked her face-to-face on the kitchen table; he fucked her on the couch, where she could ride him to orgasm. He pressed her up against a balcony window so that if anyone happened to glance up at the second floor, they'd see a naked woman bedecked in mask and beads being fucked from behind. Liz pressed her palms flat against the glass, her breasts, too—as his strong, powerful cock drove into her again and again with hard, hot strokes that made her cry out with pleasure.

And just when Liz thought perhaps their *private* little Bacchanal would draw to a close, her lover surprised her one last time. Withdrawing his erection, he walked to an easy chair across the room, picked up the wide ottoman in front of it, and carried it out onto the balcony.

Although the street below was not abuzz with crowds like the red light end of Bourbon, it was Saturday night in the Quarter and a few people were strolling the sidewalks beneath them. Liz stood watching her masked, naked lover standing unabashedly out on the balcony, his dark eyes beckoning to her, his hand motioning her to join him.

Somehow this was different than the other times they'd fucked on the balcony, even more hedonistic-feeling than when she'd ridden him in the Pussycat's Claw, where they *might* have been seen, but likely were not. Even so, she walked slowly toward her Mardi Gras king, who said in a deep, low voice, "This is your float. Your parade. This is where the revelers get to watch me fuck your pretty pink pussy."

There was a part of her that actually thought of protesting—the knowledge that they would certainly be seen, perhaps were already being noticed in their masks and beads and nudity—seemed to go a step too far into her fantasy. Even so, her pussy pulsed with maddening intensity, wanting still more of the sweet, hot fucking he'd been delivering to her so well. And indeed, as she glanced to the street below and realized at least one couple and a trio of guys were pausing to look up at the balcony, nothing as petty as propriety mattered any longer—nothing mattered but being fucked by her king while the crowd watched.

Biting her lip, she gave Jack a come-hither look, then climbed onto the ottoman, positioning herself on hands and knees, just like in her fantasy.

Jack approached behind her, placing his palms on her hips, sliding his enormous hard-on smoothly into her welcoming cunt. "Oooh, God, yes, baby," she purred at the filling entry.

His strokes came hard and deep and fast and pummeling, and Liz let herself cry out at each brutal thrust. She wanted the people on the street to hear—wanted more of them to stop and watch, to see her lover sliding his slick cock in and out of her while she screamed her bliss.

"So fuckin' wet, baby," Jack murmured as he continued driving his dick into her pussy. "So fuckin' incredible."

Liz kept her eyes open, focusing on the intricate wrought iron railing directly in front of her, the old brick of the building across the narrow street. Eventually, though, she dared to glance down and take in the scene below them—where she found a small crowd of at least fifteen people peering up at their show. Some looked shocked, others aroused. One man let out a deep throaty cheer of, "Oooh, baby! Yeah!"

In that moment of forbidden fucking, Liz became the strippers at Club Venus and the woman in ponytails she'd seen fucked at the Pussycat's Claw. She became Felicia, and Lynda, and every other woman who drank in the pure joys of unabashed sex without fear or hesitation. She became the woman in her parade fantasy, a sexual being who lived only for pleasure. She became Jack's Mardi Gras Queen.

The beads around her neck clicked and clanked against each other with each rough stroke Jack delivered. Another guy, somewhere below, let out a wolfish howl while another whistled. Jack's cock pounded her into oblivion, making her thighs weak, her entire body basking in a nearly overwhelming pleasure.

"They're watching us," she panted over her shoulder to her lover. "They're watching you fuck me."

"That's right, darlin'—they're watchin' you take my big cock, watchin' your pussy take it all the way in, watchin' me fuck you so hard."

And just as she'd imagined in her fantasy, the mask gave her just enough anonymity to make her feel safe in her glorious hedonism.

Even without stimulation to her clit, she felt so ready, so close to orgasm, that she could barely fathom it. So when Jack reached around to press his fingertips into the top of her cleft, she came instantly. The climax broke over her hard, wild, and she cried out even louder. "Yes, baby! Yes! I'm coming for you! I'm coming!" The intensity of it was nearly overwhelming, the length of it staggering as the spectators witnessed her ultimate pleasure.

"Baby, I can't take much more," Jack breathed in her ear as the waves of heat finally eased to ripples.

"That's okay, because I want you to come. I want you to explode inside me while they all watch."

That was all it took—then he was moaning, gripping tighter to her hips, saying, "I'm gonna come, *chere*, I'm gonna come in you!" His strokes grew longer, more forceful as he groaned, emptying himself inside her. "God, I love you," he murmured in her ear.

The words nearly paralyzed her. Even through his sweet apology earlier, even when he'd started talking about them still being together next year for Mardi Gras, she'd still never thought…never expected… He just didn't seem like a man who would say those words. And yet he had.

As in her fantasy, the people gathered below were applauding and cheering their performance, but Liz had already forgotten they were there. The moment he withdrew from her, she got to her feet, grabbed his arm, and pulled him inside, shutting the French doors, closing out the sultry night, for something that *had* to be private.

"I love you, too, Jack. So much."

Reaching up, Jack slipped the mask from her head, and then removed his own. Using the crook of one finger, he tilted her chin and leaned down for a long, sweet kiss that truly felt like a gesture of love, and she knew he meant his words.

"I think it's time you move in with me once and for all, *chere*. Not because of Todd, but because I want you here, morning and night. Forever."

She looked into the dark eyes of the man who had loosed the wildness hidden deep in her soul, and thought about that last word—forever. The rest of her life. He wanted her that long. In his world. A world where she wanted to stay.

Yet even in the sweet sanctity of the moment, she decided to tease him—just a little. "Maybe if we're settling down, you and I, we should get respectable, move out to the Garden District."

He laughed, seeming to know instantly that she was joking. "No, *chere*, you're a French Quarter girl, no doubt about it. You belong here, where things are just as wild and hot as you."

"Actually, I couldn't agree more. Although…"

"What?"

How would he take this? Maybe it wasn't even the right time to bring it up, but…she missed being honest with him, and she wasn't going to hold back her thoughts. "How would you feel, Jack, if I said I didn't want to…bring other people into our sex anymore?"

His eyes softly closed, but when he opened them, they glimmered with joy. "I was gonna ask you the same thing. I've missed you so much, love you so much, that I kinda want it to be just us from now on."

She smiled in reply.

"Of course," he said, turning playful, "that doesn't mean we can't pop into Club Venus sometimes, or fuck on the balcony, or that I can't get out your special toys, but..."

"You don't have to explain," she told him. "From the very beginning, I only wanted to have all those new, exciting experiences because they involved *you*. And now that I've done all that, well...you're more than enough man for me."

He grinned. "Is that so? Does that mean I should throw your special toys away?" He teasingly grabbed up the new mini-vibrator and held it out over the waste can next to them.

"Wait a minute," she said, laughing as she slapped her palms against his chest. "Let's not be hasty. That's going too far."

The smile he flashed was sexy and knowing. "That's what I thought. You're still gonna be wild and adventurous for me." Wrapping his arms around her, he nudged the gold toy gently into the center of her ass.

She let out a hot little sigh in reply. "I don't think I can help myself."

"Don't worry, *chere*. I wouldn't have it any other way."

"And if you can arrange that little float scenario next Mardi Gras..."

He grinned. "Yeah?"

"I would love to let the whole world see how well you fuck me."

About the author:

Lacey Alexander lives in the Midwest with her husband of fifteen years and she loves being a full-time writer. When not creating romance and romantica, she enjoys crafts, American history, and travel, and she particularly likes incorporating her favorite destinations into her novels.

Lacey welcomes mail from readers. You can write to her c/o Ellora's Cave Publishing at 1337 Commerce Drive, Suite 13, Stow OH 44224.

Also by Lacey Alexander:

Hot For Santa!

Coming Soon! The next two stories in the Hot In the City series: Sin City and Key West

Also available from Ellora's Cave Publishing, Inc.

Strength In Numbers: Double Jeopardy by Rachel Bo

Close Quarters by Tielle St. Clare

Hook, Wine & Tinker by Mardi Ballou

Happy Birthday Baby by Lynn LaFleur

Full Bodied Charmer by Marilyn Lee

Why an electronic book?

We live in the Information Age—an exciting time in the history of human civilization in which technology rules supreme and continues to progress in leaps and bounds every minute of every hour of every day. For a multitude of reasons, more and more avid literary fans are opting to purchase e-books instead of paperbacks. The question to those not yet initiated to the world of electronic reading is simply: *why?*

1. *Price.* An electronic title at Ellora's Cave Publishing runs anywhere from 40-75% less than the cover price of the exact same title in paperback format. Why? Cold mathematics. It is less expensive to publish an e-book than it is to publish a paperback, so the savings are passed along to the consumer.
2. *Space.* Running out of room to house your paperback books? That is one worry you will never have with electronic novels. For a low one-time cost, you can purchase a handheld computer designed specifically for e-reading purposes. Many e-readers are larger than the average handheld, giving you plenty of screen room. Better yet, hundreds of titles can be stored within your new library—a single microchip. (Please note that Ellora's Cave does not endorse any specific brands. You can check our website at www.ellorascave.com for customer recommendations we make available to new consumers.)

3. *Mobility.* Because your new library now consists of only a microchip, your entire cache of books can be taken with you wherever you go.
4. *Personal preferences are accounted for.* Are the words you are currently reading too small? Too large? Too...**ANNOYING**? Paperback books cannot be modified according to personal preferences, but e-books can.
5. *Innovation.* The way you read a book is not the only advancement the Information Age has gifted the literary community with. There is also the factor of what you can read. Ellora's Cave Publishing will be introducing a new line of interactive titles that are available in e-book format only.
6. *Instant gratification.* Is it the middle of the night and all the bookstores are closed? Are you tired of waiting days—sometimes weeks—for online and offline bookstores to ship the novels you bought? Ellora's Cave Publishing sells instantaneous downloads 24 hours a day, 7 days a week, 365 days a year. Our e-book delivery system is 100% automated, meaning your order is filled as soon as you pay for it.

Those are a few of the top reasons why electronic novels are displacing paperbacks for many an avid reader. As always, Ellora's Cave Publishing welcomes your questions and comments. We invite you to email us at service@ellorascave.com or write to us directly at: 1337 Commerce Drive, Suite 13, Stow OH 44224.

Printed in the United States
22111LVS00007B/73-204